Mousetrap, Inc.

Mousetrap, Inc.

Joseph Guzzo

RESOURCE *Publications* · Eugene, Oregon

MOUSETRAP, INC.

Resource Publications
An Imprint of Wipf and Stock Publishers
199 W. 8th Ave., Suite 3
Eugene, OR 97401

www.wipfandstock.com

PAPERBACK ISBN:978-1-6667-3147-7
HARDCOVER ISBN: 978-1-6667-2401-1
EBOOK ISBN: 978-1-6667-2402-8

09/29/21

For my parents, Antoinette and Giuseppe,
the finest people I'll ever know.
And for my brother, Tom, who's always had my back.

Acknowledgments

WITHOUT FAMILY, MY ENTIRE life would be built on sand. Mom, Tom, Amy, Angelica, Anthony, Uncle Ray, and Jim, I can't imagine a second without any of you. When we get together, we eat and drink too much, we're irreverent and loud, and we somehow manage to disagree even when we agree. Let's never change a thing.

Oh, and, Uncle Ray, a small confession: When you were on vacation and I slept in your house as a teenager, I read many of your books. One in particular, Philip Roth's "Portnoy's Complaint," opened up my eyes and showed me that creativity has no limits. That thought has never left me.

Dina Smith, my longtime boss and friend, thanks for your relentless decency and kindness. You make the world a better place.

I'd like to thank Matthew Wimer and the team at Resource Publications and Wipf & Stock for making this book a reality and for always being there to answer my numerous questions along the way.

Thanks, Brendan McLaughlin, for your finely honed copy-editing skills and years of friendship. Our professors taught us well, eh?

Michael Ayoob and Brad Powell, thanks for being my first readers and constant sources of encouragement. Above all, though, thanks for your consistently awful football picks. I'm winning again, aren't I?

And, above all, none of this is possible—and none of this matters—without my wife and son. Even though you had no idea what I was doing, Maria and Joseph, you are my constant inspiration, my heat and my light, and you have no idea how much I love and admire you. Your innate goodness makes me a better person.

Oh, and one more: To my girl Friday, who knew but never said a word. Rest in peace, old friend.

Okay, one more: Thank you, chocolate, my lifelong friend, for always being there for me. I can never repay you.

Jack Gardner's idea deserved a better hand of fate. Sam and Rachel knew it. And, in her heart, I wanted to think Andrea did, too.

I remember asking Andrea once how she got started in the business. She chuckled, placed her cigarette down, and said, "Young man, you know that expression about being able to sell ice to Eskimos? Well, I could sell ice to the same group of Eskimos every day for a month." She took a long draw from her cigarette. "And at the end of the 31st day, they'd still be thanking me.

"But how did I get started? I have a gift for convincing people they need whatever it is I'm offering. Girl Scout cookies? That was child's play—literally and figuratively. Three years in a row, I outsold every other girl in my group, and by a huge amount. The other girls hated me and figured I had my parents selling them at work.

"Hell, no. I sold them all—every damn box of them—door-to-door, and my success rate was close to perfect."

She then proceeded to give me the rundown of her entire work history—from the newspaper route she had through high school, to her brief, and successful, stint selling department-store cosmetics, to the sales job that led to her current position as CEO and owner of the company that employs me.

"And that," she said, sweeping her arms in the direction of the bank of windows that lined the far wall of her ninth-floor office and gave her a beautiful view of Downtown, "all led to this."

"Play your cards right, young man, and you could find yourself in my shoes someday." She winked.

I forced myself to smile. Being in Andrea Bianco's shoes was the last thing I wanted. I stood there, realizing that the greatest sales job she ever performed was convincing herself she was a legitimate business tycoon.

There really was no justification for our existence at Mousetrap, Inc. ("Build a better mousetrap, and bring it to our door!") There were a multitude of excuses, of course. The top rationalization was economics. We were in the middle (why do people say "in the middle" when, chances are, they probably weren't exactly halfway through something? For all we knew, it was the beginning of the recession, or, conversely, the next day, we would wake up and bright, shiny new jobs would be there to greet us.) Anyway, we were enduring a recession, whose depth and breadth we had no way of gauging, and that was as good a reason as any to stay out of Andrea's sight and pretend to be busy. Secondly, we knew that if the three of us left, three new stiffs would be there to take our places. Even in the depths of an economic slowdown, Mousetrap had no trouble attracting clients. (Case number 7418, "The Beeralyzer," sat atop my in-box.) And, lastly, we had an unwritten pact that none of us could leave separately.

I was the last to arrive in Mousetrap's graphic production department, almost two years earlier, in 1990, and as a recent college grad, I wanted to make a strong first impression. I had spent six miserable months largely unemployed (I'll get to that in due time), and I was ready to accept any job, as long as it meant a paycheck and a reclamation of my damaged pride. ("So, Nick, what kind of work are you in?" "Well, right now I'm looking . . ." This conversation would always be followed by a concerned look and a mumbled platitude—"Well, you're a smart guy; something will turn up soon." How much more I would have preferred a brutal, if incorrect, assessment—"What are you, lazy or a moron?" Alas, most people tend to be polite.)

I knew about Mousetrap, Inc. through its late-night commercial. Perhaps you remember it? The spot opens with a man in a cheap gray wig and a suit to match portraying Thomas Edison at a large, wooden desk furiously scribbling into a notebook. A voiceover intones, "Where will the next great idea come from? Have you ever walked into a store, picked up a product, and said, 'Why didn't I think of that?' or, even worse, 'I had that idea years ago!' Well, we're here to help. At Mousetrap, Inc., we turn your dreams into reality. Call 1–800–2INVENT for a free, no-obligation brochure. Don't let this happen to you . . ."

And the commercial cuts to a young woman in a department store picking up a nondescript package and slapping herself in the head in the classic "Boy, am I a dumbass" maneuver. The commercial closes with Edison dancing a jig in front of his phonograph. I remember laughing at the stupidity of both the commercial and the people who got roped into such nonsensical schemes. Yet, in the spring of 1990, 13 months out of college and six months out of a job, here I was, sitting across a desk from Sam Wiatt, graphic department supervisor.

I arrived for my interview about 10 minutes early. It was a beautiful spring day—sunny, maybe 75—and Pittsburghers were enjoying the rare combination of blue skies and warmth. My appointment was for 2:00, and with neither orange construction barrels nor snow to slow it down, my bus arrived on Liberty Avenue around 1:30, which gave me the chance to stroll through Market Square and back and enabled me to remember that Pittsburgh women actually did possess legs. Strolling through the Square, I struck up a conversation with one of its regulars—a homeless man named Spice, whom I hadn't seen since graduating months earlier. I fully expected him to be there, on his usual park bench, feeding the pigeons and scaring the humans. Spice, however, upon seeing me, acted like I had just returned from a good war.

"Niiiick," he yelled as I turned the corner past the "O." I waved, and as I got closer, a twinge of guilt surged through me. I saw Spice practically every day for four years and never noticed how bedraggled he looked—his salt-and-pepper beard, bare in some spots but out of control in others; his tattered winter coat, half its collar gone, one of its sleeves seemingly defying gravity. He looked ghastly, yet he was in better spirits than I was. And his two cats, Pete and Friday, looked as healthy and disinterested as ever.

"Where the hell you been, man?" he asked me. "I figured you got some fancy job elsewheres."

"No, I'm just about ready to join you on this bench if I don't get a job soon," I said.

"No can do, Nick. Seat's got a waiting list longer than the one for Steeler tickets," Spice said.

He laughed, as always, heartily at his own jokes, which caused people walking by to stare at him—and at us. I long passed the point of caring what people thought when they saw us. That wasn't always the case. I first met Spice my freshman year of college, when I was a scared 18-year-old and found myself living in the dorms of Sharper College, in the heart of downtown.

My family moved me into my dorm the Saturday before Labor Day, and the next morning, I woke up hungry and had to venture outside because the school's kitchen wasn't going to open until Tuesday. I went to McDonald's because it was close—my goal was to avoid encounters with anyone or anything—and the only other person in the place was a gentleman in a long, gray winter coat hunched over the counter.

I stood about five feet from him, weighing my breakfast options, when a cute young woman cheerily asked the other patron what he would like. "How much for a blowjob?" the man asked before laughing out loud, clapping his hands, and departing. I was trying not to join him in his mirth, but at the same time, I felt terrified.

"What would you-you like, sir?" the young woman then asked me. The nonexistent side of me wanted to either a)play the scene like James Bond and utter something that would 1)defuse the tension, 2)make her chuckle, 3)get her phone number, all in an effort to 4)get what the homeless guy ordered; or b)mouth something crude, like, "No, really, how much do blowjobs cost, and shouldn't they be called 'McBlowjobs?'"

But the realistic side of me chose option "c," which was this: I muttered "Egg McMuffin" without making eye contact, hurried out the door, and looked both ways before proceeding to make sure the crazy bum was nowhere near. I made it back to my room, ate, and read the paper, hoping such encounters wouldn't become a regular part of my life.

A few weeks later, walking through Market Square, I heard a voice yelling, "Hey, blue shirt, get over here." I kept on walking, and the voice kept yelling, "Blue shirt, stop." I walked a few feet more before realizing that I was wearing a blue shirt. I looked around, and there was Mickey D's patron of the month, sprawled out on a bench, with the requisite brown bag at his feet. I froze.

"That was rude—what I done the other day," he said. He had genuine remorse in his eyes, but had it not been the middle of the day, with hundreds of people around, I would have run like hell. I got closer.

"Listen—you're a young boy, and I don't want to set a bad example for you," he continued. "That's no way to talk to a pretty young lady. You hear?"

"Y-yes, sir, I hear you," I said. "Thanks."

"The name's Spice. You got a name?"

My first reaction was to make up a name—Steve Austin, Michael J. Fox—whatever. But then I realized there was no danger in telling a vagrant my first name, so I mumbled "Nick."

"Nick, glad to meet you. This here is Pete and Friday."

I was confused for a second and then assumed the worst. In the minute or two I was standing there, I stared straight ahead without moving my head an inch. Now, I figured if I looked down, Homeless Guy would be Pantsless Guy. Before seeing the two kittens playing on the bench, I pretty much assumed he had named his balls.

"Kittens," I said, a little too excitedly. I had never been so happy to see kittens in all my life.

"You must be one of Pittsburgh's finest, Nick."

"No, actually, I'm—

"I'm kidding, dummy. I have moments—like in McDonald's. That was a moment, wasn't it?" Spice chuckled.

"I guess you could say that." I had nothing else to say, and I really wanted to leave. I started moving slowly backwards.

"You have a good day, son," he said. "Be on your way now."

I feebly waved at him and his kittens and carried on.

"By the looks of it," Spice said, "you either got yourself a job, or you're trying to get yourself a job."

"Trying, Spice. Place called Mousetrap, Inc."

"Never heard of it. What do they do—extermination work?"

"Sort of—they kill people's dreams," I said.

"That what you went to school for, Nick?"

"No, but I gotta do something." I sat down. "Something bad is better than good for nothing."

Spice looked at me approvingly. "I like that—'better than good for nothing.' Well, go get 'em, man. But stop by before you go home, all right?"

"Yeah, no problem." I gave him a punch on the shoulder, slipped a fiver in his pocket, patted the cats on their heads, and went on my way.

Mousetrap, Inc. occupied the top four floors of the Penn-Liberty Building, which sat on the corner of Penn and 10th Street. It was a stately building, almost 100 years old, and a few years earlier, much to the chagrin of area architects and historians, Andrea commissioned a local artist to change the gargoyle that rested outside her window into a mousegoyle. The city's Historic Preservation committee did all it could to prevent the desecration, but Andrea was at her spellbinding best when she appeared before City Council, and, once again, she got her way.

It was my first introduction to Andrea. The local media covered "Mousegate" with the intensity usually reserved for kidnappings and post-office shootouts, and Andrea did all she could to feed the monster. She got her picture in the papers day after day, and though far from beautiful, with her long red hair, her designer dresses, and her ever-present cigarette, she possessed nearly all the characteristics of an ugly beauty. Not in the present—after all, she was in her early 60s—but at one time, no doubt, Andrea Bianco was the kind of girl whose popularity with boys baffled other girls. "But she's sooo ugly," the girls would say behind

6

her back, or, knowing young girls, to her face. Her teeth were crooked, her hair always needed a thorough brushing and her body was nothing spectacular. Yet every male she's ever met has instantly known one thing about Andrea Bianco: She'd throw you a good one.

And the press loved her because she was always quotable. "Oh, heaven forfend we alter the beauty of a gargoyle," she would say. On another occasion, when a reporter asked her if she felt any remorse altering the original design of the building, she said, "I believe in progress. With change comes progress. My granddaughter picked up a black disk at my house last week and asked me what it was. I told her it was an album. Blank stare. I explained to her that albums were old-folk versions of CDs. She was amazed!" And another time, a radio talk-show host asked her if she was concerned about the proposed mousegoyle being larger than the building's gargoyles. "I have a reputation for making things get bigger," she said, causing the host to laugh uncomfortably.

As I approached the building, I couldn't decide what horrified me more: getting a job offer or not getting a job offer. On the one hand, I craved a job like a Boy Scout yearns for a merit badge. But I couldn't erase the moral dilemma that existed concerning my prospective employer. I pulled open the door, took a deep breath, and entered the next chapter in my life.

I ARRIVED ON THE ninth floor about five minutes before my interview and spent my time admiring the artwork that adorned the drab gray walls. Above the framed images were the bronzed words "A Gallery of Success." And to the side of each picture, like the placarded explanations in an art museum, was a brief description of each success:

- *Luck o' the Lottery Scratcher:* Want to scratch that gambling itch but can't find a coin? Toss one of these in your wallet or purse and watch your luck change! Invented by Marge Hecker of Portland, Maine, this shamrock-shaped scratcher has sold over 5,600 units since 1987.

- *Toasty Pet:* Bob Simpson of Eugene, Oregon, got tired of sharing a bed with his 100-pound Lab on cold winter nights. His solution: a round bed with a heating element designed for pets everywhere. No more "three dog nights" for Bob!

- *CountRope:* Emily Stromski of Roanoke, Virginia, couldn't help her mind from wandering when she exercised. "I would always lose track when I jumped rope," she confesses. And then one day, it hit her: "What if I could incorporate a counting mechanism into the rope?" Now her mind can wander onto other great inventions while she jumps rope.

I was all set to read about The Hinge Binge when a tousle-haired guy, two or three years my senior, approached me. "Admiring our gallery, huh?" he said. He was a few inches taller than me, and I gathered instantly that though he was smiling, this man wanted to be elsewhere, anywhere.

"You must be Nick," he said.

"Uh, yes, I am," I sputtered. "You're Mr. Wiatt?"

"Oh, please. Call me Sam. This is an informal"—he emphasized the word as though he were describing a hillbilly wedding—"setting, and we all call each other by first name. Come this way, please."

Sam led me through a maze of offices and cubicles. I couldn't help but sneak a glimpse at an incredibly built blonde dressed more for a night of clubbing than a day of working. Her tight skirt rested several inches above her tanned knees, and as we approached, she bent over slightly to point something out to a coworker. This prompted my second look. Unfortunately, as I was in mid-gawk, Aphrodite caught me. I found myself showered in her sneer.

Finally, we reached Sam's office. The graphics department was tucked away in a far corner of the building. His office was spacious, and it featured a bank of windows that overlooked the Convention Center. On his credenza were the usual office belongings—a picture of an attractive woman I presumed was his wife, a photo of some young children, a signed baseball—but I also noticed some framed abstract artwork. All I know about art could fit on the tip of a pencil, but to me, this work looked intriguing.

Up the hallway from Sam's office were two facing offices. One was unoccupied, and in the other resided a woman my age working at a computer. She nodded in our direction, and Sam gave her a quick hello wave.

Though I hadn't been interviewed yet, my feelings toward the job had improved greatly because of Sam's ambivalent feelings about the company and the hideaway location of the department. My mood brightened considerably; I had found home.

"So," Sam asked, "what do you know about us?"

The question threw me. He asked me as though he were a cheating spouse coming clean. What was he going to follow up with—"When did you find out" and "How much did you see"?

"Well," I said, "I've seen your commercial I don't know how many times. It seems like an interesting industry."

"Be honest—what do you think of the commercial?" he asked.

I chuckled for what seemed like five minutes in order to come up with an answer that would be funny but not insulting. My extended chuckle, however, did me no good.

"Well, it certainly is, um . . ."

"Cheesy?" Sam said.

"No, no," I protested, "I wouldn't say that. Not at all. It gets the point across."

"It does. Exactly. We try to make people's dreams a reality, and it would be foolish of us to waste an exorbitant amount of money on a polished commercial," Sam said.

He said this so perfunctorily that I glanced at his desk to look for a 3x5 card.

He then asked me a series of standard interview questions, and he responded to most of my answers with a disinterested "Good, good" before explaining to me what the position entailed. My job, if I were the candidate chosen, would be to write product descriptions for the New Product Reports (NPRs) that they sent unrequested to product manufacturers.

Sam walked over to the "in" bin on the corner of the credenza and handed me a three-page form with an illustration stapled to the front.

"This will be the writing portion of your interview," he said. "You've done well on the prelims, but this test will account for 65, 68, possibly even 70 percent of your final grade.

"I want you to write the copy for what Carl Wexford of Terre Haute calls 'The MediTimer.' Good luck."

He left me alone, and before plunging into a description, I perused Mr. Wexford's application. It saddened and disgusted me, and I had half a mind to run out of the building. But I really needed a job, and Sam seemed like a good guy. Plus, as I was sitting there, contemplating my decision, the tanned, blond goddess walked past the door. As soon as I realized who it was, I shot my eyes down. Even though I was staring at the carpet, I knew she was smiling.

"Her name's Missy, she works out eight days a week, she's married to a bodybuilder, and you don't have a chance," Sam said as he poked his head back in. "In case you were wondering, I mean." He was smiling.

"Thanks. It's not my place, but don't most companies have dress codes?"

"This isn't most companies," Sam said. "You'll find that out when you start. I mean, if."

At Sam's verbal gaffe, I knew the job was mine if I didn't screw up the product description. I got to work.

From Carl Wexford's application: *The MediTimer will help people from dying by mistake. My mother is 88 years old, and she needs something to make sure she remembers to take all her pills. She takes seven pills, and Jesse and I can't always be there to make sure she takes them. My device will have a lot of slots and a loud alarm for her to hear it. Thank you.*

There you have it. And what was Mr. Carl Wexford of Terre Haute paying Mousetrap to pursue his invention? A cool $8,500. I wanted to cry. I wanted to run. I wanted to bang Missy through Chinese New Year. But what I really wanted was a paycheck. I picked up my pen:

"Medications can do wonderful things—but only if you remember to take them. How many times have you—or an aging loved one—forgotten to take your pills? With the MediTimer, you'll have one fewer thing to worry about. Capable of holding up to a dozen different pills, this revolutionary device will let you know when it's time for your medication by sounding an alarm. It's as easy as setting a clock. And it could save your life."

I handed it to Sam, we shook hands, and he said he'd contact me within a week. I felt good, but in a negative way. I left the building without scoring the Missy trifecta. On the bus ride home, I remembered that I was supposed to say goodbye to Spice.

MY HEAD WAS HALFWAY through the front door when I heard my mother say, "How'd it go, honey?" I finished my entrance and said, "I think it went well, but who knows?"

"Oh, you didn't get it, did you?" she said at the same instant my father was entering from the garage.

"You didn't get it? They told you on the spot?" my father said.

"No, I don't know if I got it. They'll call me," I said.

"But it doesn't look good, I guess, huh?" my father said.

I wanted to sprint headfirst into the fridge and end it all, but I took a deep breath and tried to explain that a)The interview went well and b) I think I got it. Over dinner (ditalini with meat sauce, braciole and garlic bread), I told them about the interview (minus the Missy parts) and that I had some moral reservations about the company.

"You're not going to take it?" my father asked.

"No, I'm not saying that, Dad. It's just seems that what they do is borderline immoral."

"It's a job, honey. Everyone has to start somewhere," said my mother.

"You'll make it honest work, Nick," said my father.

I had been unemployed for six months. In my father's eyes, this was akin to being a serial killer or a Republican. Even my mother would occasionally wonder aloud, "Did we do something wrong?"

My father began working around the same time he began walking. This was in Italy, in his father's cabinet shop. Dad came to this country in the late fifties, and in my lifetime, I never remember him taking a day off, except for a family funeral. My six months of unemployment simply baffled him. In college, I had a steady stream of jobs and internships, and I was even editor of my school newspaper. Seeing my name—which was also his name; I was a junior—in print made him proud. But all those years of goodwill I had built up were razed by my current situation. I was enduring Nixon-during-Watergate levels of popularity in the Adano household.

For the next few days, every time the phone·rang, my heart raced with anticipation. Usually it was an annoying relative or an even more annoying telemarketer. Finally, three days after my interview, Sam called to offer me the job. I accepted without any hesitation, and we agreed that I would start the following Monday. After six months of doing nothing, I finally could relax for a few days.

DAY ONE OF MY new life began with a thunderclap. The storm was of the typical spring variety—brief and fierce. Unfortunately, it didn't cease until I was on the bus. My mother's ironing was for naught, but at least I had time to dry off before arriving at the office. I informed the receptionist of my arrival, and she told me that Missy would be right with me.

Believe it or not, I had forgotten about Missy the past few days. But there she was, approaching me with a manila folder and beckoning me into her lair. I followed her but had to strain my head to make eye contact. Of course, as I followed her up the hallway, I had no trouble gluing my eyes to her backside. Sheathed in a painted-on lavender skirt, I hasten to add. She also was wearing lavender stockings and matching lavender shoes.

I sat down in her office, still embarrassed about our first meeting. I tried smiling, but when I consciously think "I must smile now," I end up looking like a singer in a televangelist's choir.

"Look," she said. "Do you think I'd work out so much if I didn't want men to peek?" She winked and then chuckled.

"No, no, I, me, wouldn't"—she let me stammer for a few more seconds—"I just, it was, me, wrong." Without warning, I had turned into Tarzan.

Somehow, I regained my composure, apologized and filled out the paperwork. "There are two types of guys I worry about," Missy continued. "The ones who don't look and the ones who are too smooth to get caught."

"Thank you," I wanted to say, "for noticing that I'm an inept heterosexual."

When I reached the graphics department, I was formally introduced to Rachel, who couldn't stop laughing with Sam about a product proposal. It was for a perpetual-motion machine, and, apparently, it wasn't the first time some genius had submitted this as an invention idea.

"I set aside these NPRs, Nick," Sam explained. "I'm a collector."

Sam went on to explain that they get at least eight of these a year, each one funnier than the last.

"This one's powered in part by bat guano, and I think it shoots with a bullet up to second place all time," he said.

"Dare I ask what's in first place?" I said.

Sam looked at Rachel, and they both suppressed their laughter.

"In due time, son," Sam said as he headed back to his office.

"Oh, before I forget," Sam said as he spun around. "We'd like to take you to lunch, this being your first day. Sound good with you?"

"Of course," I said.

"Cool. I have a meeting to attend, so why don't you meet with Rachel, and she'll explain the procedure."

Rachel was maybe a year older than me and quite attractive, but in an approachable way. Her short, curly hair accented her crescent face, and her lithe, athletic body was highlighted by her pianist's hands.

"Welcome aboard," she said to me with a smile.

"Thanks. You been here long?"

"About 15 months. Sam's great. It's a lot of fun."

"That's great."

If there's anything I'm worse at than small talk, especially with someone I barely know, I don't want to find out what it is. It's moments such as these that I actively wish for tornadoes to strike, for terrorists to invade, for Jesus to return, for me to suffer a massive heart attack.

"So," I continued, "you like it here?"

"It pays the bills. Why don't I give you a quick tour, and then I'll go over what your role in the department is, okay?"

We spent the next 15 minutes walking around the office, where I was called "new guy" no fewer than a dozen times ("Hey, New Guy") and was told "Welcome aboard" closer to 20 times. A few of these overlapped. ("Hey, welcome aboard, New Guy.")

The only people who made an impression were the attractive (Elaine, a lovely brunette with a plump rack and a smile so kind and inviting that I nearly proposed marriage. I believe she worked in research, but to be honest, I stopped paying attention after "Hi. I'm Elaine") and the grotesque (a salesman named Sheldon, who by the looks of it, slept in his clothes and was in desperate need of upgrading to the next size. I was waiting to be assaulted by the buttons of his soon-to-be exploding shirt.)

When Rachel and I returned to my office, she began explaining to me how I would be spending my days. She had prepared a memo:

1. A prospective client calls our 800 number or reaches us by mail.

2. Mousetrap sends out Information Packet to prospective client. This Packet contains some promotional brochures and endorsements from satisfied clients, plus a form that allows the potential client to explain his/her product.

3. Andrea reviews each form and gives a thumbs-up or thumbs-down.

4. The accepted forms are turned over to the sales department. A salesperson contacts each prospective client to discuss rates, chance of success, etc.

5. When a new client agrees and fills out the necessary paperwork, the sales coordinator brings us all information pertaining to the new client's invention.

6. I create a graphic image, based on the client's information, of what the invention looks like.

7. It will be your job to describe the invention.

8. The copy and graphic are then combined in the New Product Report (NPR), which is then sent to appropriate potential manufacturers after the research department does its work.

Rachel expanded on the above items and gave me a great overview of what was expected of me. Our entire conversation was conducted so professionally that I actually felt like a real, live adult for the first time in my life. She then showed me how to use the phone, the fax, and the copier, and before we knew it, Sam returned and told us it was lunchtime. The first morning of my first day on my first real job was complete, and I was so overcome with manly feelings that I had to suppress the urge to pat someone on the back and proclaim, "Great job on the Patterson account, Jim" as we departed for lunch.

We went to a little hoagie joint on Liberty Avenue, around the corner from our office, called Big Lou's Hoagies. Behind the counter, appropriately enough, was Big Lou himself. Lou's nickname was not one of those ironic monikers. No, Lou weighed about 350 pounds, and though the place wasn't that small, Lou's girth made everyone unconsciously gasp for sweet oxygen.

The far wall was lined with autographed pictures of celebrities and local sports heroes who had supped at Big Lou's. Granted, these often weren't the A-list celebrities ("Great grub, Lou!"—Scott Baio; "I pity the fool who don't like hoagies!"—Mr. T.) but the pictures added the right charm to the grease pit. And besides, where else could you find a picture of Mr. Rogers ("You're a great neighbor!"—Fred) next to a picture of Madonna with her stomach exposed and her hand dipping past the waistband of her unbuttoned jeans ("Great freakin' place!"—Madonna)?

"What'll it be, losers?" Lou asked us.

"Like you don't know, genius?" Sam responded.

"Ah, go to hell already. You got a new guy with you. What am I, a goddamn psychic?"

Lou laughed at his own joke and lit a fresh cigarette. "So, new guy, what'll it be? Are these questions too fucking hard?"

"Um, I'll have the steak hoagie with onions," I said.

"Fries, pal?"

"Uh, no, that's all right."

"No fries? What are you, a homo? Jesus, Sam, you guys hiring homos now?"

Apparently, in Lou's World, not ordering fries with your hoagie was tantamount to sodomy.

"Give him a break, Lou. It's his first day."

"Ah, his first day. You know what I did on my first day of the first job I had?" Lou was asking me.

"I have no idea."

"I fucked my boss for three hours!"

During this whole conversation, the other patrons, all regulars, were encouraging Lou's shtick by laughing at his every attempt of humor. They all seemed to be enjoying my hazing tremendously.

"So," I said, "I guess you don't get fries with your hoagies, either."

Suddenly, the only sound in the joint was the sizzling of the meat on the skillets. I stood up to Lou on my first visit and had upset the balance of nature.

"My boss, homo, was a lady," Lou said. He got to within an inch of my face, gently slapped it twice, and then said, "Well, she was a lady till she met me!"

He roared with laughter, and everyone was allowed to resume breathing. I passed the test. I had been accepted into Lou's fraternity, and I would henceforth be greeted as "Homo" every time I ate at Lou's.

The hoagie was delicious and dripping grease, and Sam and Rachel had their usual—a Monte Cristo that they shared. Imagine making a Dagwood Bumstead sandwich and then deep-frying it. That's a Monte Cristo. They also split an order of fries, and after tasting one, I never again made the mistake of not ordering fries with my hoagie.

"I was gonna warn you about Lou," Sam said as he bit into his deep-fried decadence, "but nobody warned me, and I didn't want to deny you the pleasure. You handled it brilliantly, by the way."

Rachel nodded in agreement, her mouth too busy to speak.

"So, how's the first day treating you?" asked Sam.

"Everything's great—pretty much what I expected, I guess," I said. As I looked around, I saw grease literally running down the chins of nearly every client. It was like watching a nature special where bears load up on fat before their long hibernation.

"Well, if it isn't Needle-dick and Ass-breath!" bellowed Lou as two middle-aged suits walked in.

"See?" said Sam. "It could be worse than 'Homo.'"

"I feel lucky," I said. "So, Rachel, I'm almost afraid to ask, but what name did Lou stick to you?"

"Ah," Sam said before Rachel could respond. "That's the beauty part. Lou is nothing if not a gentleman."

"'Pretty Lady,'" said Rachel.

"Lou's nickname for you is 'Pretty Lady'?"

"Yep."

I wasn't quite sure how to respond to this. If I laughed, it may have implied that I felt Rachel was a Hideous Monster, which wasn't true in the least. But if I indicated that I agreed, it would seem that I was making a play.

"That's sweet," I said. It went over well, which is to say that the subject was dropped without any further discussion.

Sam picked up the tab, and we departed to the sounds of Lou screaming, "See ya, Loser, Homo . . . and Pretty Lady!" His voice went from gruff to late-night deejay at "Pretty Lady."

It was such a perfect spring day that Sam suggested we take a walk up Liberty instead of going straight back. We agreed (what the hell was I going to say?), and we took a walk past the porn shops that lined a good chunk of the broad avenue before hanging a right on Seventh and heading back to the office.

I was glad to see Rachel not blanch at the sight of Ye Olde Pornne Shoppes, and the three of us were laughing so much that it felt like they had been my co-workers for years.

"You drew the mousegoyle!" I yelled at Sam, as he regaled me with the inside scoop of "Mousegate."

"Damn straight I did," Sam said. "And not just once, friend. Andrea was never satisfied. I did mousegoyle profiles, I did action mousegoyles. I even drew up a mousegoyle holding an American flag."

We finally arrived back at the office, and I was ready to help bring the dreams of our clients to life.

Client: Lenora Hockstader

Idea: Cabinet Cards

I quickly scanned Ms. Hockstader's form. She was a retired schoolteacher, and she wanted to bring the concept of baseball cards to presidential cabinet positions. My immediate thought was that this wasn't the most marketable idea ("Hey! I'll trade you a John Foster Dulles for an Andrew Mellon!"), but I was being paid for a service. So I began.

Ah, the joys of summer and childhood. Hitting the swimming pool . . . chasing the ice-cream truck . . . and opening up that first pack of baseball cards. Here's a card collectible that will educate as well as entertain. The idea is called Cabinet Cards, and each card features the image of a former or current presidential cabinet member. On the back are the vitals: name of administration served in, time of service, and other pertinent facts about the cabinet member. Perfect for educational settings, these cards could also become hot collectibles for kids of all ages.

Product Highlights:

- *Educational*
- *Instant familiarity with concept of sports cards*
- *Fun*
- *May appeal to children and adults*

I noticed that Rachel had drawn an image of Alexander Haig for the NPR. There was Al, in a suit, directing a meeting while a bunch of other suits gave Al their undivided attention. On the back, Rachel listed his career accomplishments. I hoped that she had taken the route of baseball-card designers from the seventies, who often included some inconsequential fact about a ballplayer on the back of cards ("Johnny Bench once ate a pizza at second base in Double-A ball!") with an accompanying cartoon drawing (you'd see Johnny standing at second base with a slice in his hands). Of course, she played it straight. ("Al Haig once declared himself president!")

I put our information in Sam's bin and picked up my next assignment: Choco-Rogies.

Client: Mike Sapulsky

Idea: Choco-Rogies

Mr. Sapulsky took the idea of the pierogi and substituted potatoes with "my secret chocolate sauce recipe. I'm also working on a secret peanut-butter sauce, and I may soon branch out into the fruits–secret banana sauce, secret strawberry sauce. I'm also concocting something I like to call 'secret secret' sauce."

Mr. Sapulsky was kind enough to include pictures of various family members and friends beaming at the camera while they ate his treats.

"My friends and family can't get enough of these things," his letter continued. "So I figured, why be so selfish? I want the world to enjoy these things."

This idea made Cabinet Cards seem visionary, but I started writing.

Mmm . . . a rich, velvety chocolate sauce . . . enveloped by a tasty, flaky dough that melts in your mouth? Who wouldn't love that? Served warm or room temperature (they're even great straight from the fridge!), Choco-Rogies bring a new idea to an ethnic favorite. Perfect for a holiday dessert, ideal for an after-school snack, Choco-Rogies will bring a smile to chocolate lovers everywhere.

Product Highlights:

- *Innovative twist on ethnic classic*
- *Great for chocoholics*
- *Line can be expanded to other flavors*

Sam poked his head into my office.

"Nice work on Cabinet Cards, Nick. It looks good to me. Why don't you run this up to Elaine in research so those folks can do whatever it is they do, okay?"

My brain started to turn: Elaine . . . firm breasts . . . nice smile. "You bet," I said, as I quickly grabbed the info from Sam's hands and made my way to research.

I rode the elevator up to the ninth floor, walked through the double doors, exchanged glances with people I had met earlier in the morning (and got a few more "Hey, New Guy" greetings), and finally found my way to Elaine's office. It was decorated in typical nice-girl fashion. A few plants lined the windowsills. There were pictures of nephews and nieces in polite frames on her desk. And, saddest of all, in the corner of her desk sat a Family Circus calendar.

"Hey, Nick!" she said. "What brings you here?"

"I have this NPR for you, and Sam asked me to bring it up," I said.

"That's super. Let's have a look."

And here's the weird part: Elaine, owner of well-kept flowering plants and a Family Circus calendar (did I mention the cat-doing-the-chin-up poster on the far wall?), bent over to procure the NPR from my hands. In doing so, she gave me a wonderful shot of her plump globes. It was fleeting, and when she sat back down, she continued her happy-girl talk as though nothing had happened. Obviously, I had to go along with this façade, as well.

"Well, hey, I better get back downstairs," I said.

"Everything looks good here," she said. "I'll be sure to pass this along!"

I took the steps back down to the second floor. Jogging down seven flights of stairs took care of my thoughts and the accompanying protuberance.

"Everything go well upstairs?" Sam asked upon my return.

"Yep," I said. He was laughing in his eyes, but we weren't nearly close enough to have an honest conversation yet.

"Glad to hear it," he said.

I was just starting my next invention (a perfume called Amore) when Sam yelled, "Quittin' time!"

It was 5:10, and I was exhausted, the way I felt after the first day of school. I said my goodbyes, headed toward my bus, then figured I'd better check on Spice.

I walked up Liberty and into Market Square. There, on his favorite bench, was Spice, holding court with two of his pals. He saw me approaching and let out the trademark "Niiiick" yell.

"Hey, Spice. How you been?"

"You're looking all spiffy. Got work?"

"Yeah, I said. "That job I interviewed for? Today was my first day."

"You were supposed to visit me that day you interviewed," Spice reminded me.

"Sorry, I plumb forgot."

"That's all right. Wasn't like I had pearls of wisdom for you, son."

I felt bad. "So, really, how have you been?"

"Great. It's spring now. This is the easy time of year. Hey, now that you're a bigshot, don't forget your old friends, you hear?"

"I'm no bigshot, Spice. And I'll visit as often as I can."

We shook hands. I gave his associates friendly nods and headed home.

THE BUS RIDE WAS uneventful. In the 40 minutes it took to get home, I scanned the sports page (the Pirates won last night, the Steelers expressed hope about their draft picks, the Pens vowed to make the playoffs soon), associated dirty dialogue with a severe-looking brunette sitting three rows up from me ("Let me help you with that uncomfortable-looking bulge, Mr. Adano . . .") and watched a well-endowed blonde in a short, tight skirt sitting in the back corner fall asleep numerous times. Every time she nodded off, she lost control of her motor skills, and I couldn't help but watch as her skirt rode higher with each bout of sleep. I also viewed every other guy in the vicinity sneaking a peek. Gentleman that I am, next time Sleepy Sue started getting heavy in the eyes, I ruffled my paper loud enough for her to hear. She perked up and casually fixed her skirt. I hated to put an end to such free entertainment, but it felt like the right thing to do.

I opened the front door and was greeted with the parental press conference.

"How was your first day, honey?" asked Mom.

"So, do you like it there?" asked Dad.

"Are the people nice there?"

"They treating you okay?"

"Did you eat lunch?"

"How was the bus ride?"

"Yes, everything went well," I said, finally putting their barrage to a halt. "They seem very nice. The bus ride was fine. Hey, eggplant parmigiana."

"Your mother makes your favorite for one day of work. I've been working since I was 5. What do I get?"

"Yeah, keep talking. Your father ate half the casserole, honey. I don't think he minded so much."

Both my parents had the habit of talking as though the other weren't in the room.

"Oh, and Nicole called," said my mother. "I told her you weren't home from work yet. It felt so good to say that, honey."

Nicole. My on-again, off-again girlfriend. We dated since our second year of college, and until I found myself out of work, I always thought she was the one. We did everything together, worked on the school paper together and were a great match. And then I lost my job, and things started to fray.

Soon after graduating, I landed a job in the school's alumni affairs department. I worked for a woman named Liz Greenwall, who possessed the dual misfortune of being mean and incompetent. Nonetheless, she and I tolerated each other, largely because I needed a job, and she needed my services. I put together the alumni newsletter, organized alumni outings, and dealt with any problems and suggestions the alums had. The pay sucked, but it took care of the bills until something better came along. Then in December, the school decided that my job could be filled with a couple interns, who would work for free. Merry Christmas, Nick!

So I became unemployed. In the best of circumstances, it's not easy finding a job in December. Throw in a recession, and what you're left with is an unemployed young man whose popularity is going the way of the Hula Hoop.

"So, what did you do today?" was often Nicole's opening line during our tortured phone conversations.

My responses vacillated between anger ("Take a fucking guess, Nic") to sarcasm ("The Pens are looking for a new coach, so I figured I'd throw my hat in the ring") to self-pity ("Scanned the want ads, didn't see anything good, took a nap.") Apparently, I never offered the right answer, or perhaps she would have stopped asking.

I ate dinner, read the local paper, and gave Nicole a call.

"Hey."

"Hey, how was your first day?"

"It went better than expected, actually. Sam and Rachel seem really nice. We ate lunch at this bizarre hoagie joint."

"Where was that?"

"You know on Liberty, that little triangle of buildings. It's one of those. I guess we never had the courage to walk in."

"Oh, you mean by the sponge place?"

"Yeah, and that scary-looking porn shop with the green windows. Big Lou's."

"That's cool. So, did you actually do anything, or was it just filling out paperwork?"

"No, I did real work. I wrote up descriptions for a couple of stupid inventions. Met the staff. Saw Spice on the way home."

"Jesus. How is he?"

"I think he's getting worse, actually. But he seemed happy because it's finally warm."

Nicole never felt comfortable around Spice, but I know she always admired me for befriending him. She admired me for a lot of reasons before I became unemployed, and I was going to have to work like hell to get her respect back. But she was worth it.

"Well, I had a rough day, so I think I'm going to head off to bed, Nick."

"That's cool. When am I going to see you?"

"I don't know. Friday, I guess. What are we doing?"

"Beats the hell out of me. Catch a movie, grab some dinner. Think about it, okay?"

"Okay. Good night."

At least we were still talking. We had broken up at least twice during my unemployment. (There was a third breakup, but it was over so quickly that I can't honestly count it). I was determined to be the best damn copy-writer in the universe, even if it was for a company whose morality was, at best, questionable.

By my second day, the New Guy greetings diminished sharply, and I was addressed as Nick or "Hey," as in "Hey, how's it going?" I poked my head in Sam's office, gave him a wave, and continued with my next invention, something called "Amore."

Client: Vince Olsen

Idea: Amore

Mr. Olsen's submission offered a breakthrough in the world of fragrances. His idea? Combine the usual perfume scents with those from the culinary world. "After all," his letter explained, "I don't know any guy who likes the smell of flowers. To me, nothing beats the smell of a hunk of meat basting in some nice rosemary or basil. To me, that's love. Or, as the foreigners might say, 'amore.'"

Who doesn't love the smell of oregano, curry, rosemary, and other spices? Well, why limit their use to the kitchen? With Amore, you can smell as great as last night's dinner! The right blend of cooking spices mixed with a hint of flowers and honey makes for a most unique fragrance. But be careful you don't put it on your pot roast!

Product Highlights:

- *Unique fragrance for the modern woman*
- *Appeals to men, unlike most traditional scents*
- *Could be sold at upscale food markets*

No, it couldn't, actually. Two days into the job, and I was on my way to becoming an accomplished liar. "Honey, could you pick up some brie on the way home? Oh, and get me a bottle of that Amore, too. I want to smell like dinner . . . just for you." Vince needed counseling. Instead, he was giving us $8,500 to help bring his dream to the marketplace. The thing is, I knew this product—and the ones I worked on yesterday—were never, ever, under any circumstance going to be sold to the public. These were either stupid ideas or ideas whose time would never come. Still, after I passed my work on to Sam, he gave me his OK, and I was given the green light to make another trip to see Elaine. Any moral qualms I had were immediately given a respite.

"Hey, Nick. What have you brought me this time?" said Elaine. She was wearing a conservative white blouse, buttoned to her neck, and a blue skirt that went several inches past her knees. No show today.

"I have 'Amore.' I mean, that's what the product's called."

"Yeah, I figured." She laughed. "Sit down. I need to check something."

As I sat there, waiting for her while she rummaged through her file cabinet, I saw that she had taken off her shoes and was moving her right foot back and forth toward me, each time crinkling her toes as though she were waving at me with her feet. Then, as soon as she found what she was looking for, she spun around, took the file from my hands, and acted as if everything were normal, like I somehow didn't notice her foot dance.

Oh, and today's Family Circus calendar featured a panel drawn by Billy. It was filled with Billy's famous malaprops, like "Ronald Raygun." Do you have any idea how weird it is to witness a foot come-on and a Family Circus cartoon in the same field of vision?

I made it back from the ninth floor and picked up my next assignment, SpeakerPlanters.

Client: Liz Orosco

Idea: SpeakerPlanters

Ms. Orosco hates the giant stereo speakers that her doofus husband insisted on buying. She says they "ugly up the house," and she thinks she has the solution.

Don't you hate big, boxy stereo speakers? Are you tired of how they clutter up your living room or den? Don't you wish there were a way for you to get great stereo sound without sacrificing design? Well, now you can—with SpeakerPlanters. This great idea enables any homeowner to disguise those huge speakers with beautiful plants and flowers. Simply treat SpeakerPlanters like any planter—add your favorite flowers and greenery. Inside, the speaker unit works the same as any standard speaker. What about watering? Not a problem. Inside the speaker unit lays a protective wooden panel that will prevent water from ever touching the components.

Product Highlights:

- *Beautifies any home*
- *Doesn't affect speaker quality*
- *Appeals to anyone who owns a stereo system*

I began to realize that client submissions would fall largely into two categories: just plain stupid or pointless. SpeakerPlanters fell into the latter category. It wasn't an awful idea, yet who in his right mind would want stereo speakers that double as a begonia pot?

Over the next several months, my life became that of a regular adult. I put in my eight hours, went home, ate dinner, went to bed, woke up, and began the cycle anew. On weekends, I went out with Nicole (things had improved greatly between us—so much, in fact, that she mentioned weddings every chance she had). And Sam, Rachel and I had become quite the team in the few months we worked together. One day, after completing my work on Ink Well, which consisted of a tub of ink that the inventor promised would refill any pen at a fraction of the cost of buying a new cartridge, Sam asked me if I wanted to join him for a beer.

"Ever been to the Steel Pussycat, Nick?" he asked.

"Oh, yeah, but I had to wait till my senior year. I finally turn 21, right? It's a Saturday, we start drinking—well, we never stopped drinking from Friday night. So some pals and I hit the Cat around 6:00, and what do I do? You'll never guess."

"Uh, got signed up to perform? Attacked a dancer? What?"

"Threw up. On the stage. Missed the two lovely ladies who were performing by inches. I literally got thrown out. I mean, literally. The 400-pound bouncer picked me up and threw me on the pavement."

"But your buddies stayed?"

"Well, they poked their heads out the door long enough to laugh at me, but, yeah, the assholes stayed."

"So, is there a picture of you on a wall with a red slash through it, dude?"

"No, I made my triumphant return a few weeks after the incident. I gave each of the ladies a red rose and apologized. They thought it was cute."

"They thought nearly vomiting on them was cute?"

"No, the fact that I was apologizing. Have you ever tried appearing humble in front of a naked babe who's virtually a stranger, Sam?"

"Can't say that I have. So, anyway, you wanna head over there and grab a beer?"

"You're married. Karen won't allow it," I said.

"And who's gonna tell her? I can fire you, you know." He laughed.

I hadn't been inside the Cat since the night before I graduated college. And to be honest, strip joints weren't my favorite places in the world. They always reminded me of chewing gum. Initially, there's a burst of intense flavor. But within minutes, the flavor evaporates, and what you're left with is monotony. Gentlemen, put your hands together for Candy . . . for Sherri . . . for Juicy Fruit . . . for Keisha . . . for the Doublemint Twins . . .

Still, the boss was buying me a beer. Why argue?

"You've really done some good work for us, Nick," Sam said as we sat at a table near the stage. A lovely dark-skinned woman was sashaying to "Caribbean Queen." The patrons sitting around the stage couldn't get out their dollars fast enough.

"What'll it be, fellas?" asked our matronly waitress, who, thank God, was fully clothed. Her name was Irene, and, legend has it, she was one hell of a burlesque dancer in her day. As the times changed, the Cat transformed into its current manifestation, and about 20 years ago, Irene and her husband bought the joint. Her husband passed away a few years back, and it was now run principally by Irene's son, who, by the looks of his impeccable suit, was under the impression he was working for a bank.

"A couple of Rolling Rocks, Irene," Sam said.

"Sure thing, dear," said Irene. She winked at us before heading back to the bar.

"Can you imagine working here as long as she has?" I said.

"I can only imagine," Sam said.

"No, I'm serious. You don't think it would get tiring day after day after day?"

"Yes, and I'd also hate it if some guy showed up at my house every day with a bag full of money. That would completely suck."

"All right, all right, but I'm telling you I'm right."

"Nick, you can honestly say you would ever tire of this?" and he pointed at the stage. The stripper—Clarice? Beech-Nut? Teaberry?—was swinging around the pole, her leopard bra partially off, exposing one perfect breast as her ass, which, needless to say, was tight and round and flawless, pointed right at us. I wanted to lunge mouth-first.

"I'm a complete asshole, aren't I?" I said.

"Yes, yes, you are, Nick-O. But you're fitting in really well at work."

"I'm glad to hear I'm doing well. Thanks, man. I appreciate it." I desperately wanted to ask him his true opinion of Mousetrap, but I wasn't sure if this was my opening.

"So, now that you have a few months under your belt, Nick, what do you think of your employer?"

Okay, this was my opening.

"Here ya go, dears." It was Irene. She placed our Rocks and a couple of glasses on the table. "Can you believe I used to look like that?" she asked, pointing toward the stage. She then put up a hand to the side of her mouth and whispered, "Maybe even better!"

"You still look great, Irene," I said.

"You're a dear. Maybe the next round will be on me."

I could have let the moment pass, and Sam and I could have sat there for the next few hours, talking about the Penguins and enjoying the scenery. But I really wanted to know how he felt.

"You were saying, Sam?" I said.

"Yeah, tell me. Be honest. What's your assessment of Mousetrap?"

"Well, I'm not sure what to say. You are my boss, after all."

"Uh-oh," Sam said.

"No, it's just . . . I don't know. We seem to take people's money pretty easily."

"Ya noticed?" Sam said. He was smiling. I relaxed.

"The word 'sleazy' comes to mind sometimes, Sam. And it's nothing against you or Rachel or anyone in particular. It's just that people pay us thousands of dollars for ideas that usually suck."

"I'm so glad you said that, Nick."

"You are?" I said.

"It now confirms that I made the right choice when I hired you. Rachel and I both feel the same way—what you just said. It's just that getting a job ain't easy right now. So we're sort of stuck. Plus, our coworkers are, for the most part, decent people."

"They are," I said. It was true. From human resources to the computer geeks and everyone else in between, Mousetrap employees were hardworking, God-fearing, taxpaying people, it seemed. So how the fuck did we all get hired by such a nasty outfit?

We finished our beers, bid adieu to the dancers, and headed out into the September night.

"So," Rachel said to me when I entered my office the following morning, "welcome to the club." She then winked at me conspiratorially before dropping a fresh stack of hopeless dreams into my bin.

At first, I was confused, but I quickly realized that Sam had informed her of our conversation the night before. To be honest, a corrupt burden had been removed from my conscience.

"Can I ask you a question, Rachel?"

"First, we're in a recession. Second, I'm getting married in nine months, and we need the money. Third, this is a fun place to work if you can forget that we're sleaze. Does that answer your question?"

Had it been later in the day, I would have been able to think on my feet and say, "Actually, Rachel, I was going to ask you about my relationship with Nicole. I could really use a woman's perspective." But being that it was 8:14 and I was still groggy from having fallen asleep on the bus, all I could muster was a meek head nod.

Since our offices were somewhat physically isolated from the rest of our coworkers, the three of us liked to fantasize sometimes that we were working at a hip ad agency. But then I'd look at my bin and see something like "Eterno-Sharp," and reality would slap me in the face like an abusive parent.

Client: Brian Marks

Idea: Eterno-Sharp

Mr. Brian Marks, a Toronto shop and mechanical-drawing teacher for 27 years, has "had it up to here" with his students wasting valuable class time at the pencil sharpener. The solution? A pencil that never needs sharpening, one that "through a patented crumbling, wood-like material" simply disintegrates as necessary, leaving the user in possession of a fully sharpened pencil at all times.

I was sure that manufacturers of crumbling, wood-like materials would jump at this idea, so I quickly got to work.

Is there anything more important than educating a child? And shouldn't we do everything we can to ensure that every minute a child spends in school is used for learning? Well, here's a simple device that will help keep kids where they belong—in their seats. It's called Eterno-Sharp, and it eliminates those time-wasting trips to the pencil sharpener that can eat up a clock quicker than a Dean Smith four-corners offense. (It was with this entry that I occasionally started injecting bizarre analogies and personal notes inside the NPRs. I figured if people were actually reading what I was writing, the least I could do was give them a chuckle.)

Product Highlights:

- *Great for educational settings*
- *Home-use applications as well*
- *Teachers will love it*

I had just placed my work for this revolutionary product in Rachel's bin when Sam poked his head in and told us that Andrea had called an emergency meeting that was beginning in five minutes.

We all gathered in the large conference room, and no one seemed very concerned. Some of us were discussing our upcoming Thanksgiving plans, and I got into a friendly yet heated conversation with our head of marketing about the Pens' chances to make the playoffs. Andrea walked in, looking more severe than normal, and for the first time in all the months I knew her, she wasn't smoking. Something was up.

"Thank you all for taking a few moments from your schedule to meet with me. First of all, I want to tell you how pleased I am at your hard work," she said. Opening up with a compliment was, of course, the way to begin a headlong descent into bad news. "Over the past few days, however," she continued, "I've had to make one of the hardest decisions of my career. Early this morning, I had to temporarily—and let me stress that word, people—lay off six of your coworkers."

Immediately, we all snuck furtive peeks around the room in an effort to determine who wasn't there. I quickly figured out that it was three administrative assistants, a secretary, and two salespeople who after five months of employment had yet to net a sale. Sadly for the men of Mousetrap, one of the administrative assistants let go was Missy.

"It is my sincerest hope that we will be able to rehire these fine people within the next few months. But after meeting with my board last week, we decided that we needed to do a little tightening around here in order to grow stronger in what promises to be a magnificent 1991."

With that, she saluted us, told us to get back to work, and informed us that there was no need for any of us to ask her questions, since she had told us everything we needed to know.

When we got back to our nook of offices, Rachel and I both looked to Sam for answers.

"Guys, I'm as surprised as you are—honest. You know Andrea. It's not like she consults with management before she does anything. Listen—don't worry. I'm sure if either of you were in jeopardy, she'd have the decency to let me know."

Rachel and I kept staring at him, waiting for a better response.

"All right, it's somewhat fucked-up sounding," he finally confessed. "Lord knows we're busier than ever. Maybe it's what Andrea said—it's just a matter of belt tightening. She's older. Maybe she's getting greedy."

Sam promised us he'd delve into the matter and find out more, and he assured us he'd keep us informed. Satisfied, we went back to work. Still, the more I thought about it, the less I liked it. I decided to ask Sam if he wanted to go to the Pens game with me that night. Nicole called me earlier in the day and told me she probably had to work late, so I figured I'd put the extra ducat to good use.

Sam and I walked at a brisk pace as we headed up the hill toward the Arena. Even on a relatively mild November night, the wind whipped through us and made it feel more like January—in the Antarctic. When we finally reached our seats, Sam looked at me point blank and said, "Something's not right, Nick."

I had been racking my brain all day trying to devise a smooth entry into what happened at the meeting; fortunately, I didn't need to use it.

"I mean," he continued, "about 10 days ago, I saw a couple of stiff-looking suits sitting in Andrea's office. They weren't clients, they weren't potential employees, and they sure as hell weren't old friends."

"Who do you think they were?" I asked.

"Beats the hell out of me. But let's face it. You and I aren't employees of Honest Company USA."

Prison. Images of me grasping onto closing bars suddenly shot through my mind. My immediate hope was that, at the very least, a kindly judge would make Sam and me cellies.

"Do-do you think we're in trouble?" I asked.

"Yes, we're going to prison for the rest of our lives, Nick. No! Not us, anyway. We're just pawns. Who the hell knows what Andrea has going on? Look at the obvious, Nick. Our company openly engages in sleazy dealings. Imagine what we don't know."

That wasn't reassuring in the least, but my Pens were battling the Calgary Flames, and within 20 minutes, our attention turned to the game, where it stayed for the next two and a half hours. There is no better comfort food than sports.

THOUGH IT WAS EARLY in the 1990 campaign, my beloved Pens looked good. Coming off last night's win against Calgary (John Cullen scored the game winner with seconds left, in case you cared), they posted a record of 8–6-1, and once again I began to imagine the impossible. You see, growing up in Pittsburgh in the seventies meant one thing—the Pittsburgh Steelers. Everyone—and, honestly, I mean everyone—was a Steelers fan in the seventies. They won four Super Bowls in six years, and the fans' intensity could have rivaled that of even the most diehard Manchester United supporters. Even the Pirates, who won two World Series in the decade and featured legends like Clemente and Stargell, played in the shadow of Art Rooney's team.

Naturally, I took the Pens to my heart like a child finding an injured puppy. This was due in part to my father having lived in Canada for a few years and being indoctrinated into the religion of hockey. But the rest was all me. I loved the Steelers and Buccos, too, but the Penguins? They were the stepchild of the Pittsburgh sports scene, and I embraced them fully.

Next up, another entry from Bad Ideas Weekly. Let's give it up for FrigiPots.

Client: Jane Schiffman

Idea: FrigiPots

Mrs. Schiffman, an elderly homemaker from New Orleans who "raised two fine boys and helped raise seven grandchildren," has burned her hands one too many times with conventional potholders. Her solution? Potholders lined with a special cooling gel that you could keep in the refrigerator. I wanted to send her a letter saying, "Hey, Jane, here's a thought. Perhaps those potholders you purchased when Truman was in office have grown a little threadbare." Sadly, though, I plowed on and came up with this . . .

Ouch! Is that you taking a hot cake out of the oven? Are you tired of running to your first-aid kit every time you cook or bake? Wouldn't it be great if you could take things out of the oven with confidence? Well, look no further—FrigiPots are here! Lined with specially designed cooling gel, these mitts will keep your hands cool every time. And what's even better—when you're done with them, toss them back in the fridge! Amazing. Reliable. Safe. FrigiPots.

Product Highlights:

- *Keep your hands burn-free*

- *Reusable*

- *Great for kids in the kitchen*

I sincerely hoped that Mrs. Jane Schiffman had $8,500 to blow on her stupid idea. My fear was that she would be spending the rest of her days eating cheap cereal out of the box. In the depths of my conscience twisting, however, I devised a two-word solution: Visit Elaine. I grabbed the stack of complete NPRs and headed upstairs.

My voyeuristic hopes were dashed the second I entered her office. She looked as though she had just found out a favorite aunt had a terminal illness. "What's up?" I asked her gently.

She shook her head slowly and twisted a lock of her dark-brown hair. "There's bad things going on here, Nick. Did you see the suits meeting with Andrea today? They looked like freakin' pallbearers."

I did notice a glum-looking bunch of men heading toward Andrea's office earlier, but I thought nothing of it.

"Yeah, I saw them. What are they, investors?"

"No, lawyers. One of them, anyway. I heard him say his name to Connie when they arrived."

"All right. Don't take this the wrong way, Elaine, but so what?"

"Well, the lawyer's name is Don Sakowski. My cousin is a lawyer in Mr. Sakowski's firm. They specialize in troubled companies," Elaine explained.

"Troubled how?"

"Well, legal troubles. I mean, none of us are idiots. I know we're not exactly finding a cure for cancer or even selling aluminum siding here. But geez."

Two things coursed through my head: One, obviously, was the fear that we were all going to be herded into paddy wagons and thrown into jail for a long time. The other thought was to give Elaine a down-to-the-bone massage, which would lead to me clearing everything off her desk—even the Family Circus calendar; hell, especially the Family Circus calendar—and making sweet, illicit love to her. After all, if we were a sleazy company, shouldn't we all start acting the part?

I snapped out of it.

"Listen," I said, trying to reassure my friend. "Andrea's cagey as hell. Maybe she's just trying to nip things in the bud. We had a few layoffs, and maybe she just wants to get things back in order."

"I hope you're right. Do you have an NPR for me?"

"Yeah, right here. It's a gem."

"Aren't they all?" she asked. I handed her FrigiPots, she scanned it, rolled her eyes, and said, "Maybe it wouldn't be such a bad thing if when we arrived tomorrow morning there were giant padlocks on the front door."

"Please don't say that. I wouldn't wish unemployment on my worst enemy."

I really wouldn't. At first, being unemployed was no big deal. It gave me a chance to unwind from college life, and I figured my unemployed status would last, at most, two or three weeks. I was a little off. By the third month, I had come up short in several interviews, my confidence was destroyed, and most upsetting to me, my family had given up hope that I would ever find employment. I truly wanted to take a running leap off the Smithfield Street Bridge.

It got so bad that I started fixing the grammatical mistakes in rejection letters I received and returned them, thus eliminating any chance I would ever get hired by Companies I Deemed Unworthy of Me Because They Forgot a Comma. I was growing into a full-blown jagoff, but I had a good reason: My family and Nicole were driving me absolutely fucking nuts. Sample conversation:

Dad: How'd the interview go?

Loser Son: I think it went well.

Mom: Did you talk?

Loser Son: Uh . . . yeah?

I went on a number of job interviews, and while I may not have blown anyone's socks off with my radiant personality, I did grasp the fundamentals—you talk a little about your personal life, you mention goals you'd like to achieve, you say at least once that you're a team player, you ask questions about the company, you shake hands firmly, you smile.

Apparently, after I had "failed" a number of interviews, my parents had an image in their heads that I showed up in a tank top and cutoffs and mumbled incoherently into my armpit. What drove me nuts about this was that in college, I had been editor of my school paper, worked as an intern at one of Pittsburgh's daily newspapers, got elected to student government (well, all right, I didn't actually run a campaign and win the confidence of my fellow students. What happened was two friends of mine wrote my name in for Junior Dorm Representative, and I was the only person to receive any votes. Hence, I became an elected school official) and graduated magna cum laude.

A mere six months later, I had festered into Shameful Pete. On top of this, Nicole, who saw firsthand how hard I worked in college, behaved no better. Sample conversation:

Nicole: What happens on these interviews?

Shameful Pete: Dancing, mostly. We usually drink a few beers, too.

Nicole: You see? That's your problem. Maybe you're not taking this seriously enough.

Don't you just want to punch someone in the face when they say the magic words "that's your problem"? How could she have believed that I wasn't taking job interviews seriously enough? I would have killed someone for a job. Was she under the impression that I liked sitting at home day after day getting woeful looks from my parents? How could she even ask me such a moronic question? Allow me to continue:

Shameful Pete: You don't think I'm taking this seriously enough?

Nicole: I don't know. I mean, I got hired. Our friends have jobs. No one's going to hand you a job, you know.

Shameful Pete: They're not? Damn.

Nicole: See? There you go again with the sarcasm. I hope I don't have to tell you that people hate sarcasm.

Shameful Pete: Ya think?

Nicole: Honestly, Nick! That's it, isn't it? You mouth off during interviews.

Shameful Pete: Yes, and I throw punches, too. In fact, the last interview I had? I stabbed a woman with her letter opener. Didn't you hear?

Nicole: I got to go. It's getting late.

I know, I know. They meant well, right? That gave me little solace. In fact, it gave me no solace at all. These people should have been on my side, and they let me down. I forgave them, but it took a while. And finally, I got a job. The job you're reading about right now. The job where I help people's dreams get no closer to reality and in the process take sacks of their money. I'm so fucking proud.

Two weeks before Thanksgiving, on a sleepy Monday morning bereft of character, Sam, Rachel, and I were snapped from our slumber by the sounds of Andrea's nicotine-coated drawl and what can only be described as a hyena being sodomized by a lion.

The conversation, from what we could ascertain, was one-sided. Andrea would say something, and this mystery beast would howl instantly. The weird thing was that they were having this discussion in a small, unoccupied office adjacent to Sam's. As if on cue, the three of us met eyes, and all thought the same thing.

"No, that's not moving in, is it?" Sam asked.

Before Rachel and I could confirm his fears, Andrea brought our new neighbor over to meet us.

"Gentlemen and lady," Andrea said, glancing Rachel's way, "I'd like you to meet your new neighbor, Alice Legato. She will be joining us on a temporary basis to help me address some issues that have arisen recently."

We all exchanged pleasantries, and before the conversation lull grew into an uncomfortable canyon, Alice and Andrea departed.

When they were out of earshot, Rachel and I turned to Sam.

"Again, guys, I'm not privy to every secret thing that goes on around here. You've known Alice as long as I have. But, if I had to guess, I'd say she's Mousetrap's legal counsel."

"Really? I was hoping you were gonna say interior designer," said Rachel.

"Guys, what the hell did we do to—"

"Nick, don't panic. Companies have legal representation for a million reasons. Maybe there's a sexual-harassment suit going on. Maybe it's nothing that important."

I was on the verge of reminding my friends that we worked for a company that takes people's money and, for all intents and purposes, sets it on fire. I held my tongue, though, because there was no need to bring the mood down and the anxiety up any further. Besides, I had a pile of NPRs on my desk awaiting me, and who was I to hold up production on ideas that would change the world?

Client: Ken Burchfield

Idea: Radio Stay-tion

A Mr. Ken Burchfield of Atlanta thinks he's created the ideal portable radio for sports fans. Let's turn it over to Ken. "I am so sick and tired of fiddling with dials every damn time I want to hear the Braves game. Half the time, I turn it on, and I damn near burst an eardrum with the rock and roll blaring. See, I have kids, and they always want to play with Daddy's radio.

"Then one day, I got to thinking. What if Daddy's radio could play only one station? I bet they'd leave it alone then. So, that's my idea, in a nutshell."

And what a fine idea it is—a product that gives consumers fewer options and for almost no reason. Who wouldn't love this? Why stop there, Ken Burchfield of Atlanta? How about a car that goes only one speed? Or a phone that dials only one number? Wasn't the Radio that Plays Only One Station an inhabitant of the Island of Misfit Toys?

As a wise person once said, necessity is the mother of invention. But sometimes, all it takes is bratty teens! How many times have you flipped on your radio, only to be assaulted by the volume of your kids' "music"? And all you really wanted was the score of the ball game! Well, here's a solution that's genius in its practicality: the Radio Stay-tion. Programmed to the station that broadcasts your favorite local team, the Radio Stay-tion will put a rest to anyone changing the station—and keep your ears safe, too!

Product Highlights:

- *Deters others from using radio*
- *No more fiddling with dials*
- *Practical and affordable*

It wasn't even 10:00 on a Monday, and already I wanted to leave. But then I considered the alternative—the return of Shameful Pete—and I soldiered on. Immediately, though, I felt a real sense of déjà vu.

It seems a Ryan Kloski of Elmhurst, Wisconsin, finds himself quite concerned about his parents' ability to maintain a strict pill regimen. He's so concerned, in fact, that he's created the Tick-Tock Pill Clock. This wondrous device can hold numerous pills and set off alarms when it's time for the user to take specific medications. This was just another in a long line of pointless ideas, except for one thing: When I applied for this job, one of the tests I was given was to write a description of something called the Medi-Timer, which was virtually the same as the Tick-Tock Pill Clock.

I poked my head in Sam's office and asked if he had a minute. The Hyena continued her assault on our once-quiet environs.

"Are you here to puncture my eardrums with a fork, buddy?" Sam asked.

"What the fuck is that?" I asked.

"It's been going on for almost an hour," Sam said. Maybe Robin Williams is in there with her. Really, that's the only explanation. Anyway, what's up?"

I explained to Sam the similarities between the two NPRs and wondered why a manufacturer would be interested in a product they rejected months earlier.

"It's money-grubbing, I guess," Sam said. "It's not like Fred Schmuckley of wherever is gonna meet Ed Douchebag of wherever and discover they've hit upon the same idea. Easy money."

"We're all going to hell, aren't we?"

"Hold that thought, Nick." He buzzed Rachel on the phone. "Rache, could you come here a sec? Thanks."

Rachel entered, and Sam proceeded to catch her up to speed on the situation I encountered.

"Young Nick here thinks we're all going to hell."

Rachel shook her head. "No, Nick, Sam and I have had this conversation before. Purgatory, almost certainly. But not hell for this."

"Look, Nick, if we weren't here, three other stiffs would be," Sam explained. We have no contact with these sad-sack clients. We don't smooth-talk them into sending us thousands of dollars. We're simply the last step in a dreadful procedure."

"Blaming us would be like blaming the mortician for death, Nick," Rachel said.

"This is clearly wrong, even for this company," I said.

"Then quit," Sam said.

I was a little taken aback by the abruptness of the easygoing Sam. Even Rachel shot him a glance.

"Look, all I'm saying is that we're all in the same boat. There have been mysterious layoffs, I have a fucking hyena sharing a wall with me, and then you come in like St. Nick of Pittsburgh."

I apologized, but Sam even cut that off.

"Aw, fuck it, guys." He chucked his eyeglasses on the desktop. "On top of everything else, Karen and I have been trying to start a family, and now I'm terrified that Karen might be pregnant."

Both Rachel and I congratulated Sam and encouraged him that everything would work out.

"You guys hungry?"

Seeing that it wasn't even 10:30, we weren't, but Rachel gave me a quick glance, and I figured the politic thing to do would be to join my boss and associate for lunch. So off to Big Lou's we went.

"Loser, Homo, and Pretty Lady!" Big Lou screamed. "Isn't it a little early for an artery clogging?"

"We've had a rough morning, Louis," Sam said.

"It's 10-fucking-30—pardon me, Pretty Lady—on a Monday morning!"

"You want our business or not, lardass?" I said. Yes, in only a few months, I was comfortable insulting Big Lou without the fear of him sizzling my face.

He chuckled, then started on our orders.

"Well," Sam said, "she's definitely a lawyer. I could hear enough of her conversations to figure that out."

Before Rachel or I could pepper him with questions, Sam raised his right hand and continued. "And that's all I know right now. There's a managers' meeting today at 2:00. When I find out more, I'll tell you."

Our food arrived, and except for a few grunts of "mmm," we ate in silence. Even after we finished, the silence still lingered, and, being the junior member of the department, I didn't think it would be proper protocol for me to break it. Fortunately, Rachel took care of the situation.

"Well, Daddy," she said, "I need to get back to work." We all chuckled, and Sam seemed to breathe a sigh of relief for the first time today. On the way back to the office, which was only a block away, we chatted aimlessly before being greeted by the Hyena as we reached our offices.

"Hi, guys!" the Hyena yelled. We all waved and managed to plaster big, phony smiles on our faces. I inferred from her appearance that Alice was a good lawyer. She wore huge glasses and, judging by the color of her skin, spent virtually all of her time indoors. Why did a pasty complexion make her a good lawyer? Well, I assumed that she spent most of her time hitting the books and didn't have time for any outdoor endeavors. Also, Rachel pointed out that her clothes were hopelessly out of style, therefore adding to my notion that she spent literally all of her time with her nose in a law book.

Or, perhaps, Sam chimed in, she's just a fucking geek who laughs like a hyena and is ashamed of her hyena laugh and doesn't leave the house much out of embarrassment. Sam was in a foul mood, and 2:00 couldn't get here fast enough for us.

I decided to kill the time by working. I figured that nothing would distract me better than an awful idea whose inventor had pissed away junior's college fund in the hopes of becoming the next Rubik's Cube dude. The problem in the inventors' thinking, of course, was that the Rubik's Cube was actually fun. What I was staring at—Spice-tisserie—was, in its best light, mildly retarded. But we'll let Sue Labeck of Minneapolis explain:

"I am so tired of handling those little spice jars," writes Sue. "So I got to thinking. Why not have one big spice jar? Then, I realized that wouldn't work, so I got to thinking. Why not have like an artist's palette of spices, all at the ready? You could even have small, medium, and large ones, depending on how often you cook. It could have a whole bunch of holes."

A spice Frisbee. Sue thinks a spice Frisbee is a great idea. Yes, what chef wouldn't want to hold a giant circle of spices? How convenient that sounds. Nevertheless, my attempt at putting a good face on this idea would help me drown out the Hyena, who was laughing so constantly and so rhythmically—ha ha ha Ha ha ha—that I didn't know whether to fall asleep or slash her throat.

Client: Sue Labeck

Idea: Spice-tisserie

How many times have you felt like you needed three hands in the kitchen? Tired of making numerous trips to your spice rack because you forgot about that dash of cinnamon? And, of course, you remember only when your hands are covered in dough! Well, here's an idea that will rid you of that aggravation once and for all—Spice-tisserie! Simply load up this ingenious device with the spice bottles you use most, and never again will you have to play hunt-the-spice.

Product Highlights:

- *Saves time*

- *Saves cleanup*

- *Saves patience*

Well, that brought me to 11:30, and, to make matters even worse, I was now hungry for something cinnamon. I decided to take a quick trip to the bakery up the street when Sam summoned me into his office.

The first words out of his mouth—"Don't panic"—made me panic.

"Andrea wants to see us in her office right now."

"Wh—

"Not a clue. Let's just go."

Visions of unemployment tore through my brain. I was already preparing explanations to my parents and Nicole. "I think it's a temporary layoff. I'm not sure what's going on, but I think it might be a legal situation. No, I didn't do anything illegal. No, Mom. No, I'm not going to jail."

I had been in Andrea's office only a few times and never for more than a minute. Upon entering this time, though, it felt like stepping outside in February without a coat. Behind a haze of smoke sat Andrea. She looked even more bedraggled than normal, corpse-like, even, wearing a black dress that she had worn at least three times in the past week. We were about to get canned by Miss Havisham's evil twin.

"Gentlemen," she said, slapping a smile on her face. Her eyes bored into me.

"I have a project for you, young man."

At the word "project," I resumed breathing. Whatever the project was—putting new shingles on the building's roof, becoming roommates with the Hyena—beat the pants off Shameful Pete, the Return.

"The government is trying to fuck us over," she continued. "The FTC, to be specific. You know what FTC stands for, boys?"

I wasn't sure whether to answer or not.

"Fuck Those Cocksuckers!" she yelled.

I was glad I didn't and made a mental note to myself that the right answer isn't always the right answer.

She smashed her cigarette into an ashtray and promptly lit another. I normally hate cigarette smoke, but mentally, at least, the little bit of smoke generated from her Camels was cutting down on the tundra-like coldness of her office.

I was staring at Joe Camel, since it's my nature to avert my eyes when someone's in the middle of a blood-curdling rant.

"I'm sorry, boys. Pardon the French. Let me cut to the quick."

She proceeded to tell me and Sam that the FTC was essentially try-ing to put Mousetrap out of business. And for what? Let's let the govern-ment handle this:

"Mousetrap, Inc., based in Pittsburgh, is an invention-marketing company that has for years misrepresented the nature of its operations. Its purported ties to industry are virtually nonexistent, and its success rate—i.e., inventors who have turned a profit—is close to zero.

"The nature of the invention-marketing industry has long been one prone to deception, but even by these low standards, Mousetrap, Inc. is in a class by itself, charging clients anywhere from $3,750 to $9,750 for its services and doing next to nothing toward bringing client ideas to fruition.

"As a result, effective immediately, clients of Mousetrap, Inc. will be rewarded refunds based on how much they invested, and henceforth the company will be required to provide potential clients with information pertaining to its success rate.

"To pay for potential client refunds, Mousetrap, Inc. will be levied a fine of $1.2 million."

Keep in mind, it took Andrea the better part of a half-hour to get through this governmental beat-down, pausing numerous times for em-phasis, putting out and lighting three more cigarettes, and, at one point, even throwing her hands up into the air, evangelist-like, to make her point.

I still wasn't sure where I fit into this, but all thoughts in my head were consumed by one thing. It was as cold in Andrea's office as Three Rivers Stadium during a Steeler playoff game, and I had to piss something fierce.

"Nick, I'm putting you in charge of writing this horseshit success-rate bullshit nonsense that we have to put in our client brochures. And, Sam, I wanted you to know since you're Nick's boss.

"Well, Sam," she continued. "That's pretty much what we're going to cover at 2:00, but please come, anyway. I don't want any of the other managers suspicious as to why you're not there."

"That's all, gentlemen."

And with a wave of her cigarette hand, we were allowed to leave the Arctic ice station and resume our normal bodily functions. By the time we got back to Sam's office, our brains thawed, and we realized the sever-ity of what Andrea just dropped on us.

"Rache!" yelled Sam. "Get in here."

Sam proceeded to catch Rachel up-to-speed. "We're doomed, right?"

Sam and I looked at each other. I offered him a shrugged-shoulder agreement with Rachel's assessment.

We sat in silence for a moment, none of us sure what to say.

I decided to break the ice (no, not the ice that had formed on my extremities from an extended stay in Andrea's office. I'm talking figurative ice here).

"Sam, do you think I could have some business cards printed up that say 'Horseshit Writer' on them?"

He smiled, as did Rachel. The facts, though, were ugly. I was going to write up a document that would tell potential clients this: For the love of God, don't give your money to us! Are you familiar with Three-Card Monte? Seriously, you have a better chance getting money off a street swindler than you do from us. We are low-down, deceitful, money-grubbing bastards, and we will take thousands of your dollars and give you nothing back! Please sign below! And thanks!

Here was the challenge: Make the awful truth sound palatable. Don't call a disease a terminal illness. Call it a life challenge. Don't call it a tax increase. Call it revenue replenishment. Don't call it unsound business practices. Call it governmental compliance.

I was more nervous about creating this document than I should have been. After all, we didn't suspect that Mousetrap would survive more than six months after potential clients discovered we had a success rate worse than that of the Washington Generals. Still, I looked at it as a challenge, and seeing how Andrea was on the verge of full-blown lunacy, I felt it was my duty to give her my best.

After numerous false starts and a few soul-searching walks through Downtown streets, this is what I came up with:

HOW DO WE DEFINE SUCCESS?

It all starts with you, of course—your ideas, your aspirations, your dreams. We at Mousetrap want to take those ideas and turn them into your reality. For the past 11 years, our number-one goal has been guiding your ideas through the right channels in an effort to bring life to your inventions. Have we always been successful? Of course not. After all, what business is successful 100 percent of the time? But know this: We put forth 100 percent effort on every one of your ideas, from the second we receive your proposal to the minute we work your case file through the proper channels.

In these past 11 years, almost 7,100 clients have brought us their hopes, and 68 have seen their ideas go from paper to reality and have turned a profit on their initial investment. That's a success rate of nearly 1 percent, which doesn't sound very promising until you dig a little deeper.

Why do most of our clients' thoughts never gain traction in the marketplace? Any number of reasons—bad timing, unimaginative manufacturers, and sometimes, frankly, ideas that just don't hit the mark.

In addition, our success rate is based almost entirely on the ideas potential clients send. All we can do is apply our industry know-how and utilize our seasoned professionals to bring your inventions to fruition.

The bottom line, though, is this: You can't put a success rate on the American dream. Who's to say that you're not that special 1 percent who, with our help, can see your idea become reality? *Our next success is one stamp away.*

Mousetrap—100 percent effort for the special 1 percent.

My dirty work was done. I felt good about it, but in a queasy way. I ran it by Sam, and while he was reading it, I sensed the same feeling of nausea overwhelming him. "She'll like it," he said.

"But you don't?"

"Honestly, no, but don't take that the wrong way. You did what you were assigned."

"Ah, the old 'I was only following orders' defense, right?"

"Look, Nick. It doesn't matter what any of us do or don't do. The jig's up on this place, anyway. Don't feel guilty. She'll love it."

He was right. What we did was irrelevant. Yes, I sugarcoated the fact that Mousetrap's success rate was way south of the Mendoza Line. Still, people would see that 1 percent, and bells would go off in their heads saying, "Stay away. Step back from the checkbook, please, and no one gets fleeced."

To the tundra I proceeded for a meeting with Andrea. She wasn't smoking, and while she was again wearing the same black dress she'd seemingly been wearing for weeks on end, she styled it up a bit with a pink shawl. At first, I saw a Grinch-like smile cross her face as she read my copy. This was followed by a small hand pump. Next came blown kisses in my direction. Finally, she leaped to her feet and yelled, "Bravo, Nick!"

Her euphoria was quickly replaced by Nixonian anger, as she again vented about the FTC and the government and how they were killing her.

I quietly excused myself while she was in mid-rant, and she managed to give me a thumbs-up as I departed.

That following Sunday the headline of the *Pittsburgh Press* read: Invention Company Faces Compliance, Heavy Fines

Mousetrap, Inc., a Downtown invention-marketing company, has been slapped with a $1.2 million fine, the result of a two-year Federal Trade Commission investigation into such companies nationwide. Also, the company will be forced to include its success-rate information in any literature it sends to potential clients.

Andrea Bianco, Mousetrap's president, denied any wrongdoing. "We've been in business for more than 11 years, and we've never one time done anything illegal. My employees work very hard, but the bottom line is this: You can't put a success rate on the American dream."

I damn near choked. She liked the bullshit I wrote up so much that she was using it herself.

The article continued:

According to FTC documentation, Mousetrap has done work for more than 7,000 clients, and only 68 of them have made a profit or at least seen their inventions reach the marketplace.

The report continues: "The nature of the invention-marketing industry has long been one prone to deception, but even by these low standards, Mousetrap, Inc. is in a class by itself, charging clients anywhere from $3,750 to $9,750 for its services and doing next to nothing toward bringing client ideas to fruition."

Bianco, however, sees this investigation as "emancipating."

"Look," says Bianco. "I'm not delusional. I never had any thought that our success rate would be even 10 percent. We cater to a very special group, that 1 percent that says, 'You know what? I might have a crazy dream, but I'll never stop pursuing it.'"

Bianco declined comment on whether the impact of the fine and having to reveal the low company success rate will lead to immediate layoffs.

"We will continue to put forth 100-percent effort for that very special 1 percent pursuing their American dream," she said.

Mousetrap is located on Penn Avenue and a few years ago gained notoriety when Bianco insisted on altering the gargoyle outside her window of the almost 100-year-old building into a "mousegoyle." She ultimately won the right to do so.

The article continued, and there were a few more comments from Andrea, but two things bothered me more than anything: first, she twice used my words to her advantage and second, the reaction of my parents upon learning that their son was about to be unemployed again.

To my pleasant surprise, my parents were supportive and understood I was doing the best I could to remain employed. That was reassuring, but an awful thought gnawed away at me, and even the Steeler game couldn't displace it from my brain: What if I did too good a job on the success-rate insert? What if this doesn't kill the company?

By the end of December 1990, the results were in: There was a mere 5-percent reduction in clients from December 1989. Mousetrap would survive. Yes, the $1.2 million fine and the slight reduction in our client base would lead to a few more administrative layoffs, and yes, there would be no raises for any of us, but the company would survive. Hooray.

Andrea celebrated by wearing a new dress for our interoffice Christmas party. In years past, I was told that Mousetrap's holiday party was quite a blowout affair, usually held at a fancy hotel. Booze and food were doled out in copious amounts, and the standard rules about behavior during such gatherings—such as don't get shitfaced in front of your boss—didn't apply, seeing how Andrea was usually drunker than anyone.

So this was a low-key affair, with trays of lunchmeat and bread set up on a buffet table along with some appetizers and Christmas cookies. But all of us mingled happily, myself included, knowing that we probably had weathered the worst of the government and could resume breathing again.

When the party began winding down, Andrea, drunk and happy, clapped her witchy hands and yelled, "What would a Christmas party be without presents?" For a second, I think we all had expectations of receiving something useful or inspiring, but those hopes, like all hopes here, quickly died as Andrea unveiled the T-shirt she was holding for all of us to see. On the front of the shirt it simply read "Mousetrap." On the back were the words, in I'm guessing 500-point type, "The Special 1 Percent."

The kiss-ups began applauding. The rest joined in. I fought the urge to vomit or impale myself with a cake knife. For reasons of competitiveness and job security, I spun what should have been the death knell for this company into a positive. But Andrea? Fuck, she turned it into a line of clothing. Part of me admired her; the rest of me wanted to tear off her head.

But I had to remind myself of a very simple thing: I had a job. I also had a girlfriend who was probably expecting a marriage proposal for Christmas. Looking back, I understand why women are so persistent in getting men to walk down the aisle. The truth is this: I was 24 years old, had a job that paid poorly, was living at home rent-free, and had an Italian mother who cooked and did my laundry. And Mom didn't just cook out of some maternal instinct. No, she loved to cook for me—or anyone. So why would I leave that to get married and probably have to cook for myself and do my own laundry?

So, now I get it. But back then, I didn't, and every time Nicole mentioned the "M" word, I tried my best to change the subject or bring up anything negative I could concerning matrimony. ("Hey, did you hear about that guy who decapitated his wife and killed his entire neighborhood because she overbaked the ziti?")

After Christmas passed and there was no ring on her finger (apparently the sweater and some books didn't cut it), Nicole started becoming more direct in her line of marital questioning.

"Where do you see this relationship going?" she asked one January night.

"What is this, a job interview?"

"Oh, that's right." she said. "You do lousy on those. I forgot."

"Come on, Nic. We will get married. You know it. I just don't think I make enough yet to feel stable. And besides, did you hear about that woman who set her husband on fire for hiding the remote?"

"Maybe we should call it quits," she said.

That one caught me by surprise. "You're kidding."

"No, Nick. You're the one with the jokes all the time, as if these are fates that await us. If it makes you feel better, we can write our own vows, and I'll say, 'I, Nicole, promise to honor, obey, and never set my beloved ablaze.'"

"Yeah, that's the spirit!" I said. But she wasn't laughing. Or smiling. Fuck, she was crying. A crying woman to a normal man is what kryptonite is to Superman. It was over—no, not our relationship. My freedom. My bachelorhood. My mother's eggplant parmigiana (which, honestly, you would pay $50 for a dish of and feel it were a bargain). Still, I clung to some sense of dignity and managed to say . . .

"Honey, I love you so much, I'd whisk you off right now and we'd get married tonight. But let's step back and think for a minute. Allow me to surprise you. I'm totally unprepared. I've never bought an engagement ring before, you know?"

I didn't say a lot of dignity, just "some." Maybe 1 percent?

Still, it bought me time—a few weeks, anyway. Lord knows she would be expecting the ring on Valentine's Day. I hated the thought of doing something so conventional—go to some nice restaurant (no coupons tonight, honey; we're getting hitched!), have the waiter bring out the ring on a dessert plate or some such nonsense, cue the tears and hugs and applause from fellow idiot patrons—and then, three years later, watch as the husband takes a carving knife and—oh, fuck it. I was about to join the ranks of the married, and I would have to expunge all marriage horror stories from my mind.

I asked Sam and Rachel to help me shop for a ring. They were a big help, although Rachel kept insisting I spend more money than I wanted to, seeing how "it's the most special day in a woman's life." I decided upon an honorable ring and chose a week before Valentine's Day to spring the question.

That entire day, Friday, February 8, I was nervous, even though I knew what her answer would be. I couldn't concentrate on work, and even Andrea yelling "1 percent" at me as I passed her office didn't make me wince, as it usually did. Finally, 5:00 rolled around, and I met Nicole in front of a great Italian restaurant a few blocks from my office.

We exchanged pleasantries, discussed how our days went, the usual. I was trying to act normal, but Nicole knew something was up, seeing how we didn't usually go to nice restaurants for the hell of it. We ordered drinks and appetizers, heard the night's specials, and for a second, as I was debating between the spinach ravioli and veal Romano, I almost forgot about the night's main event.

I took a deep breath and then began my remarks. "Nicole," I said, I no longer want you to be my girlfriend."

"You don't?" said Nicole. She was onto me.

"No, I want you to be my wife. Will you marry me, Nicole?"

"No."

I was halfway done opening up the jewelry box before Nicole's "no" sunk in. I wasn't sure what to do, but here's what I did: nothing. I sat there, with a half-opened jewelry box in my hand, and stared at my girlfriend. Nicole grasped my confusion and to help me repeated her answer very slowly: "No, Nick. The answer is no."

I closed the box and put it back inside my sport coat. We were sitting in awkward silence as the cheery waiter returned with our appetizers and drinks and asked if we were ready to order. My head was spinning, and my heart crushed, but Nicole went ahead and ordered, as if a weight had been lifted from her soulless shell of a skeleton. When the waiter asked if I was ready, I had a one-word response: Steak. Why steak? Because it was the most Neanderthalic thing on the menu, and I felt like nurturing my inner caveman at the moment. I wanted a giant piece of meat, the bloodier, the better. I wanted to rip a leg off the table and use it as a club and start beating not only Nicole but every patron who saw my proposal get shot down. And after I was done clubbing people, I wanted to light the end of my table leg with the candle of a nearby wall sconce and torch the place to the ground, thus killing anyone who was a possible witness to my destruction.

Then, I would cook my own steak on the embers and laugh maniacally until the police came.

What I actually did:

"Do you want to tell me why? I think I deserve an explanation."

"I'm afraid this is just a ruse to string me along, quite honestly."

"A ruse? It's a fucking ring!" Yes, people were looking openly now. I no longer cared.

"Do we have a wedding date?"

"That's your department, isn't it? Isn't that what women do? What's the norm, a year and a half?"

"See! That's 18 months! That gives you time to back out. That's forever!"

The waiter returned with salads. We did our best not to have our scene turn into a full-on conflagration.

"Plus," she continued, "what kind of stability do you have with your job?"

"Well, I really don't mean to brag, but because of me, the company seems like it's going to survive. And that makes me want to vomit."

"You'd rather not have a job?"

"No, as I've said to you a thousand times, the job I have is better than not having a job at all. It pays the bills until something better comes along."

We ate in silence. I was now in the weird position of fighting for something I didn't want in the first place. The truth is, I did see myself married to Nicole. She was smart, decent, sexy, and the most honest person I've ever known. Frankly, I couldn't imagine my life without her. But I was young, and my low-paying job was with a company that had no future. As I ate my manly dinner, I realized I had two choices: Fight for Nicole's hand like I've never fought for anything in my life or let her go and be lonely and full of regret.

"Nicole, name the date, and I'll be there. This isn't a delay tactic. You are my heart. I just thought weddings took months and months to plan. That's why I said 18 months."

"Let's talk about something else."

I took a pen and piece of paper from my pocket and started writing.

"What are you doing?"

"I'm writing down the date and time. This is the first time in all the years we've been dating that you haven't wanted to talk about marriage. It needs to be recorded."

Nicole tried not to smile. "It's just . . ."

"What?"

"I feel like I've forced you into this"—

"Ya think?"

"See! Then we shouldn't do it. I'm an idiot."

"No, Nicole. Yes, you mention marriage every chance you get, and I try to change the subject when you do. But I don't want to lose you."

We finished our dinners without causing any more scenes, got in Nicole's car, and stared straight ahead.

"So, what do we do?" Nicole asked.

"I propose to you again, you say yes, we live happily ever after."

"Or?"

"I propose to you again, you say no, I go on a violent rampage, starting with the dashboard of your car."

"So this is all or nothing?"

"I guess it is. You either become my fiancée, or you stick with your original answer, break my heart, and throw us away, which will no doubt lead to my boozing and landing in the gutter, only to emerge triumphantly in seven years' time, but with great heartache and no liver."

"I wouldn't want that to happen."

"Will you marry me, Nicole?"

"Yes."

You know the rest—ring, tears, hugs, promises, hopes.

Nicole and I arrived at my parents' house and told them the good news. They were surprised but did a good job of hiding their dismay. I was their baby, and the thought that I would be leaving the nest probably horrified them. Still, they liked Nicole, and they figured I probably could have done much worse.

After a celebratory drink, I walked Nicole to her car, and we made plans to see each other the next day. She was genuinely happy, and my marital fears, to my surprise, began to dissipate. I was engaged to be married. I felt like an adult. Now if only I had a grown-up job to go along with my impending marriage.

The next day Nicole showed up at my house around noon armed with wedding magazines the size of a New York City phone book. She and my mother began discussing ideas, and, in the process, Nicole told us she had a date picked out—November 16.

"Oh, that soon, honey?" said my mom. I did the math. It was nine months from now. Not the 18 months that I figured, but also not the three months that I feared.

"Well, I thought about a Christmas wedding, but you never know with the weather. And I'd hate to wait until spring or summer after that. What do you think?"

"It's fine, Nic. But, seriously, does that give us enough time to get everything together?" I asked.

"If we start soon, sure." She wasn't being pushy. She was just excited. And maybe it was good for me, too. Helping to plan a wedding would take my mind off Mousetrap. I hated it there so much that if a doctor told me I had an incurable disease, I probably would have reasoned, "Well, at least this will take my mind off Mousetrap." I even grew to hate the word "mousetrap." Whenever I'd meet someone at a party and the inevitable, "So where do you work?" would arise, I'd always mumble and hope they'd heard me say "Monsanto" or "Mellon" or "IHOP" or anything else other than the truth.

"I'm a commercial pilot! I'm a lifeguard! I'm a pastry chef! I'm an astronaut! I peddle drugs to elementary-age schoolkids!"

Please, anything but the truth. The truth always elicited a cocked eyebrow. Oh, how I hated that cocked eyebrow. The eyebrow that said, "Oh, I get it! You're sleazy. I've often wanted to talk with sleaze but never had the chance. Continue, please."

Keep in mind, because of Andrea's unique personality, people in Pittsburgh knew her and her company. I worked for a high-profile company, but not high profile in a good way, like "Mr. Rogers' Neighborhood." No, this was high profile like one of those legalized Nevada brothels.

The topper, of course, was that I played an instrumental role in keeping Mousetrap afloat. Nicole and I spent most of the weekend discussing the wedding, and I awoke Monday to four inches of snow, ceaseless gray, and work.

ON THE TOP OF my in-box:

A product proposal from Allison Park of Las Cruces, New Mexico, for something called Prescript-i-Clock. Says Allison: "My poor grandmother must take I don't know how many medications. Plus, seeing how she's up in years, she can't remember which one to take when. She even tried to come up with some song to help her remember ("Take the blue at two and the green at three.") But she got frustrated when she couldn't find rhymes for yellow and orange. Anyway, I think if we could make a specialized alarm clock for elderly pill users, it would be great."

Allison was nice enough to include a sketch with her proposal of what looked like a standard alarm clock with a series of drawers around it.

"I also think," the letter continued, "that if some sort of trigger device could pop out the drawers, that would be even better."

This was now the second time—at least—that this idea had been presented to us. But we were still taking Allison Park's money, knowing damn well her idea was never going to see the light of day.

I felt bad for her senile, pill-popping grandmother, but, to be honest, I felt worse for myself.

And I felt even worse when I showed Rachel the proposal.

"Ah, another one. We get one of these about every six months, Nick," she said.

"So this isn't just the second time?"

"Well, as I said, we get about one every six months. So that would be the second time this year, if that makes you feel any better."

"How does it make you feel?" I asked.

"Like shit. That's why I'm doing this."

She brandished a handful of envelopes to which she was applying stamps. "The sad thing is, only a few of these are from want ads I saw in

Sunday's paper. The rest I'm just sending out unsolicited and hoping for a miracle.

"How about you? Any bites on a new job?"

"Nothing. And now that I'm getting married, I'm in the position of dreading the fact that I work here and dreading even more if the job disappeared."

"This won't last forever, you know, Nick."

"My God, Rache. What if—No, I can't say it."

"What?"

"Well what if, unbeknownst to us, we died—maybe we all had one hoagie too many—and this is it? This is purgatory. We're forever condemned to write about and draw people's awful ideas for eternity."

Rachel chuckled, and it made me feel better to see her pleasant face smile. But, like most things at Mousetrap, this pleasure was short-lived, as the Hyena heard my little speech and thought it was the funniest thing she'd ever heard.

Her cackle treated our moment of pleasure the way a guillotine treats a head.

"Listen, Nick." The Hyena stopped laughing long enough to speak. "Things are on the upswing here, thanks in no small part to you. The worst is truly behind us, and we all expect 1991 to be a banner year for us."

She then good-naturedly punched me on the arm twice and went back to her office. Rache and I stared at each other, nonplussed.

"The Hyena gives pep talks, Nick."

We smiled, and I trudged back to my office to work on Ms. Park's brainchild.

Client: Allison Park

Idea: Prescript-i-Clock

We all have elderly loved ones who take medications to address serious needs. And, as we all have experienced, sometimes they forget. The solution? Prescript-i-Clock. Yes, it's a handsome and reliable alarm clock. But it's so much more. It's designed with a series of small drawers around it that are triggered to open at certain times of the day so that our older generations will not only remember to take their pills, but take them at the right time, as well. This product addresses something that truly is a matter of life and death.

Product Highlights:

- *Trigger device pops out drawers*
- *Also accompanied by standard alarm*
- *Works as a normal alarm clock*
- *Can be made in any color to match décor*

I placed my latest masterpiece on Rachel's pile and noticed there was a stack of done NPRs that needed to be taken up to Research. This meant a trip up to Elaine's office, which I thought would bring a little light to an otherwise drab February Monday in Pittsburgh. She didn't disappoint.

I entered her office. She gave me a cheery hello. Again, it was Billy's turn at the drawing pad for Family Circus. Again with the malaprops— "gorilla warfare," "precedent of the United States," "prostrate cancer."

Yeah, that last one probably wasn't in the strip, come to think of it. Anyway, Elaine was wearing a red turtleneck and longish skirt, so I figured this would be a pretty empty visit. But, again, she managed not to disappoint when she casually put away some folders in a file cabinet and just had to bend over to do so, giving me a wonderful view of her backside with just a hint of her back showing, as her turtleneck rose ever so gently.

Keep in mind, she and I were having a typically mundane office chat while she was putting on her little show, as if nothing were amiss. I left inside of two minutes and couldn't decide if she really was an exhibitionist or if I was just imagining things for my own amusement. I mean, it wouldn't be possible for a woman dressed as conservatively as Elaine to behave in such a manner. And yet . . . Damn, was it a game, or was I a pig?

I figured I knew Sam well enough now to confront him about this and get his opinion.

"Got a minute, Sam?"

"As far as I know, no one's being canned today, Nick. Oh, and it's entirely thanks to you." He chuckled.

"Then give me a raise, you bastard."

"Let's not push it. What's up?"

"All right, I'll get right to the point, and if I'm wrong, please don't hold it against me. Every time I'm in Elaine's office, she—

"Exposes herself."

So I wasn't crazy. I laughed, as did Sam.

"Yeah, I've been waiting for this day, Nick. It feels so good to not harbor this dirty secret alone. It's like a weight's been lifted."

"What do you make of it? I mean, she seems so conservative."

"That's the sick, twisted—and yet scrumptious—part, isn't it, though? The covering clothes, the Family Circus calendar, the cat poster, and then . . . the tits or legs or whatever she feels like displaying."

"Today it looks like ass is the featured entrée. Do you think she's aware of what she's doing?"

"No, Nick, a tiny robot has infiltrated her brain, and she's completely under its evil influence. Fuck, I don't know. I'm not a psychologist."

"Maybe someone should tell her, though."

"Go ahead, Nick. In fact, put it in memo form and distribute it company-wide, just in case anyone else feels like exposing themselves."

"It is the company's policy," I began, "that employees do not expose themselves to each other during the normal course of business. It's been brought to our attention that a certain female in Research likes to bestow upon certain male coworkers the occasional cleavage shot, foot come-on, and bent-over-rump looky. We are concerned for the mental state of our employees and request that if this behavior continues, proper psychological treatment is sought.

"Furthermore, in addition to being improper for the workplace, behavior such as this makes the aforementioned male coworkers horny and unable to concentrate. Again, we emphasize: Please see to it that this behavior ceases immediately. If necessary, wear a suit of armor hence.

"Yeah, I suppose you're right. I guess we'll have to keep this to ourselves."

"Keep what to yourselves?" Nice timing, Rache.

"The fact that Elaine likes to expose herself to me and ugly boy over here."

"Sam, I thought we agreed—"

I was stopped by the look of total disgust that enveloped Rachel's face.

"You know, that's such typical guy bullshit. Right, every woman here is just throwing off their clothes every time you're in their presence."

"No, really, we came to our conclusion independ—"

"And you're trying to become a father! And you're getting married soon!"

"That doesn't make us blind," I offered.

Rachel grunted and then left, shaking her head. I felt bad, but I genuinely believed that Sam and I were right. This wasn't some mindless guy notion. This was real, and it was deliciously weird.

LATE FEBRUARY BROUGHT THE usual to Pittsburgh—gray, snow, ice, cold, sunsets at 4:00 p.m. But it also brought the heartbreaking. On a routinely bleak Wednesday, a man by the name of Ron Leechburg visited the Mousetrap offices. When I heard our secretary, Connie, refer to him as Mr. Leechburg, it took me a few minutes before I remembered where I had heard that name before.

Mr. Leechburg was the inventor of the Dual Horn System, an especially stupid invention idea that I had worked on a few months prior. Here's what I wrote for the NPR:

Client: Ron Leechburg

Idea: Dual Horn System

Haven't you ever wished your vehicle's horn came with options? A blaring sound to ward off imminent danger. A happy sound to say "thank you." A mellow sound to give the driver ahead of you a nudge if he's still stopped at a green light. Well, here's your answer: the Dual Horn System. This is the perfect aftermarket auto accessory that could not only save aggravation, but lives, too. The system would also come with a simple tricolored sticker that could be affixed to the steering wheel to indicate to the driver which area to hit to produce the desired sound effect. By hitting the green area, the driver would produce a happy sound; the yellow area, a gentle nudging sound; and red would produce the standard blare to alert someone to danger.

Product Highlights:

- *Wonderful aftermarket auto accessory*
- *Prevents aggravation/violent confrontations*
- *Snazzy sticker makes system a snap*

Yeah, auto manufacturers weren't convinced until I sold them on the "snazzy sticker." "Ferguson, this idea might be the most retarded thing I've heard in years, but—hey, did someone mention snazzy stickers? Onward!"

So there sat Mr. Leechburg, looking as stupidly hopeful as a turkey in November, clueless to the fact that the $7,500 he gave us is long gone and ain't ever coming back. He wore an ill-fitting herringbone jacket and no overcoat. His brown slacks were too short, his graying mustache unkempt, and I guessed he was about 50 and that he had staked a hell of a lot on us.

I slumped back to my office.

"Nick, who died?" Sam asked.

I explained to him who was in our lobby and gave him a quick synopsis on the poor bastard's invention.

I was no sooner done giving Sam the lowdown as Andrea and Mr. Leechburg were standing at my office door.

"Ah, gentlemen, we have a special guest here today with us. I'd like you both to meet Mr. Ron Leechburg. He's one of our treasured local inventors, and I believe you both worked on his splendid idea for transportation safety."

And now allow me to translate that into words Sam and I understood:

"Ah, workers, buck up, put smiles on your faces, and meet this dumbass. He's a local guy, which is irrelevant save for the fact that if we all don't play nice-nice, he'll visit again and possibly go crying to the fucking papers, which means you two and everyone else will be out on the pavement in cold-ass fucking Pittsburgh in February."

"Ah, yes, Andrea," Sam said, "Nick here was just telling me about that. He heard Connie talking to Mr. Leechburg in the lobby. In fact, Nick is the person responsible for describing your product to potential manufacturers."

Again, allow me to translate:

"I'm your friend, Nick, but I'm still a guy, and I'm just having some fun fuckin' with you right now."

"Yes, that's right. In fact, I believe I worked on that right around Christmastime, which means hopefully by spring we'll hear some feedback. Would you like to meet the illustrator responsible for the schematics of your idea, sir?"

Ah, nothing like passing the buck to get out of an uncomfortable situation. Plus, I owed Rachel for that whole defending Elaine/protecting womanhood speech she laid on us a few days prior.

During this whole time, Mr. Leechburg seemed happy. He spent much of the visit nodding his head while Andrea blathered on, introducing everyone by name and acting as though Mousetrap was just your regular, everyday company staffed by hardworking men and women who did their best every day to bring positive results for clients.

To be fair, most of us did work hard. To what end, outside of getting Andrea and her husband richer? I haven't a clue.

We had largely survived the visit unscathed—Andrea seemed happy at our complicity, and a happy Andrea is a nonfiring Andrea—until Mr. Leechburg gave us a parting shot.

"You all seem like nice folks," he began. Unfortunately, he continued. "I've had this idea for years, you know. I don't have much. Hell, I gave you my life savings. But it's my dream. Henry Ford had a dream. What if he never pursued it?"

His speech hung in the air. The four of us were speechless. My mind quickly scrolled through a variety of replies:

"Yeah, but Henry Ford was a genius, and you're a yinzer."

"No, sir, seriously, auto manufacturers won't be getting back to us in spring. There is no spring for your idea—only the death of winter."

"For the love of God, Andrea, give the man his money back right now. Perhaps then we all won't hell-rot for eternity."

"Hey, the Pens are playing some surprising hockey these days, aren't they? And wait till they get Lemieux back. This could be the year!"

Fortunately, Andrea rescued us. She looked at the sap square in the eyes and said, "I believe—we believe—in the power of ideas and the poetry of tomorrow." She said it with such sincerity that even Sam and I, at least for a moment, believed her. I have no idea what the fuck "the poetry of tomorrow" meant, but I have to admit I liked it.

Mr. Leechburg also got some parting gifts from the 1-percent line— a leftover T-shirt, a pen, and a button, all emblazoned with the 1-percent logo. He seemed genuinely content as he left the lobby.

If Andrea noticed our disgust, she kept silent about it. "It's always nice to come face-to-face with the people who pay the bills, huh?" she asked before heading back to her arctic lair.

We all nodded and mumbled our assent before shuffling back to our offices.

It's not like I didn't know real people sent us their money and their dumbass ideas. It was just that until now, I never fully made the connection. We were ripping off actual humans—people who had hopes and desires, like the rest of us. This guy really thought he was going to be the next Henry Ford with the idea for a three-part horn that would undoubtedly make the roads a more dangerous place. What he really was, was one in a long line of suckers, whose only purpose was to make Andrea Bianco a wealthy woman and to keep us employed.

I figured before I caught the bus after work, I'd see how Spice was holding out during the recent cold spell. Before heading over to Market Square, where he was no doubt holding court, I made a quick stop at the Candy-Rama and bought a bag of Snickers for him.

Surprisingly, he wasn't around. I saw one of his pals curled up on a park bench under a ratty comforter and asked him if he knew where Spice was. He shook his head and then tried speaking but couldn't make out the words. Finally: "Spice died the other night, man. He couldn't take the cold anymore."

As I left Market Square, fighting back tears, I noticed Pete and Friday poking their heads out of their new owner's comforter.

So this is it, huh? A decent person who never gets the mental help he desperately needed dies on a fucking bench in Market Square in the dead of winter, while another man, probably equally decent, pins his hopes and aspirations, not to mention his life fucking savings, on an idea that's as dumb as Spice was crazy.

I shared the Snickers bars with my bus mates and tried to think of the laughs I'd had over the years with Spice—the weird stories, the offbeat advice, our first encounter. It gave me a little solace, as did the Snickers bar I was furtively munching. It crossed my mind that I should visit a McDonald's tomorrow for lunch and order a McBlowjob, in tribute to Spice.

SEE, HERE'S THE THING about Pittsburgh (and, I suppose, the entire Northeast) in the winter: It's relentless. The sun is merely an idea. You go to work in the dark. You leave work in the dark. And on good days, it doesn't snow, and you escape without hearing the incessant pinging of sleet against a window. Living in this part of the country, though, gives you certain knowledge that residents of, say, Arizona lack. For example: Freezing rain falls from the sky as rain and freezes upon hitting the frozen ground. Sleet, however, falls from the sky as ice. I suppose it's more committed.

Nonetheless, they both produce the same effect: turning pedestrians into Brian Boitano (assuming he was experiencing a never-ending epileptic seizure) and producing horrifying vehicular accidents.

No, relax. This isn't foreshadowing. No one in this tale of deception dies, or is even injured, in a car, truck, SUV, or 18-wheeler. (You'll notice I didn't mention snowmobiles). This story, however, will at some point feature rampant, embarrassing nudity. So there's something to look forward to, in case you've hated everything up to this point.

My point, however, is this: Our moods match the weather. It's difficult dealing with a boss/spouse/annoying child when there's a foot of snow on the ground and the wind chill is 8. No, more to the point: It's difficult dealing with the aforementioned on a beautiful day in July. It's damn near impossible doing so in winter.

On a positive note, March was finally here. Realistically, March weather is usually as nasty as February's. Psychologically, though, it's March! Spring is upon us! Flowers, sun, miniskirts! (Historical note: March 13, 1993, was the date of what meteorologists dubbed the "Storm of the Century." Millions died and something in excess of 400 inches of snow blanketed the U.S. from Maine to Tennessee. Plus, sustained winds exceeded 300 miles per hour. Entire cities were reduced to piles of bricks, wood, and Pog collections, and a renegade leader known only as Xanto declared himself king of the land and ruled with an iron fist for nearly 11 years. I got these facts and numbers from Wikipedia. Actual facts and numbers may vary.)

Plus, my beloved Penguins were playing about as well as they ever had in their star-crossed 24 years of existence. (Briefly: The Penguins were incorporated almost the same day of my birth, and I've had a life-long love affair with them. They managed to break my heart dozens of times over the years, but I always believed. In addition, the ownership threatened to move the team seemingly every year, and the team even declared bankruptcy once. How bad was the organ-eye-zation's luck? Their mascot penguin, Slapshot Pete, died of pneumonia. Still this year, I had reason for hope).

So, to summarize. Good: Springtime, Pens playing well.

Bad: Reduced company income, more layoffs.

No, not me or Sam or Rache. We again survived Andrea's ax. Sadly, Elaine wasn't so lucky. Her research duties were to be split among her three subordinates. I felt horrible. Elaine was sweet, kind, and decent. And yes, I'd be totally lying if I didn't admit that part of what made me feel bad was all the free shows I'd be missing.

In addition, a few people in H.R. were let go, and Andrea informed us all that instead of occupying both the second and third floors, we would all be located on the third floor. She explained that doing so reduced the rent and kept one more of us employed. Somehow, the task of moving everyone from two to three largely fell to Sam and me. This wasn't as bad as it sounds. Believe me. It was better than dealing with what I got paid to do. Plus, when I did return to my actual job, there probably would be a stack of work waiting for me. It would force me to work diligently and not linger on the idiocy of what I was reading.

Still, for Andrea, this had to be wake-up call. Mousetrap in its hey-day was located on floors 9 through 12. Then, a potential tenant asked the building owners if it could have the top floor, and the owners gave Andrea a sweet deal to move from 12 to 2. Still, her company was on four floors. Then, when she first got wind of the FTC's investigation, she got rid of the 11th floor, which was largely for meetings, anyway, and consolidated her company on three floors. And then the first layoffs hit, and she needed only two floors—the second and third.

And then there was one. I think she decided to stay on three instead of two because two was closer to the exit, and she couldn't bear the thought of relinquishing her fiefdom.

A few days after we were all settled onto one floor, Andrea called a company-wide meeting and expressed confidence in the future. She looked beaten, but not quite yet defeated. And I have to admit a begrudging admiration for her. Was she the owner and founder of a company that would do society a favor by disappearing, a company whose best days never existed? Yes. Was she, at times, withering, nasty, scornful? Oh, yeah. Were hygiene and the generally accepted new outfit/new day tradition that most of us adhere to high on her list of priorities? No, and allow me to highlight now the benefits of smoking: Cigarettes stink, yes, but they do a wonderful job of masking standard body odor.

Still, the government was trying to take away something she adored, and the fighter in me had to tip my hat to her. At a certain point, I think, Andrea started believing her own bullshit and genuinely thought she was the legitimate CEO of a respected Pittsburgh institution. She was too far gone to see the truth.

But, yes, part of me was in admiration of a foul-smelling lunatic prone to profanity-laced rages. Call me crazy, but also call me employed, along with my other 30 or so coworkers who sat quietly, waiting for Andrea to finish her cigarette before she began to address us.

"You are survivors," she began. Her eyes slowly landed on each of us as she made her way around the conference room. "You are survivors."

"I am a survivor." Again, a pause. "This company is a survivor." Only seconds passed, but it felt like hours.

"And I'll be damned if some unnecessary governmental agency puts us on the street."

With this utterance, she slowly pointed a skeletal finger toward the window and gradually glanced in its direction, as if she were afraid to look, perhaps fearful that a 15-foot-tall FTC lawyer would meet her at eye level and begin laughing at her.

Her next statement, however, made us realize that no, Andrea wasn't scared of some government suit. She was merely building up the drama.

"Beginning the second I adjourn this meeting, I will once again be joining the ranks of the consultants. Ah, I see you're all a bit surprised."

We were. Before she started her own invention-marketing company, Andrea was a consultant for a rival firm. Within the industry, she was legendary. She was always top salesperson, and even Mousetrap's best consultants, in their peak years, were only about 80 percent as successful as she had been. So, this was probably a positive for the company, but a blight on our souls.

"Now, if you'll excuse me, ladies and gentlemen, I have some consulting to do." And with that, she grabbed a visor she had hidden underneath the table and placed it upon her dirty red hair. Emblazoned across the front? The phrase "1 percent." Does my shame know no end?

WITHIN THREE WEEKS OF resuming her sales career, Andrea bagged 17 new clients. This was the criminal equivalent of Wilt Chamberlain scoring 100 points in a game. If there were a Corporate Deceit Hall of Fame, this accomplishment would merit its own informational kiosk, complete with subtitled video and informational brochures.

She hand-delivered her sales to me, slapped them on my desk, winked at me and said, "Now work your magic, young man."

Don't you hate it when facts get in the way of a great story? I mean, here she is, the owner of a company that's getting its ass kicked from the government. But she's plucky and resourceful, and she picks herself up, dusts herself off, and leads her company back to profit. Hurrah.

And when I looked at her first new sale, I wanted to run down the hall, kick in the door of her tundral (not a word; ought to be) lair, and rip off her head. There in front of me sat an idea called "Alarm Rx." Need I continue? Must I put you through the torture of an idea you by now know so well? Yes, I must.

It seems a Becky Stroman of Indianapolis has come upon a wonderful idea that will no doubt help keep her ailing mother—and millions just like her—alive longer. And what, you ask, does this life-saving contraption purport to do?

Come on. Say it with me now: It's an alarm clock that can be programmed to remind users when to take their medications! And how much did Andrea fleece this woman for? About $6,500.

My head was moving in a thousand directions. Do I quit on the spot? Do I go talk to Sam? And why are so many people coming up with this same idea? Really, maybe the marketplace could use this device. I decided to have a chat with Sam, who had been expecting me.

"What's the difference," he began before I crossed the threshold of his office, "between new bad ideas and regurgitated ones?"

"What, you're psychic now?"

"No, I was in Andrea's office this morning, and she was brandishing it about. I caught a peek at the name of the invention and kind of figured out what it was."

His question briefly stumped me. After all, what was the difference?

"Still, Sam," I said, "doesn't it seem somehow more wrong to promote an idea we already know has failed countless times? At least with a new idea, there's always that hope, small as it may be, that it could become reality."

"Fuck, I don't know. Maybe I'm trying to rationalize it. The baby's due in July. Maybe that's assuaging my guilt a bit."

"And I'm getting married in eight months."

We both looked at each other, as if to say, "In other words, we're stuck here, because the thought of being a jobless parent or newlywed is not an appealing one. So, suck it up, shut the fuck up, and get back to work."

I shrugged my shoulders, spun, and went back to tackle Alarm Rx.

Client: Becky Stroman

Idea: Alarm Rx

People are living longer nowadays due to the miracles of modern medicine. And that's a good thing. But with every advance in science and technology, unforeseen problems arise. Take the space program, for example. If you grew up in the seventies, like I did, you probably ingested gallons of Tang because, after all, that's what astronauts allegedly drank. But think about the last time you craved a big glass of Tang. I'm gonna go with "never" as being your answer. You know why? Well, two reasons, actually. First, Tang is no longer made. And second, it tasted like shit. The thing is, I thought space travel was so cool that I convinced myself that I liked it. I even thought it might help turn me into an astronaut. I still find the wonders of space to be never-ending, but the reality is that millions of kids suffered through the seventies drinking an orange-like powdered drink. Adults of the seventies had to endure disco, leisure suits, and Vietnam, but if you've ever drunk a glass of Tang, you'll realize they got off easy.

Alarm Rx is an idea that tackles the problem of elderly folks forgetting to take their meds. After all, while medicine certainly helps keep the elderly alive, what good will it do if they neglect to take it?

And this idea is ingeniously simple. Essentially, it's an alarm clock that sounds a series of different tones at different times of the day for up to 10 medications. A buzzing sound, for example, might mean it's time for

Grandma to take her cholesterol pill, while a chirping sound four hours later might remind her to take her high-blood pressure medication. And the best part about this idea? It will save lives.

Product Highlights:

- *Based on an existing, easily modified product*
- *Great idea for increasingly number of elderly*
- *Could be made in any color to match décor*

"Could be made in any color" was usually my way of saying, "I got nothing." Did I really think that was going to make a difference? Was some potential manufacturer going to read this and say, "This is the stupidest thing I've ever heard, but . . . hey, it could be made in hunter green? Bingo!"

Yet this was only the beginning of Andrea's Cavalcade of Sleaze. Next up? Honey Butter, a honey/peanut butter concoction submitted by a woman from Utah who "just knows" her family recipe will sweep the nation if it's mass-marketed; Grilled Pepper Stuffs, a stuffed-pepper dish sent in by a "committed, lifelong griller" from Florida, who, like the Utah woman, was sure his idea was the next great thing in food marketing; and something called Warm Little Piggies, which was some sort of microwave-heated slipper thing whose developer was certain she was on the verge of striking gold. "After all," she opined, "who likes cold feet?"

This invention pissed me off because a) it, like most of the others, was dumb as a mitten and b) the phrase "cold feet" reminded me of my impending marriage. To be fair, I was growing content in the knowledge that I would be married soon. What bothered me was trying in vain to find a nice way to say "I don't care" to the relentless barrage of questions Nicole assaulted me with on almost a daily basis concerning our big day.

"What do you think about purple for my bridesmaid dresses?"

"What about flowers? Should they match the dresses or just be fall colors?"

"Band or deejay?"

"Sit-down dinner or buffet? Homemade cookies or bakery?"

My pat answer was, "Honey, you do what you think is best. I have complete faith in you." And when this failed, I tried my best—and usually succeeded—at divining which answer Nicole preferred. So, things were going swimmingly concerning our wedding plans, not unlike Andrea's revived career as a consultant. She was even sporting a bounce in her gait these days and possessed the intensity of a hungry bear. And though it bothers me to admit this, her passion was contagious. Sam, Rachel, and I were a lot more focused because we had much work to do, and for a while it almost felt like we were working for a real company and doing honest work.

I banged out Andrea's first 17 NPRs in two days' time, and Rache did the same for the artwork. Never mind that of the 17, roughly 17 were ridiculous. The point is this: It felt good. I felt like an actual, live adult with an actual, honest-to-goodness job. Not even something called Dough-Nuts! (balls of fried dough shaped like cashews; the exclamation point came with the invention) could bring me down.

What finally brought me down? Perpetua. Andrea's first 17 sales annoyed me. They were bad ideas submitted by honest, misguided, and soon-to-be poorer folks. But her 18th pissed me off. One quick glance of the inventor's submitted artwork told me all I needed to know. It contained a bunch of wheels and magnets and was covered top to bottom in nonsensical mathematical formulas. It was Bill Doddey's idea of a perpetual-motion machine. Had it also possessed a way to dispense medications at certain times of the day, I swear I would have killed everyone in the office before turning the gun on myself.

Andrea couldn't possibly take this guy's money, could she? Perpetual-motion machines are the Ponzi schemes of the scientific world. Doesn't everybody know that? Well, everyone except Bill Doddey, I guess. I mean, even da Vinci tried his hand at a perpetual-motion machine before realizing such a thing couldn't exist. Just to make sure I wasn't crazy, I took a trip to a nearby bookstore on my lunch break to read up on perpetual motion. Here are some definitions I came across:

1. *Any device that continues its motion perpetually without decreasing. This is a literal interpretation of the words.*

2. *Any machine that violates laws of physics, or postulates speculative theories.*

3. *A machine that perpetually puts out more energy than it takes in.*

My favorite phrase from above is "violates the laws of physics." Not only were we violating the law in general; we were now violating the laws of physics. Any goodwill I had felt about my job the past few days was hereby vanquished. I hated bothering Sam with another one of my righteous-indignation moments, so I figured I'd run it by Rachel first to get her take.

"She broke her own vow," was the first thing out of Rachel's mouth.

"What do you mean?"

Rachel explained to me that it was a known fact in the office that about two or three times a year someone submits an idea for a perpetual-motion machine and that Andrea has always made jokes about them. She buzzed Sam's phone, and he came over instantly.

"What's up, guys? Uh-oh, Nick's got the look."

Rachel handed him the submission.

"We're accepting this?" He froze for a moment, and then he chuckled.

"Well, Rache, on a light note, I guess now is as good a time as any to tell Nick what Mousetrap's number-one all-time invention is."

"Oh, God, that's right." She started to laugh.

"Nick, three words: Perpetual-motion vibrator."

So, that was it. Mousetrap's all-time bad invention was a sex toy "designed" by what I can only imagine was a terminally horny woman who was tired of spending money on batteries. We all laughed, but we also realized that Andrea had crossed a line. Granted, it's like going from embezzlement to larceny, but an imperceptible line had been crossed. Andrea was now officially playing on the dark side, willing to take money for any stupid idea that landed in our mailbox. And I would get to see them all.

I tried cajoling Sam into confronting Andrea about the perpetual-motion machine. He shot me down but told me I was free to confront her myself. I laughed his response away initially, but that night I tried to think of the pros and cons of going head-to-head with the woman who signed my paycheck.

On one hand, I was curious to confront her, just to see what her reaction would be. I didn't think she was the type to fire someone on the spot for asking a question, painful as it may be, but I also wasn't sure I wanted to put my theory to practical use.

The next day, I asked Sam if he was serious about my talking to Andrea.

"It's your funeral, bub," was how he responded. I told him I was serious.

"Then you have my permission. Shall I fetch the sweater for you?"

"The sweater" was a cardigan Sam kept in his office for whenever he had a meeting in Andrea's frozen lair of an office. It came in handy year-round, and it gave us a chance to feel like Mr. Rogers. As I was putting on the sweater, Sam serenaded me with a few bars of the "Mr. Rogers' Neighborhood" theme, substituting the word "neighbor" with "ex-coworker."

I took a deep breath, adjusted the sweater, and headed to the Arctic Circle. Andrea was on the phone but summoned me to come in. This is the scenario everyone entering her office dreaded: having to sit there freezing while she blathered on about Lord knows what on the phone. Fortunately, the conversation lasted only a few more minutes; hypothermia probably wouldn't set in.

"Nicholas, what brings you here?" She was giddy. Well, as giddy as a poorly dressed, unattractive, chain-smoking 60-year-old woman could be, anyway.

"Perpetual motion." There. I just blurted it the fuck out. Why not? How do you lead up to it, anyway? What was I going to say? "Well, Andrea, it's come to my attention that a client's submission perhaps fell through the cracks and landed on my desk. I can't imagine a woman of your integrity would ever accept money from someone whose idea is fundamentally flawed and has been the scorn of science for the better part of, oh, I don't know, forever."

Nah, fuck it. Let's have at it, girl. Perpetual fucking motion, ya skeezy, smelly entrepren-whore.

"Well, what can I say, Nick?" She chuckled and looked off to the side. I sat there, frozen by fear and, well, frozen in the conventional sense. Why didn't I pee before I got here? Sam and that stupid Mr. Rogers' song.

"You caught me." She said it in a whisper.

"I guess you're aware that perpetual-motion machines are something I've laughed at over the years, right?"

I nodded, perhaps not vigorously enough for her to see.

"Right?" she barked.

"Yes," I chirped.

"Well, Nick, we're up against it. You know that as well as I do. Our numbers are down, even with me selling. The fact is, if we don't reconfigure our policies, or, at the very least, tweak one or two, you and all your friends will find yourself on Penn Avenue faster than I can say 'Boo.'"

She shot me a piercing look. Yet before she spoke and broke eye contact, she cocked her eyebrow.

"I shouldn't have told you what I just told you, Nick. It's in your best self-interest not to go blabbing to your coworkers about what I just said. I like you, and I respect your courage for confronting me on this.

"It's also in your best interest to never do this again. Now get back to work on helping make dreams come true for that special 1 percent."

I got up, nodded, and walked as quickly as I could back to Sam's office.

Rachel was there, and they were both waiting for me to spill. I told them the truth, figuring that they were good with a secret. I then hung up the sweater back in Sam's closet and got back to the next NPR. I had incurred Andrea's wrath yet had survived. Of course, she admitted to me that she was being openly sleazy in her business dealings and that I better shut the hell up about it.

Still, weirdly, I felt good. My conscience was, at least momentarily, assuaged. And the next idea on the pile, I was glad to see, was merely conventionally stupid, not the bane of the scientific method:

Client: Beth Sewickley

Idea: Fabrocs

Have you ever noticed that garden rocks come in one of two colors—white or gray? How boring is that? What gardener or homeowner wouldn't love to color-coordinate a rock garden to match the décor of his or her home? Fabrocs makes this possible. Fabrocs are rock-shaped balls of material that can be assembled in virtually any color or design to match a home's outdoor color scheme.

But wait . . . what about holiday decorating? Red-and-green Fabrocs for Christmas, black-and-orange for Halloween. The possibilities are endless.

Product Highlights:

- *Add color to any yard/garden*
- *Can be made to withstand any weather conditions*
- *Appeals to people who, like the inventor, have too much time on their hands*
- *Attractive as a seasonal product*

I couldn't resist the jab. Mine were the last set of eyes that would read the copy on the NPR. Sure, someone in administration folded them and put them in envelopes, but they never bothered to read the copy. And in the off chance that someone in the recipient's office even bothered to open the envelope, the worst thing that would happen is that he or she might get a chuckle.

By the end of April, we had fleeced 44 new clients, all of whom were waiting for a letter or phone call that would never come, all with visions of their face plastered on jars in supermarkets across the country, their stories in *Fortune,* inspiring others to follow their dreams. I felt bad for these folks, but I also questioned their intelligence. No matter how much we (and when I say "we," yeah, I mean "me") tried to conceal the fact, the 1-percent brochure included with every packet to a potential client didn't hide the truth: We're as close to completely unsuccessful as a company can be. And yet they still sent us not only their ideas, but their money. Perhaps part of me just didn't understand their mentality, since my dreams are much more attainable—a good game on TV and some nice pie to go along with it. When's the last time you heard someone say anything bad about pie?

Of the 44 new clients, Andrea was responsible for half of them, and the seven remaining consultants came up with the other 22. Fun fact about most of the consultants: They used aliases in the workplace. I'm guessing this was done both for safety and legal reasons. And I could never decide which consultant type alarmed me more: the ones who were openly sleazy and laughed at their clients, or the ones who seemed earnest in their client dealings. You would hear them sometimes on the phone as you passed their offices, kindly encouraging inventors to keep their heads up and that success would strike like a lightning bolt—"You just watch!"

Since we had fewer clients, I had more time to dedicate to my inner-office lark: writing a series of ridiculous stories called "The Terrible Towel Murders," which involved my serial-killer protagonist, Chapel Fox: by day, a respected lawyer; by night, a lunatic who seeks revenge on those who utter anything anti-Pittsburgh. He especially hates anti-Steeler sentiment and strangles all his victims with his beloved Terrible Towel, which he loves to remind everyone is "an original version, circa 1976, signed by Myron Cope himself."

It was a normal Wednesday in the office. Chapel Fox had seen his usual number of clients, typically well-heeled women hell-bent on squeezing every last dime from their philandering, good-for-nothing lumps of proto-plasm they previously referred to as "husband."

Spring was trying to break through winter's maniacal stranglehold on the area, and that at least brightened Fox's otherwise dour mood. That, and he noticed at lunch they were having a half-off sale on men's suits at Kaufmann's. He figured he'd swing by after work. After all, a lawyer can never have enough dark suits.

He assumed the rest of his day would be routine—meet a few more clients, make a few phone calls—until she stumbled in.

Yeah, that's right—stumbled in. Sure, she was gorgeous, and in all the ways you'd assume. (If you prefer blondes, make her a blonde; do the same for any other preference. If you want her to be a Latina midget with jet-black hair, have at it.) But here's why she stumbled, all right? She wasn't used to wearing high heels, and so as she entered the office, she tripped.

Fox laughed at the sight of a (Latina midget, blonde goddess, brunette centerfold-type, whatever) stumbling toward him, and he lent her a hand before she landed face first at his feet.

"You must be Mrs. Gutierrez, (or Mrs. Washington or Mrs. Goloski; you get the idea), my 2:00," said Fox.

"Well, they say first impressions are lasting ones," she replied, trying to laugh off her embarrassing entrance.

"Please, ma'am, come this way. And, Beth," he told his secretary, "please hold all my calls."

Fox had never married, but he knew what he liked. And he liked Mrs. Gutierrez. (For the record, since Fox has a penchant for chesty brunettes, she'll be referred to as Mrs. Gutierrez hence. But, like I've said, this is an interactive story. If you prefer, say, the Charlene Tilton or the Tina Turner look, adjust accordingly. Or the Harrison Ford look, for that matter. We're not picky here).

Fox got through the pleasantries—"Coffee or tea, ma'am?"—before approaching the reason she was sitting across from him, taking in the wonders that were his office. Yes, divorce was good for Fox and afforded him an office that would be the envy of any cubicle dweller. And the view from this 15th-floor office manse? He overlooked the Allegheny River and the Station Square complex and had tried, unsuccessfully, over the years to abate his insatiable inner rage by looking at the gently rolling river.

"It's my husband," said Mrs. Gutierrez.

"I kind of figured," said Fox. If he had a nickel for every time a client stated the obvious, he would have been able to purchase even more suits at Kaufmann's.

"He's been cheating on me, it seems, for years. I thought we had"—

She began to cry. When he was a young lawyer, Fox used to feel genuine sadness at this point of the proceedings. But now, after all these years, he knew it was just part of the routine, as if there were some publication called "Divorce Weekly" that offered tips on how to get maximum benefits.

Still, he pretended to be moved and handed her the box of tissues that he always kept at the ready. It occurred to him, too, that his monthly Kleenex outlays also bit into his suit-purchasing power.

After she regained her composure, she rattled off the usual litany of complaints, the biggest one, of course, being the ongoing infidelity and how she literally caught them in the act—and in her bed, no less.

She wanted everything—the cars, the house, the investments, the Steeler tickets.

"You a fan?" asked Fox.

"Lifelong," she replied.

The dark hair and giant rack had already won him over. But this bit of information was almost too much.

"I'd love to see them draft a receiver this year," said Fox, in an effort to test her football acumen.

"Eh, I don't know. Lipps is terrific. Hell, I think he's better than Swann. Don't you think Swann was overrated?"

Damn it. He was crestfallen. How could this conversation have gone downhill so quickly? One minute, he's envisioning this Latina goddess in his bed. Now? Well, Fox was left with no choice. After all, asking Chapel Fox if Lynn Swann was overrated was like asking Julia Child if wine's popularity was a bit overblown. It was like asking the Pope, "So, what's this God guy done lately, huh?"

Sure, she was still physically attractive, but to Fox, her soulless body was riddled with tumors—tumors of stupidity. Lynn Swann was a fearless receiver who constantly went over the middle, knowing full well that Bradshaw was leading him to danger. But time and again he went, picking up first downs, jumping what seemed to be 20 feet in the air and sticking a dagger in yet another defense. Louis Lipps better than Swann? "No wonder your husband was banging some other broad," he thought. "I hope he banged your sister, too. And your best friend."

When he first laid eyes on her and then found out she loved the Steelers, he figured dinner was in the works. And, yes, to be sure, they would be meeting again tonight, but under quite different circumstances.

He didn't let her linger too much longer in his office. The sight of her tumor-riddled soul was beginning to sicken him. Plus, he now had plans for that night.

After work, he went to Kaufmann's, of course, and picked up two new gray suits. No need to let an unplanned homicide get in the way of a good sale.

He parked a few blocks from Mrs. Gutierrez's residence and waited till 11:00 to pay the Swann hater a visit. He had ascertained from their meeting that her husband had moved out. It would be smooth sailing.

She was surprised, but certainly not alarmed, to see him standing on her porch. He was holding an accordion-type folder under his right arm. He motioned to it, indicating there was some paperwork that couldn't wait for morning.

She let him in.

"Listen," he began. "I'm really sorry to bother you at this time of night, but I want to start processing your paperwork first thing, and as I was leaving the office, I noticed you hadn't signed a few things. So, if you wouldn't mind . . ."

"Oh, sure, no problem. Let me just grab a pen."

"What humdrum last words," thought Fox.

As she turned to get a pen, Fox, with catlike grace, grabbed his trusty Terrible Towel from the accordion folder and secured it firmly around her neck. She never knew what hit her.

"Lynn Swann is overrated, huh?!" Fox yelled. "You stupid cow."

Within a minute, Mrs. Gutierrez was no longer and crumpled to the floor. Fox, who had made sure not to touch a thing in the house, used his elbow to undo the latch on the storm door and vanished into the night.

Her body would be found in two days by her husband, who, of course, would end up being the number-one suspect. Fox? Sure, a detective paid him a visit, seeing how she was at his office the day of the murder, but what motive would he have? She was about to fork over to him a nice chunk of change.

He would have to be crazy to have killed her.

Pleased with my time-killing stupidity and the knowledge that it looked as though I were busy working if someone walked by my office, I dashed off to the copier to make 10 copies for my reading-club members. I figured they could use a laugh and a distraction. I had my own distraction: My beloved Penguins were in the semifinals of the NHL playoffs. Hell, they weren't just in the semis. They were on the verge of beating Boston and reaching the Stanley Cup finals for the first time in their 24-year history. Plus, it was May. Color was returning to this part of the world. The sun had reblessed us with its appearance. I heard the laughs from my coworkers as I walked the halls. They were enjoying the newest Chapel Fox story. Things were—well, to be honest, they were okay. The Pens playing deep into spring worked like a 24-hour endorphin on me. In addition, Sam bitching about Karen dragging him to birthing classes and his increasing nerves over becoming a father provided an endless source of entertainment for me and Rachel.

And in mid-May, work picked up again, thanks in part to Andrea's salesmanship, both inside and outside Mousetrap's walls. Sure, she was still the top salesperson, but her numbers had inspired the other consultants to pick up the pace, too. By May 15, we had 30 new clients. These numbers were downright pre-1 percent, FTC numbers. Andrea was ecstatic, and we were happy to be busy and employed.

THE END OF MOUSETRAP began with a very loud fuck. No, not the physical kind. The verbal kind, as in the psychotically cheerful Alice screaming the word as though she were ablaze.

She yelled so loudly that Sam, Rachel, and I all left our desks and headed toward her office, certain that she was in imminent physical danger. She looked at us, frozen, her hand on the receiver. Her usual smiling face had turned to stone, and, again, she yelled the word. We didn't know what the hell to do. Finally, Sam said, "Are you okay, Alice?"

She looked at him and again yelled the word, though this time she dragged it out, as though she were trying to make it more conversational. She then brushed by us and headed toward Andrea's lair, yelling "Fuck" with every step she took.

She slammed Andrea's door behind her, and the three of us crept as close as we could to see if we could pick up any of the action. When we heard Andrea unleash a thunderous "Fuck" of her own, we knew that all this fucking was company related and that we were the ones about to be screwed.

The three of us of had a meeting in Sam's office and discussed what the possibilities could be:

1. It was a reporter asking for a quote about a story being run concerning a disgruntled client who decided to blow the whistle on our deceptive ineptitude.

2. A friend called Alice to tell her that she just read an article in the *New England Journal of Medicine* that indicated a connection between senseless laughing and cancer.

3. The FTC got wind of our "admission" and is demanding full, honest compliance with its edict.

We figured it probably wasn't Number 2. We hoped it was only Number 1. We secretly knew it was Number 3.

We were right.

About 20 minutes after Alice's fuck-fest, Andrea buzzed me and told me she wanted to see me. It looked like Mr. 1 Percent was going to be called on again to make his tasty brand of hiding-the-truth lemonade.

I grabbed a pen and notebook and, blessedly, remembered to hit the men's room before entering Frostbite Falls.

As soon as I stepped foot in her office, I knew the FTC had found us out. Andrea had a faraway look on her face, the kind you see young widows sport. Disbelief, hurt, with a hint of rage quaking beneath the calm surface—it was all there.

"Well, Nicholas, the bastards found us out."

"The FTC, Andrea?"

"What other cocksuckers do you think I'm talking about?"

I was there to listen, not to ask questions.

"That wonderful insert you wrote—the 1-percent thing? Well, it's not good enough for the bastards. They want it stripped down to the raw numbers—clients, successes, etc. And, in addition, they've levied another $50,000 fine on top of the previous one for noncompliance.

"Non-fucking-compliance for their asshole demands, the cocksuckers. How dare they?!"

At which point she picked up a stapler and threw it against the nearest wall. Well, actually, that's not quite accurate. She threw a stapler, but it fell several feet short of the wall, seeing how years of smoking and eating only to survive had left her as physically capable as a woman twice her age.

This feeble display apparently was too much for her, and as we watched the stapler roll once before coming to a stop, she started sobbing. And then the tears came. I approached her, and as I did, she stood up, threw her arms around me and started wailing.

So, there I was, in possibly the most uncomfortable moment of my youngish life. A smelly, deceitful, chain-smoking, morally bankrupt lunatic was crying into my shoulder. As she continued to cry, her makeup started to run, and I honestly thought for a second that her whole face might start to disintegrate, like that scene in "Poltergeist."

Within a minute, though, it was over. She tried to regain her composure and issued me my command.

"I want you to write it, Nick. And this time, the f—the bastards want to see it first. Play it straight."

I nodded, left her office, and went back to tell Sam and Rache the bad news. They weren't surprised, naturally, and Rachel mumbled something about spending the rest of her day sprucing up her résumé before trudging back to her office.

"Hey," said Sam with mock enthusiasm, "I'm gonna be Unemployed Dad!"

"And I get to be Unemployed Newlywed," I replied.

"Yeah, but I also get to be Unemployed Husband, so I totally kick your ass." He then sighed. "I'm sorry for getting you in this mess."

I looked at him quizzically.

"Hell, I was the one who hired you, remember? I'm sorry. You deserve better than this."

"There's no reason for you to apologize. I accepted the job knowing full well what I was getting into, first of all. And if I wanted to, I could leave right now. This isn't the mafia."

"No, you're wrong, Nick." Sam was suddenly sporting a very determined look. "You know too much now. You leave . . . you die."

Perhaps I had been a Mousetrap employee for too long and could no longer differentiate truth from deception. Perhaps it was the fact that my mind was more focused on writing a straightforward insert and my impending unemployment as a result of it. Or perhaps I'm just slow on the uptake. But for a second, anyway, Sam got me, and the terror that gripped me only was released when Sam threw his head back and started howling at me.

"Thanks, buddy," he said. "I really needed that."

"Glad I could oblige, bastard."

"Listen. Let's head over to the Pussycat sometime soon and let off some steam, all right? After all, you're not going to be single much longer."

"And you're not single at all," I reminded him.

"Yeah, but I'm gonna be a father soon, so that entitles me to look at naked women who aren't my wife. It's in the by-laws."

"What by-laws?"

"The marriage by-laws," Sam said. "You didn't know? On your wedding day, your priest will give you a copy of a 'Husband's By-Laws,' which you are to follow all the days of your life."

I wasn't buying a word of this, but I wanted to see how far he would take it. "And in these by-laws," I said, "that are given to a groom by a priest, it says that a husband with an expectant wife is allowed to visit strip joints."

"Well, not in those terms exactly. Don't be ridiculous."

"Well, then, what does it say?"

"It says something to the effect of, 'Don't you have a fucking thing to write for those ass-cock, midget-brain, piss-drinking FTC douchefucks?'"

Sam uttered that last line in a dead-on impersonation of Andrea, and as we laughed our asses off, we heard the unmistakable cackle of Alice Legato joining in. Boy, did that kill any momentary happiness.

"Sam," she whispered, "That was hysterical!" Okay, good. She wasn't going to go running to Andrea. I guess sometimes funny is funny.

"Listen, Nick. I just wanted to remind you that the FTC thing has to be a 'Just the facts, ma'am' document, okay? And run it by me when you're done."

"Sure, Alice."

And with that cue, I returned to my office and began to lay the groundwork for the destruction of Mousetrap.

I briefly scanned my original insert and realized the task ahead of me was quite simple: remove the bullshit and keep the facts. My 1-percent insert did possess all the information any potential inventor would need to know, of course. I just happened to do an effective job of obscuring the facts with hopeful nonsense.

So, therefore, what was originally written as this: *In these past 11 years, almost 7,100 clients have brought us their hopes, and 68 have seen their ideas go from paper to reality and have made a profit on their initial investment. That's a success rate of nearly 1 percent, which doesn't sound very promising until you dig a little deeper.*

Now became this: *Mousetrap Inc., which has been in business for 11 years, has served almost 7,100 clients. Of these clients, 68 have seen their ideas turned into market reality and have made a profit off their initial investment. This is a success rate of .0095 percent.*

And that was it. The rest of the words I had written in the 1-percent insert were nothing more than barren hopes and promises never meant to be kept. I printed it out and brought it to Alice's office.

It took her five seconds to scan it. "Boy, I guess that's all we can say, huh? I wonder if we can maybe include a brief description of some of our successes."

She buzzed Andrea to find out.

"No!" came the quick reply. "And the bastards want us to print it on bright paper, too, and put the whole thing in huge, bold type."

Andrea sounded drunk, which didn't come as a shock. Alice looked up at me and wasn't sure what to say. Amazingly, though, she wasn't laughing, either, which was a refreshing change.

"Well, I guess this is a go, then, Nick. I'll, uh, run it by Andrea before we proceed printing it."

We faxed it over to the FTC the next day, and they approved it almost immediately. From that day on, we were to include the new insert with every information packet we sent out to a potential client.

Andrea had sobered up and came around to tell us there would be a company-wide meeting at 2:00 to discuss the latest FTC actions. She possessed an Olympic figure skater's look of determination at the beginning of her long program, and I knew she wasn't going to let her company go without a fight.

Which was noble, of course, but we couldn't escape the obvious: Beginning today, we were inserting in every packet we mailed to potential customers a handy, postcard-size, bright-as-the-sun slip of paper that all but proclaimed, "We are comically incompetent at what we do, we're deceitful about it, and we'd really, really like it if you wrote us a check for, say, 6 or 7 grand. Sound good?"

I was, though, perversely looking forward to the meeting. If nothing else, it would at least be great theater.

She didn't disappoint. We gathered in the large conference room and began idle chit-chat, mostly about the Pens, and waited for Andrea to make her grand entrance.

Everyone seemed relatively happy, and only Sam, Rachel, Alice, and I knew that never again would there be three dozen Mousetrap employees gathered in the same room, unless it was a room featuring a bench, a judge, and a mad-as-hell jury.

Five minutes passed. Then ten. The small talk got a little louder and more animated. Suddenly, we witnessed the closet door fly open. Silence. "No longer will we live our business lives in a closet, ashamed of what we do!"

She took two steps from the closet and stared at us. "And if any of you feel ashamed of working for my company, then get . . . the . . . fuck . . . out . . . now. By window, by door, I . . . don't . . . give . . . a . . . fuck."

Half of me wanted to leave, and the other half wanted me to run up to the imaginary stage she was standing on and hand her a bouquet of fresh-picked spring flowers. I was sickened and enthralled. I hated everything she stood for and loved the fact that rarely, if ever, would I be in the presence of somebody who could accurately be described as larger than life.

No one left. Hell, no one twitched a foot or tapped a pencil. We weren't going anywhere. Well, most of us would likely be canned soon, but 90 percent of the people didn't know that yet.

"I love this company. It is my life. I awake every morning thinking of ways to make people's dreams real." She chuckled ruefully and lit a smoke. "Of course, the government begs to differ."

A few people let out tentative chuckles.

"No, please, laugh. Laugh at the government. We will laugh now, and we will laugh later, and we will laugh last. Ha-ha-ha-ha-ha-ha-fucking-ha!"

She was now coming across as slightly deranged, and what I first viewed as great theater was now turning Hitlerish.

"Nick!" she yelled.

Oh, for the sweet love of fuck, why did she just say my name? How about I just run headfirst through the window, and maybe you can sue the FTC by pinning my suicide on them?

"Yes, Andrea?"

"Why don't you tell your coworkers what the FTC is making us do starting today?"

I wasn't sure why Andrea was making me the bearer of bad news, but I was sure of one thing: 72 eyes boring holes through me. I was so tempted to say something nice and happy, like, "The FTC is demanding that Mousetrap provides free cake for all employees every Friday! In fact, FTC now stands for Find the Cake, and the employee who finds the hidden cake each Friday not only gets the first slice but $1,000, too!"

"Well, folks, they want us to, uh, be more direct in our presentation of the number of successful clients we've had."

"And they want it in bold type! And they want it on paper so bright, we should enclose a pair of fucking sunglasses, too!" She was now spitting.

"Here's what they really want, people. They want us gone. But are we going to let them?"

Most of shook our heads, which apparently wasn't enough.

"Are we going to let them, Alice?"

"No, Andrea."

"Sam, are we going to let them?"

"No, Andrea."

She did this for every employee. After the first dozen or so people said, "No, Andrea," the rest started jazzing it up by offering the occasional "Heck, no," which advanced to "Hell, no," which inevitably led to Sheldon, a consultant, and the last employee asked, bellowing out, "Fuck, no, Andrea!" She loved it.

This was Andrea Bianco's idea of team-building—crazy, dictator-like speeches, punctuated with cigarettes and swearing. Most companies go on rafting trips or climb mountains. Not us. We're the special 1 percent.

"So, before you go back to your offices, I need you to keep this in mind: This company is in jeopardy. I'm not going to sugarcoat it. Your livelihoods are in jeopardy. We need every new client we can get, and I will personally see to it that our company guidelines are changed to reflect our current situation."

Translation: More perpetual-motion machines.

"But don't leave here with a heavy heart. Fight. Fight with me. You don't want to lose your jobs, and I don't want to lose my company. Now let's go out there and fight twice as hard for what truly is that special 1 percent."

So, that was it—Andrea's rah-rah speech. She was clinging to an illusion, of course. Maybe the majority of our clients weren't members of Mensa, but I assumed that even the vast majority of them would figure out we were no damn good.

On a completely unrelated note: The Penguins, my beloved Pens, won their first Stanley Cup on May 25, defeating the Minnesota North Stars 8–0 in the deciding game. Something I had waited for literally my whole life had finally happened, and it took the sting out of the impending train wreck that was Mousetrap.

May was a good month for Mousetrap, too: It ended up with 49 new clients. Of course, the new disclaimer insert started to go out the last week of May. By some point in June, we figured, the FTC could at the very least start chiseling the M-O-U on our corporate tombstone.

June 1991

BY THE FIRST WEEK of the first month of summer, the glow of the Pens' Cup triumph had largely been suffocated. Of the first six NPRs that passed my desk, three of them—really, I wish I were making this up— were variations of the Medi-Timer: Pill-Tock, HourLife, and Medicine, Man! And yes, the exclamation point was client-provided. And yes, I'll spare you any detailed descriptions, seeing that if you don't know the idea by now, you really haven't been paying very close attention, and at this point you're just waiting for the naughty scene I promised several chapters ago.

Also, there were seven fewer of us. Andrea axed three administrative people and four nonperforming salesmen shortly after last month's spirit-building lovefest.

Initially, though, June's numbers held up pretty well, as we had figured, since most of our new clients had been spared the bright-as-Big Bird insert that was now greeting any potential marks. Plus, around mid-June, the FTC had a change of heart and decided that the insert didn't go far enough in proclaiming our suckdom. They demanded that in addition to our "success" rate, we also had to make mention that Mousetrap had been fined heavily for unscrupulous business practices.

I was beginning to really hate the FTC. No, not because of what they were doing to the company that employed me. For that, they had my total support. But, you see, every time the FTC fucked Mousetrap anew, a phone call from an angry, drunken Andrea would result, each one becoming uglier and more embarrassing than the last.

"Nick, they won't let it go. Help me!" Click.

I entered the frozen tundra of Fraud Field and began chiding myself for forgetting my Mr. Rogers ensemble when I came upon the ghastly sight of Andrea pouring Jack Daniel's into a water glass and slugging back the entire contents in one swoosh. She had been weeping, and the contents of her desk were scattered on the floor around her. A broken music box featuring a now shattered Mickey Mouse was playing the same three notes of "It's a Small World After All" over and over.

"I hate them, Nick. I hate them. I hate them. I hate them!" She was drunk, furious, and entirely wrong. I felt like I was watching the last days of Richard Nixon. Any second, I figured we'd both be on our knees, praying for the souls of Haldeman and Ehrlichman.

"So, go ahead and make a new fucking insert, Nick, and put in there how much they fined us. And put this in there, too: 'Lick my balls.'"

I looked at her hesitantly, which I knew was stupid the second the feeling overcame me.

"'Lick my balls' or out the door, Nick. Which is it?"

"I'll get right on it, Andrea."

Sure, my friends and I were soon to be unemployed. And sure, at any subsequent job interview for the next several years, we'd have to explain away the time we worked for a fraudulent company. But I practically skipped back to my office to begin work on my new assignment. This was priceless stuff, and my hands literally raced around the keyboard. I was going to follow the boss's orders to the T.

I started with the original . . .

Mousetrap Inc., which has been in business for 11 years, has served almost 7,100 clients. Of these clients, 68 have seen their ideas turned into market reality and have made a profit off their initial investment. This is a success rate of .0095 percent.

And then added in the FTC's new request:

In November 1990, the FTC levied fines against Mousetrap in the amount of $1.2 million for deceitful business practices as part of an ongoing investigation into the invention-marketing industry. It then levied an additional $50,000 fine last month for Mousetrap's failure to comply with all terms of the 1990 agreement.

Then, I got a piece of bright yellow paper, placed it in the printer, and brought it all together:

Mousetrap Inc., which has been in business for 11 years, has served almost 7,100 clients. Of these clients, 68 have seen their ideas turned into market reality and have made a profit off their initial investment. This is a success rate of .0095 percent.

In November 1990, the FTC levied fines against Mousetrap in the amount of $1.2 million for deceitful business practices as part of an ongoing investigation into the invention-marketing industry. It then levied an additional $50,000 fine last month for Mousetrap's failure to comply with all terms of the 1990 agreement.

Lick my balls.

I promptly handed it to Sam, who heard me laughing.

"Nick, don't do it like this. Come on. Don't lose your self-respect."

I couldn't stop laughing and was unable to do anything but vigorously shake my head. Sam handed my latest work to Rachel, who burst into hysterics. Alice, beckoned by the sound of laughter, came laughing into Rachel's office.

"Nick, look. I know how we all feel about the FTC, but this won't help anything."

I still couldn't stop laughing but was able to blurt out, "Andrea."

"Yes, Nick, Andrea will probably love it, but that doesn't mean—"

"No, Alice. I'm following Andrea's orders. She threatened to fire me on the spot if I didn't add the last sentence."

I then resumed laughing my ass off, as did everyone in the room. We each took turns reading it, each time laughing harder, and we all eagerly awaited our next turn holding the fluorescent yellow paper in our hand, as though it were a joint and we were awaiting our next hit of funny.

Finally, after several minutes, Alice spoke up. "I guess I have to convince her that this isn't the best idea."

I warned her that Andrea was sucking down whiskey like it was lemonade in July, and I reminded her that one cocked eyebrow almost cost me my job.

"I'm a big girl, but thanks. Anyway, Andrea desperately needs legal counsel, and I doubt she's in position to hire a new lawyer."

About 30 seconds later, Alice appeared in my doorway, handed me the paper, and said, "Just fax the damn thing as is, Nick."

I started to speak, but she cut me off.

"She may have been drunk when you saw her, Nick, but she's now reached a new level of, I don't know, 'drunksanity'? She's not making any sense, she's throwing things around, and she won't stop yelling . . . you know."

I didn't, but she kept pointing at the paper. "Oh, that." I started laughing again, as did Alice. "Just fax it, Nick." She shrugged her shoulders and returned to her office.

I gave Sam and Rache an update, and I figured they'd want to see the document transmit over to the FTC. I wasn't wrong. Seeing it go through the machine and knowing that a human on the other end was going to read it gave us all a special thrill. Sure, the FTC was right, but Andrea signed our paychecks, and, after all, funny is funny.

The FTC didn't find Andrea's prank nearly as humorous as we did. They answered back within 30 minutes to inform us that a fresh, new $100,000 fine had been slapped on Mousetrap for "further failure to comply with the November 1990 agreement."

I redid the document once more, this time updating the $50,000 figure to $150,000, refaxed the new version over, and was given permission to proceed.

Of course, it would have been very easy for us to have "forgotten" to include this slip of paper in the packet of materials we sent to prospective clients. And, no doubt, this crossed Andrea's mind. But, careful consumer, never fear: The FTC required us to supply them the names and phone numbers of everybody we sent packets to, and they informed us that they would randomly call potential clients each month to make sure that our success-rate information was included in our mailing. If it wasn't, the FTC warned, they would promptly fine us out of business, and the company would face legal action.

Since I had little actual work to do (prescription-alarm-clock NPRs pretty much wrote themselves by this point) and feeling inspired by the "Lick my balls" escapade, I thought it was a good time for another psychotic adventure of Pittsburgh's well-meaning, yet ultimately deranged, superhero, Chapel Fox.

After the Gutierrez "mishap" (internally, he never felt that what he did constituted murder; he was merely righting wrongs), Chapel Fox, for the first time in years, felt a general sense of unease. After all, the Steelers were 9–7 the year before and had missed the playoffs. And this year didn't hold much promise, either. Plus, every time for the rest of his life that Louis Lipps caught a ball, he would think of that awful woman and her ridiculous notion.

Sure, he had to admit, Lipps was a good receiver. But as good as Swann? Just thinking about it made him wish he had the power to bring his latest correction back to life, if only to kill her again.

So, what did today bring Chapel Fox professionally? Nothing out of the ordinary. A few meetings with established clients for the purposes of updates, plus a few more with prospective ones. He looked out his window. It was a beautiful June day. He then remembered the Pirates were playing the Cubs at Three Rivers that afternoon at 1:35.

"Perfect!" he thought. His meetings were either in the morning or later in the day. His mood brightened. He would enjoy a few hours of baseball on a lovely late-spring day. What could be better?

Ironically, at that exact moment, Tim Schoenfeld and Frank Plager were thinking the same thing. They were on their way to Three Rivers Stadium from Chicago to see the exact same game, and they were excited to see their Cubbies play on the road, in a city neither had visited before.

As fate would have it (and stories like this don't exist without fate), best friends Tim and Frank sat in front of Fox.

Fox could have forgiven their partisan cheering. After all, he understood fandom, and when he saw the two Chicagoans decked out in Cubswear, he thought nothing of it. He respected fans of all teams.

And he even tolerated their incessant booing of Pirate slugger Barry Bonds. Again, Fox reasoned, Bonds has the potential to be the greatest player of his generation and no doubt will be booed his entire career by opposing fans merely because of his greatness. Again, no foul.

But here's where Fox's happy, American baseball day began to sour. Let's listen in, as Tim and Frank begin their critique of Pittsburgh:

Frank: This place really is as bad as everyone says.

Tim: You said it.

You see, this annoyed Fox rather than upset him. He was looking forward to having a happy day—baseball, maybe a beer and a dog—and he genuinely was hoping that the men in front of him were merely trashing Three Rivers Stadium, which, truth be told, was a dump.

Sadly, the men continued:

Frank: I think they would have been better off leaving the smoke. At least the smoke covered up the ugliness!

Tim: Ain't that the truth!

Okay, that was it, of course. "You stupid, malignant fucks," Fox wanted to yell. "Voted 'America's Most Livable City' five years ago!"

He needed to dispatch with these morons, but he had to show restraint. Killing people in front of a crowd of 20,000 wasn't the way to go. But, good God, it was only the third inning. How much more of this was he expected to endure?

The Pirates jumped out to a 6–1 lead by the fifth, and this made Frank and Tim, now both quite drunk, berate the city even more.

Frank: And did you see the women? I wouldn't fuck 'em with your dick!

Frank, Fox reasoned, would need to experience extra pain because he was a) a drunken, know-nothing asshole and b) unoriginal and unfunny.

At best, Fox had an hour to devise a plan. Right before the seventh-inning stretch, inspiration hit. As Frank, Tim, Fox, and 20,000 others rose to their feet for the traditional "Take Me Out to the Ballgame" sing-along, Fox made sure he made eye contact with the inebriated boobs in front of him.

As they retook their seats, Fox seized the opportunity and began laying the groundwork for his unexpected, but never off-putting, trash removal.

"Excuse me, gents," he began, "but I couldn't help overhear your ridiculing our fair city."

"Yeah, what's so fair about it?" said Frank. Tim was too busy laughing at his friend's "joke" to say anything.

"Well," Fox continued, "my name is Fred Rogers, and I'm the head of the Pittsburgh Tourism Bureau. If you have no plans for dinner, it would be my great pleasure to change your mind about Pittsburgh."

Frank and Tim exchanged glances, figuring that a free meal is a free meal. Using the fake name Fred Rogers and having it not set off a warning bell or at least generate a comment from these idiots also convinced Fox that he wasn't dealing with genius material, either. Still, he felt bad misusing the name of a Pittsburgh icon for such tawdry purposes.

"Tell you what. Tell me what hotel you're staying at, and I'll meet you in the lobby at 5:30. We'll go to dinner—my treat—and then I'll give you a tour of my city that I believe may alter your lives."

They laughed at his nonjoke and resumed watching the game, little realizing it was the last game they'd ever see on Earth.

Fox had guessed right, seeing what condition they were in, that they were staying overnight. Of course, had they decided to drive back to Chicago in such a state, nature might have done Fox's job for him. But no, on this night, the pleasure would be all Fox's.

He arrived at 5:10 at the hotel and quickly ascertained what room the lumps were soiling with their presence. As he rode the elevator, he felt somewhat stupid carrying two large "Welcome to Pittsburgh!" baskets, full of Pittsburgh goodies and topped with a Terrible Towel, but he also felt the familiar surge of adrenaline, the tingling in his fingers, and, weirdly, hunger pangs. After he completed this bit of unpleasantness, he was taking his secretary to dinner. Why let reservations go to waste?

He knocked on the door, and a surprised Tim answered. "I thought we were—"

"I couldn't wait to show you my town," gushed Fox, putting on his best happy face. "One for each of you," he said, resting the baskets on a nearby credenza.

As Frank approached, still groggy from a drunken nap, Fox sprung into action and neatly planted the heel of his foot right in Frank's forehead, sending him sprawling to the floor, barely conscious.

Tim, too stunned to move, received slightly different choreography—a crushing kick to the chest, which sent him to his knees. Fox whipped the Terrible Towel from the basket of cheer, and before Tim knew what hit him, he had breathed his last.

Beautifully, Frank was conscious enough to know what awaited him but too helpless to stop it.

"You still hate Pittsburgh, you miserable excuse of humanity?"

"No, please," said Frank, barely audibly. But his pleadings, of course, fell on deaf ears, and Fox, within a minute, had sent Frank to be with his friend Tim.

He then placed the Terrible Towel back in the basket, grabbed both baskets, managed to open the room's doorknob with his foot, and vanished into the Pittsburgh evening, making sure no one saw him leaving the room.

The next day, of course, the story was front-page news, and police were baffled. Clearly, a third party had done this, seeing how unlikely it was that a person would strangle himself. But there were no fingerprints, no forced entry into the room, and the victims weren't even local. Who would want to kill these guys?

Eventually, the trail went cold, seeing how there was no trail to begin with. People had their own theories—it was a lovers' quarrel, drugs were involved, it was a mafia hit—but only Fox knew the truth.

Some people just aren't worthy of being his neighbor.

I promptly printed and copied my latest masterwork and distributed it accordingly. It made me happy—temporarily, at least—to know that I would bring a smile to the face of my equally beleaguered colleagues. And it was a hell of a lot more fun than trying to put a good face on a ridiculous idea submitted by a client who now, by late June, we could officially crown as being among the Stupidest People Alive.

Back in the halcyon days of this company, before the FTC trained its eye on it, clients could be forgiven to a degree because, after all, it's hard-wired into the American ethos that "he who hesitates is lost," and we've all been raised on the notion that we should "follow our dreams." Andrea, of course, preyed on these notions the way a heel in a TV wrestling match constantly works on one area of the body. Coupled with an over-the-top, shameless personality, it helped her build a small empire.

But now the forces of justice were snatching her empire away from her, and we all knew it was only a matter of time before Mousetrap expired. By this point, I could feel only anger toward new clients. People, did you not notice that bright-yellow paper inside your package, the one that said not only are we lousy at what we do, but we also have a habit of being deceitful and have incurred massive governmental fines because of it? How wrapped up are you in the notions that "you only live once" and that you don't want to have any regrets on your deathbed?

The unspoken corollary, by the way, to "you only live once"—and one that I've centered my life around—is "you only die once, too." Here's a partial list of things I'll never do:

1. Skydive.

2. Ski.

3. Fly in one of those tiny airplanes where I'm the only passenger.

4. Eat that Japanese fish that could kill you instantly.

5. Bungee jump.

6. Go ATVing, snowmobling, or motorcycling.

7. Light my own backyard fireworks.

Okay, there are more—millions more—but you get the idea. Call me a pussy if you want, but my feeling is that if you do any of the above things, you're pretty much poking God in the eye and just begging Him to cream you. Now, is that a smart approach to take? You versus God? I'm putting my money on the big guy.

Not to belabor this, but seriously: Let's take skydiving. And not to invoke God again, but if He meant for us to fly, we'd all be sporting wings. We don't fly, people. Deal with it. We also don't have four stomachs or the ability to change colors. Do these "limitations" cause people grief, too?

Skiing. It's cold, wet, and unless you started when you were small and close to the ground, you'll probably break a leg. Sign me up!

Small planes. Do people who pilot these or ride as passengers not see the news . . . ever? How many times a year does some "pilot" crash one of these babies into a mountainside or onto an interstate? I'm even more bewildered by a subgroup of these folks—the ones who build their own planes from kits. Building model planes and cars is great fun if that's what you're into. But you really ought to draw the line at getting in them and turning on the ignition.

"And our last special tonight, sir, is that Japanese fish that if prepared improperly will kill you and involve blood gushing from various orifices." Think about this scenario and tell me I'm the crazy one. Go ahead.

Bungee jumping? Yeah, that's a great idea. I've long been curious about how it feels to have my lungs and stomach switch places.

Snowmobiling? Okay, anything involving snow just flat-out sucks. ATVs are loud and mangle people, and motorcycles are, well, loud and mangle people.

And isn't it about time we embrace the notion that fireworks are best left in the hands of professionals? Why are there so many people out there who seem to have a death wish against their fingers?

So, in summation, I'm not one leaping before I look. Not only do I look twice or even three times, I take measurements, empanel survey groups, and consult with various spiritual advisers who will remain nameless at this time for fear of retribution. I'm as cautious as can be, and maybe that's why I've reached the end of the line with our esteemed clients, who now are being accepted at the rate of 100 percent.

There was a time—no, really—when an idea such as State Pies might have been rejected. This, however, was not that time. We're now officially in overtime. No, not in the sports sense, where the next goal or touchdown wins, but in the sense that we've passed our expiration date. We're over . . . time.

So, what the fuck's a State Pie, you ask? Well, let's let our friend Marcy Hackwell explain it: "If your kids are like mine, they don't know much about geography. And if your kids are like mine, they hate eating anything that's good for them. So I got to thinking, and I thought if I combined my world famous chicken-pot pie with educating kids, I might be onto something. Well, here goes: my chicken-pot pie recipe sold individually in state-shaped tins."

If I were the crying type, her forms would be sodden. We accepted money for this—a nice chunk of money, I'm guessing. Still, as bad as this and other ideas were, it kept me from being unemployed or writing even more Chapel Fox stories.

Client: Marcy Hackwell

Idea: State Pies

Geography has become something we've taken for granted. Yet studies have shown most school-age children today have trouble locating most states on a map. Another problem facing youth: poor nutrition.

Well, believe it or not, there's an idea that addresses both these youth-related needs in one tasty package!

What is it? State Pies. Combine a delicious, vegetable-filled chicken-pot pie, put it in an individually sized tin in the shape of a state, and you have the makings of a well-fed geography expert!

Plus, the bottom of each tin could contain facts about that state, and kids will love collecting all 50.

And if this idea takes off, as we think it will, it could be expanded to include countries of the world.

Product Highlights:

- *Helps kids learn geography*
- *Nutritious*
- *Perfect for school-cafeteria menus*
- *Could be expanded to include countries of the world*

Here's what scary: After writing the above nonsense concerning State Pies, I actually started kind of liking the idea. Why not add regional ingredients to pies? Jambalaya pie! Pierogi pie! Taco pie! Did I go back and add my suggestions to the NPR? Nah. What would be the point? You know how many sets of eyes are going to see it after we send it off? None. I could have written an NPR for Urine Pies, and it wouldn't have meant a damn thing. We had several thousand dollars of Marcy Hackwell's money, and that's all that mattered.

Well, this mattered, too, but to a much lesser extent: I decided that if I ever formed a rock band, its name would be State Pies. But seeing how, despite years of piano lessons, the only thing I'm able to do musically is play a passable version of "Fur Elise," I don't bet on that happening anytime soon. Still, I liked the idea of an announcer proclaiming, "Ladies and gentlemen, the State Pies!" Cue the screaming young women in the front row, shedding their clothes for our approval. This scenario was about as likely to happen as you seeing "Bell Tonez" on your local home store's shelves anytime in the near future.

First of all, I've never been sure what tempts marketers to misspell perfectly fine words (Froot Loops, anyone?), but apparently this disease has permeated all the way down to the inventor-wannabe level. Why did

Phil Marston use the less-conventional "tonez" spelling for his product? We will never fully know, but the bigger point is this: His idea was stupid. I felt bad for the guy, seeing how the company that employed me was taking thousands of dollars of his hard-earned money, and yet, at the same time, had Mr. Marston walked into my office at this exact moment, I would have punched him repeatedly in the face, pausing only to rain blows on his midsection. Phil Marston was keeping me employed. Phil Marston was a moron. I loved Phil Marston. I hated Phil Marston.

Anyway, here's Phil Marston's brainstorm: "If you guys are anything like me, you have good days and bad, right? Well, I've invented a multi-song doorbell that people can change on a daily basis to fit their mood for that day! I've even included mechanical schematics to help you. I call my invention Bell Tonez! Thanks!"

First of all, Phil Marston, did you really think calling it Bell Tones would have lessened its impact? I mean, the idea's the thing. If Edison had called electricity MaggotPus, we'd all still use it and love it, right? ("Dang, honey, that storm knocked out our MaggotPus. Better get a flashlight.") So, your needless "Z" does only one thing: Pisses me off more than I need to be.

And secondly, shouldn't you have called them "schematicz"? That would have been the cool spelling, right, you jackass?

Finally, what about the split-personality set? They'd be running to their doorbell switch 20 times a day.

Client: Phil Marston

Idea: Bell Tonez

Wouldn't it be nice to hear your doorbell play "Happy Birthday" on your or a loved one's birthday? How about holiday songs at Christmastime? Well, Bell Tonez allows you to pick the music that fits your mood every day of the week!

This device will attach to any existing doorbell system, and by means of a tuning device, the end user can pick one of 10 preset songs and change it as he/she sees fit.

This is a great, fun product perfect for anyone tired of the same, old "ding-dong!"

Product Highlights:

- *Fun home product*
- *Can hold up to 10 different tunes*
- *Line could be expanded to include holiday-specific tuners*

- *Really, really suckz as an idea, doesn't it?*

Then, amidst the squalor of ideas that Andrea and our sales team were now accepting, came Luckit! I started to read the description . . .

"My family and I have been playing this game for years. My father invented it, or it might even have been his father. Nonetheless, as I said, my family and I have loved this game for years, and we want to share it with the world."

. . . and I immediately began to zone out. Great. Another family idea/recipe/whatever that Jim Schnerdly of Idiotville just has to share with the world. Then, more out of boredom than anything, I kept reading . . .

"The game is fiendishly simple. It consists of two decks of cards and a die. The first deck contains 25 cards, one for each letter of the alphabet, excluding the letter X. The second deck consists of 50 topic cards.

"So, for example, let's say player one rolls a 3, picks up the letter M from one pile and a 'Movie titles' card from the other pile. He would have to say three movie titles that start with the letter M. If he does so successfully, he earns 3 points. If not, he gets zero.

"Naturally, the game's rules can be amended. We've always played by the all-or-nothing rule, but obviously that can be changed.

"Anyway, that's the idea. We think it's fun, simple, and extremely marketable."

I guess the law of averages finally hit Mousetrap. I mean, this was a good idea by any standards. But by Mousetrap standards? This guy may as well have been da Vinci.

I ran over and shared Jack Gardner's great idea with Rachel and Sam. After reading the description, they both possessed the same stunned look I had.

"Wait a minute," said Rachel. This—this idea doesn't completely suck, does it?"

"No, it doesn't suck at all," I said. "In fact, it's way too good for us."

Sam stopped scribbling topic ideas on a piece of scratch paper, and all of our eyes met.

"We can't keep this guy's money," declared Sam.

I then informed my coworkers of the good news: We only had $50 of this guy's money, and that was given to us in what he hoped would be "good faith."

In addition to having a good idea, Mr. Gardner also had a brain. He figured we were sleazy, yet he wanted to test the waters to see if we had any legitimacy or integrity at all. He wrote: "From what I've read in your informational packet, you've been in trouble with the government and seem to be staying in business by not always being on the up-and-up. Still, I'm curious to see how you folks will react to my idea. Therefore, I'm enclosing a $50 check, not the thousands you require, in good-faith money, and I await your response."

I also read aloud to Sam and Rachel the note Andrea attached: "Sheldon, get our usual amount from this guy. He thinks he's smart, okay? So turn on the charm and get every penny from this s.o.b.—nothing less than 75, 72 if you have to."

She meant, of course, $7,500. None of us knew what to do, and none of the options we had were totally satisfying:

1. We treat the product as any other. Sheldon does what he does, gets thousands from this guy, and the NPR never sees the light of day. We've had game ideas before, and we knew which manufacturers to send the NPRs to, but none of them ever got past that stage. Obviously, manufacturers treated correspondence from Mousetrap as junk mail; Luckit wouldn't have a different fate.

2. We contact Mr. Gardner directly, tell him the truth, and beg him not to send us a penny more. Of course, seeing how we have so few new clients, doing so would incur the wrath of Andrea.

3. We confront Andrea directly and beg her not to take this guy's money, unless she has contacts that could make this idea come true, which we knew damn well she didn't.

We decided that we couldn't live with ourselves if we let the first option occur. The second option seemed underhanded to us. After all, Andrea did sign our paychecks, and we owed her at least a modicum of respect. So, option three would win by default. It was the most difficult choice, seeing how we were going to beg the money-grubbing owner of our company to turn down as much as $7,500.

"Should we draw straws?" I asked.

"No, we all go," Sam said. "Power in numbers."

"And I suppose you get the sweater, then?" I asked.

"We can all take turns, if you like."

None of us made a movement toward the door. We all chuckled nervously. Then, we made our way slowly to the tundra.

"Uh-oh, it's all three of you," said Andrea as she saw us approaching. "This must be big. Enter." She seemed pleasant and sober enough. A good sign, I thought.

"What can I do for you?"

Sam spoke on our behalf: "Andrea, there's a submission in-house for a product called Luckit. It's a card game."

"Yes," said Andrea. "I put Sheldon on it. Don't worry. He'll get our money."

"Well, that's just it, Andrea," Sam said. "Let's not pursue this one."

"Let's not what?! I'm sorry. I must have missed that memo where it was stated I report to you, Sam." So much for pleasant.

I figured it was my turn to get my ass handed to me. "Andrea, the three of us think this is actually a pretty good idea." Andrea trained her eyes on me, awaiting the rest of my thought.

"And?" she said.

"And, well, we'd like to pursue it full-bore or not at all."

"Please explain 'full-bore.'"

"Well, if you have any legitimate contacts—"

"Legitimate? You question this company's legitimacy?"

"Andrea, allow me to be blunt here. A few months ago, we had a discussion about the perpetual-motion machine we accepted. Remember?"

She laughed. "Yes, okay, and allow me to say now what I said then, to all three of you this time: We need every penny we can to stay afloat. So Sheldon is going to call this moron today, and we are going to get our 7 grand. If you don't like it, then get the fuck out of my office, my company, and my life."

"He's not a moron," said Rachel. Her words almost literally froze in the air.

"Treat this client as you would any other, or quit en masse and never step foot in my office again. Now go. I really don't care what you do."

We shuffled back to our offices, proud in the fact that we stood up to the beast, but not getting the result we desired. Then Sam hit on the solution. (No, stabbing that fatass Sheldon to death wasn't it).

"Let's pursue it with all our ability," he said. "Let's make a genuine prototype and send it to the usual manufacturers, but in different packaging so that maybe they'll notice it."

"You mean, let's do what we were hired to do before the reality of this soul-sucking place beat down our creativity to the point of nothingness?" I asked.

"Yeah, something like that!"

By the end of the day, Sam and Rachel had created a couple prototype decks of cards with various topics on them. I, meanwhile, constructed the rules. And then we played. And played and played. Over the next few weeks, we started including coworkers in our games, and everyone seemed to enjoy it.

After we worked out all the kinks and decided on which design we liked best, Sam created the final prototype, and we sent it off to potential manufacturers in a tidily designed box, unlike the Mousetrap envelope we usually used.

And then the waiting game began. Would a manufacturer actually show interest? Would we end up feeling less guilty, knowing that at least we shepherded one good idea to the marketplace and made its inventor a potential profit? Or would it be tossed like all the other NPRs, just another broken dream in a long line of hopelessness?

Well, eventually, you'll find out, of course, but at least for a few blessed days in late June 1991, Sam, Rachel, and I put in honest days' work and genuinely believed we were contributing positively to the American marketplace.

One other thing you may be wondering: Why the name "Luckit"? Well, let's let the inventor explain: "The name to you might make no sense. But, according to family lore, my grandfather was a bit of a sore loser, and whenever he would lose this nameless game, he would yell out something that sounded an awful lot like, ahem, 'luck it.' Over the years, we figured yelling out 'luck it' instead of you-know-what was a nicer way to voice our displeasure, and the name stuck."

A good product, a funny family story, a nice, smart inventor—we really wanted this one to work. But however it turned out, at least we knew we gave it our best, and that counted for something in these ugly days at Mousetrap. And it was especially nice for Sam, whom Rache and I were sure was one gentle push away from insanity, with fatherhood looming over him. Putting together the Luckit prototype provided him hours of nonbaby bliss, until, of course, Rache or I would walk by his office and yell "baby" or "diapers" or some other reminder, lest he was able to have a few moments of happiness.

We spent the next few days hopeful that some manufacturer would contact us and tell us they were as excited about the card game as we were. We would feel validation and joy! We would dance in the halls! Impromptu parties would erupt! All guilt would be erased, our filthy corporate souls scrubbed clean! Andrea would lead her employees in bawdy songs, and we'd all get blissfully drunk, celebrating our success—a success spearheaded by the three of us!

Then, by the end of the week, when no call materialized, we rationalized our impending pessimism by saying that things like this take time and that good news would come soon enough. We all took turns pestering Mousetrap's lone surviving account executive, a foul-mouthed, phony, aging termagant by the name of Loretta, to see if anyone had contacted her. Each time, her "no" became increasingly curt. At its peak, the company employed six account execs. Though by far the least likable of the six, Loretta repeatedly survived the cut by being able to turn on the charm and assuage the fears of the numerous clients who would contact her, suddenly terrified that giving us several thousand dollars perhaps wasn't the best investment they'd ever made.

"You have to understand," she'd say, "that the wheels in corporate America move oh, so slowly. We believe in your product as much as you do, and I promise you I will keep you up-to-date every step of the way."

Which she would do, of course, contacting her clients to tell them that—congratulations!—your product idea has been accepted. You're on your way to your dream, Mr. Dumbass! She would follow that up with informing them of all the bullshit—your NPR is complete, your NPR has been sent to potential manufacturers, your NPR is right now in the hands of manufacturers.

Then, the checks would clear, the NPRs, at best, got turned into paper airplanes or scrunched up for some mean games of office basketball, and the clients, after waiting patiently for a few weeks, would call their account exec and meekly inquire about the status of their dream.

Now, sadly, the three of us were acting like clients, although Loretta had the good sense not to give us false hope. "In your professional opinion," I asked her, "what are the chances on this thing?"

"You're fucking kidding me, right?" She laughed unpleasantly.

"Yeah, look. I know we're not exactly swimming in success here, Loretta, but this actually is a good idea, and we packaged it"—

"And what's Santa bringing you this year, Nick? A nice, shiny set of golf clubs?

"Grow the fuck up!"

Here's the other reason Loretta was our lone surviving account exec: Talking to her coworkers, she was more witheringly critical toward the company than anyone. But in front of Andrea, she nodded her head up and down, signaling agreement, more often than a bobblehead doll during a windstorm.

And now that she was the only game in town, she didn't feel the need to be polite to anyone. She would last until there were no more clients, which, of course, was no longer a matter of if, but when. Still, by June's end, we managed to snare another 31 clients, mostly from the beginning of the month. I was amazed that we still had that many new clients, but I also knew in May we had picked up 49. We were steamrolling toward zero.

July 1991

THE FOURTH OF JULY fell on a Thursday in 1991. To us working slugs, this, of course, meant a 4-day weekend, especially for those who work for a company that's not exactly overflowing with business. So when Andrea called a company-wide meeting on the 3rd , we thought nothing of it.

The thought that this was going to be just a typical rah-rah meeting was shattered the second the three of us walked into the conference room. Behind Andrea, on the huge dry-erase board that took up most of the back wall, was a lone word, "independence," except the "i" in the word was replaced by the digit 1. It looked like this: 1DEPENDENCE.

And sitting proudly at the head of the conference table was Andrea, sporting a blue sequin jacket, white blouse, and red shiny hat. Imagine Uncle Sam, but replace his robustness with rot, throw in a half bottle of whiskey, and you begin to get the idea.

There were about two dozen of us at the meeting. My other remaining coworkers had the good sense to turn the holiday into a 5-day weekend. We were all too frightened to speak, which played perfectly into Andrea's bony hands. "Onedependence," she said, barely above a whisper. We all, in unison, almost, moved a little closer. "Onedependence," she repeated, this time a little louder.

It finally hit me, not like the clichéd ton of bricks, but maybe like a ton of bricks that possess mouths and poisonous fangs. I felt the bricks' venom filling my bloodstream and wondered if that "special 1 percent" nonsense I came up with months ago would ever leave me. It was like a chronic illness.

"We're the special 1 percent, right, Nick?" she asked. Again, she was dragging me into her filthy world. "Yep," I said.

"And what's Thursday?" she asked the room.

"Independence Day," yelled Loretta, the way the dumb kid in grade school shouts out an answer that's obvious to everyone.

"I hereby declare today Onedependence Day!" Andrea said, and, in a surprisingly quick move, she pulled out from under the table a large sheet cake, iced in red, white, and blue with the word 1DEPENDENCE in the middle. Plying people with cake, I might add, is never a bad way to win them over to your view. When's the last time you heard someone say, "Man, I hate cake"? No one hates cake. There may be those who can't have cake, but everyone loves it. It'd be like hating rainbows or music. Just not possible.

"Now, before we dig into this cake, I have some declarations to make," said an increasingly satisfied Andrea. She was putting on a show, it was going well, and even if it bombed, hell, there was cake.

She was hiding a scroll underneath her jacket sleeve, and she dramatically let it roll to the ground before sharing its contents with us.

"I, Andrea Bianco, hereby declare that on this day, July 3, 1991, no longer will my company, Mousetrap, be dependent on what society deems to be standard business practices."

"Hear, hear," piped up Loretta.

The three of us shot quick glances at each other. Did Andrea just declare that deceitful business practices were now going to be official company policy? I'm not stupid, and I was long aware that any ethics this company possessed went out the window a long time ago, but still I was stunned. People who commit acts of deception tend to be secretive about them. "Hi, honey. How was work today?" "Well, I've decided to launch my embezzlement scheme. Other than that, not much. How are you?"

"I, Andrea Bianco, hereby declare that on this day, July 3, 1991, my company, Mousetrap, will be fully dependent on fostering the dreams of our imaginative clients.

"I declare that July 3, at least in the confines of this building, will be forever known as Onedependence Day and will be celebrated each year in our offices.

"I declare that every Mousetrap employee will do his and her level best to maximize profit from every client.

"I declare that no governmental agency will ever douse the flame of our entrepreneurial spirit. And I declare that this is still America!"

Dragging America into it seemed to get to a few people in the room, and the "hear, hears" became louder. Personally, I wanted to kill almost everyone around me and eat some damn cake in peace.

"And I declare, that in the spirit of Onedependence, our Mousetrap offices will remain open Thursday and Friday, because I declare our job here is just beginning!"

It took us all a second to realize that Andrea had just taken away not only Friday, but the actual holiday itself. We were going to celebrate Onedependence Day by not celebrating Independence Day.

"Hear, hear," yelled Loretta, who no doubt wanted to rip out Andrea's spleen and spread it on the cake.

Finally, the rest of us also uttered a "hear, hear," and that's how we got to spend the Fourth of July at work. If any of us in the room had the power of telekinesis, our five or so employees who had already escaped would have been killed promptly.

For the finishing touch, Andrea brandished four sparklers, which she had hidden up her other sleeve, lit them, and decorated the four corners of the cake. Our thoughts of a relaxing 4-day weekend were gone, but finally we were going to eat the fucking cake. It was delicious. I had seven pieces. About an hour later, of course, I was still mad as hell about my weekend plans being ruined, and, in addition, I had that weird sugar-induced coma feeling that's always unpleasant.

The next day, while the rest of America was grilling and shooting off fireworks, we Mousetrap employees were greeted at the door by a flag-waving Andrea, who high-fived each of us as we entered and praised "our entrepreneurial spirit, which is the bedrock of our country."

She also told each of us that somewhere, George Washington was smiling. Yes, no doubt the founder of our country, the man who, as we were all taught in grade school, "couldn't tell a lie," would light up at the sight of a deceitful lunatic denying her employees a day off in an effort to keep her horrible company afloat. How about Jesus, Andrea? Is He smiling, too?

The Fourth of July (and the fifth, for that matter) weren't especially trying days. But we had to play the game, since it meant so much to Andrea. The best way for me to look busy without actually working, of course, was to call on my old friend Chapel Fox.

Fall was approaching in Pittsburgh, and Chapel Fox was sitting in his office, feeling depressed about the Pirates. They had fallen short of reaching the World Series, and, even worse, probably for the rest of his life, every time he attended a Pirate game, he would think of Tim and Frank . . . and how he wished he had brutalized them more before ending their no-doubt horrid existences.

Even thinking about them and their relentless stupidity made Fox want to put his fist through the nearest wall.

Fortunately, as Fox was in mid silent rage, his lovely secretary, Beth Park, poked her head through his doorway and appeared to have something on her mind.

"*May I come in?*" *she asked.*

His mood brightened instantly, as he had been carrying a flame for Ms. Park for years but was always afraid to make a move, seeing how his other line of work required a life of emotional detachment from all others.

"*Yes, Beth Louise Park,*" *he said,* "*you're always a welcomed sight. What's up?*"

She closed the door, which was odd, and possessed a very purposeful look.

"*I know,*" *she said.*

A minute passed. Fox was legitimately confused, never thinking for a second that his lovely, innocent secretary would be the one to connect the dots. The police? A detective? Sure, that was always a possibility. But Beth? Beth, who takes her grandmother to church bingo every Wednesday night? Not a chance.

"*You know what, Beth?*"

"*I know what you do.*"

Okay, now he was a little worried, and a light bulb—well, maybe not a light bulb; perhaps a Christmas tree light—went off on his head, and he nervously chuckled.

"*Of course you do, Beth. I'm a lawyer. You're my secretary. Perhaps I could introduce you around the office?*"

"*You know what I mean.*"

A million things ran through Fox's analytical brain, the first one being: "*If she knows that I'm a killer—and an excellent one, at that—what would make her confront me? Wouldn't she know that I'm capable of killing her, too?*"

"*I have no clue what you mean, Beth, but maybe you should stop while you're still ahead* (*oh, how he longed to say* "*while you still have a head,*" *but he valiantly fought the urge. Besides, the last thing he wanted to do was kill Beth.*)

"*Sometimes practical jokes aren't as funny in execution as they are in theory,*" *he said, trying to give her an out.*

"*Mrs. Gutierrez,*" *said Beth, now staring him down.*

"Yes," Fox said, "she was briefly a client. They never did figure out what happened to her, did they?"

"You killed her."

Fox laughed, a little too heartily. "Beth, seriously, what the hell is wrong with you?"

"Those two Cubs fans who died after attending a Pirate game—you killed them, too, didn't you?"

"Yes, Beth, and I also killed JFK and Jimmy Hoffa. Listen. I'm starting to get a little mad here. What the hell is this, 'Candid Camera'?"

Beth didn't move an inch. "I know about the others, too. Those three were just the latest. You're a monster."

"No, Beth, I'm your boss—your very pissed-off boss who will fire you right now if you don't apologize and get back to your desk."

What an unforeseen and awful predicament this was becoming. The only people Fox needed to kill were Pittsburgh bashers. Beth was definitely not in that group. But now he was put in a situation where he felt he had no choice. He didn't know if he could kill someone he liked. Plus, she was a wonderful secretary, and he hated the whole hiring process—taking out the ad, going over résumés, interviewing a bunch of morons. Maybe, he thought, I can goad her into saying something anti-Pittsburgh.

"It's not that simple, Chapel. You know that I know. Sure, I can return to my desk. And maybe later you'll stop by and ask me out to dinner. And then maybe we'll go back to my place. And then you'll kill me, too, right?"

Fox laughed again. "Well, I'd love to go to dinner with you tonight, and I'd love it if you asked me back to your place, since you brought up that scenario. But I could think of better things to do than, say, slitting your throat.

"I'll ask you again, Beth—what the hell are you talking about?"

"How about I call the police and tell them everything I know?" she asked.

"Everything you know about what, Beth?" Fox was still trying to play dumb. He continued. "Look, Beth. Let's forget this whole nonsensical conversation. For real, how about dinner tonight?"

"Fine. Sounds good." She still had her eyes trained on him until she finally turned, opened the door, and went back to her desk.

Fox spent the rest of the day analyzing his choices and kept on returning to what he knew the only option was: eliminate the threat to his freedom that his lovely secretary had unexpectedly become.

But Fox, for the life of him, couldn't figure out what Beth's motive was. If she were being a good citizen, she would call the police, right? Didn't she now know that she was putting herself in a perilous position by going to dinner with a homicidal maniac?

He figured he'd play it cool at dinner and act like nothing happened. Beth apparently was using the same game plan, which bewildered Fox and made him think for a minute that their conversation earlier that day had been a hallucination. Beth was her usual playful, funny self, and dinner went great.

It went so well, in fact, that as Fox pulled up to Beth's house, she invited him in. Fox had resisted Beth's charms for years, but a dark thought now crossed his murderous heart: "We may as well have some fun, seeing how this is her last night on Earth."

Right through the after-dinner drink and their furious, acrobatic lovemaking, they both acted like nothing had happened earlier, that the accusatory conversation had been a mirage.

He waited for her to fall asleep. Unbeknownst to her, he had slipped his trusty Terrible Towel under her bed earlier, sneaking it in his briefcase, which he told her he didn't want to leave in his car. He waited until he was sure she was asleep, and for the first time in his life, he felt genuine sadness. The others he had killed? Hell, they had it coming. But Beth? He could see himself with Beth for a long time. She was everything he wasn't; she was a ray of light in his dark world. He felt like crying. But he also hated the idea of life imprisonment. "Why, Beth?" he wanted to yell.

He carefully took hold of the Towel, and as it began its descent to her neck, she snapped to attention and grabbed the gold death rag in her right hand. Fox damn near passed out.

"Do you want to start talking, Chapel, or should I dial 911?"

"What? I thought you were cold—" was the best he could come up.

"Just fucking stop it. You were going to kill me."

They froze for a second, and then Beth kissed him deeply, and they had a second round, this time practically bouncing off the walls of her small bedroom. (Again, reader, feel free to add your own steamy details here. Perhaps you envision some spanking or light bondage. Have at it).

After regaining his breath, Fox fixed his gaze on his naked secretary and said, "Beth, don't take this the wrong way, but what the hell is wrong with you?"

"No," she said, equally gassed, "first, you tell me the truth."

"Okay, Gutierrez, the two Chicago fucks—yeah, I killed them. And the others."

"I want in," she said.

He was perplexed. "You want in what?"

"In your world."

Fox laughed.

"I have the goods on you. Stop laughing."

"I'm a serial killer, and I could kill you right now. I'll laugh if I want to."

"I don't think you can kill me."

She may have been right, but he couldn't let her know that. "Beth, let me ask you a question."

"Fire away, Chap."

"I've killed and have gotten away with every one of them. I haven't even been brought in for questioning. If I wanted you dead, you'd be dead, and my only problem would be finding a replacement for you."

She was maddeningly unfazed by his false show of strength. "Anyway, that's my offer. I'm in your world, or you're in custody inside of 15 minutes."

Fox knew when he was beat. Fortunately, being beat in this case meant being alone and naked with a woman he had desired for years. This wasn't a total loss, but still, he wondered and just had to ask . . .

But was interrupted by another question.

"Why'd you kill them?"

"Because they all, in one way or another, insulted Pittsburgh. I can't stand that.

"Beth, how the hell did you figure it out?"

"Every time one of these mysterious murders took place," she explained, "you acted really weird the following day. The day after Mrs. Gutierrez was offed, for example, you were uptight all day, totally not like yourself. And after the Cubs fans were murdered, some of us were talking about it in the office, and you said something like, 'Those miserable clowns probably had it coming.' Again, that was unlike you."

"Wow, Beth. That's a hell of a leap, isn't it?"

"Well, it was a hunch. I figured, what the hell do I have to lose? If I'm wrong, you'll probably forget about it, and we'll have dinner. And if I'm right . . ."

So, that was that. Chapel Fox, independent agent and defender of all things Pittsburgh, was unwillingly taking on a partner. He still didn't know what her motive was, and, frankly, he was a little bit scared of the whole

thing, but that night he slept like an infant, and in the morning, they had
a third go-round, this time cracking plaster, sending knickknacks scattering
to the floor like so many snowflakes, and snapping the bed frame as though
it were made of toothpicks.

Partnership had its benefits.

I had just finished putting the final touches on my ridiculous story
when Sam burst into my office and blurted out something to the effect of
"Water broke, baby, hospital, see ya."

For the next several weeks, the department I worked in was led by
a sleep-deprived, talented artist who knew his abilities were being pissed
away at a soul-sucking, soon-to-be-deceased enterprise. Rachel and I sat
back and enjoyed the show.

Sam, by the way, was the new father of a healthy girl, and in between
the bouts of crankiness (Sam's, not the baby's), I could tell how proud and
happy he was. This took the edge off his frequent meltdowns, a side of
which we had never seen before.

To wit: He was on my Chapel Fox mailing list, and he usually enjoyed my tales. His first day back at work, however, he called me into his
office and while brandishing the latest Fox story, yelled, "Don't you have
anything better to do?"

I figured he was joking and started to chuckle. He didn't. "Seriously,
Nick, you don't get paid to write your nonsensical stories. We pay you to
write product descriptions."

I felt really stupid, and momentarily I deluded myself into thinking I had let the company—my honorable, noble employer—down. That
thought passed quicker than a burp, but seeing how Sam was in Angry
Boss mode, I thought it best to apologize humbly and be on my way.

"You're right, Sam. I'll get back to work."

He sighed heavily, and I was convinced that my completely insin-
cere apology had pissed him off further.

He chuckled and then said, "What the fuck is wrong with me, Nick?"

I felt a little bolder. "Well, you haven't slept since the night you became a father, you work for a decaying company whose best days never
really existed, you have talent, and, if you could, you'd like to run headfirst into the nearest wall."

"Yeah, that about sums it up," he said. The tension lifted, but Sam
assured me that he would probably be having outbursts like this until his
daughter slept through the night.

"To tell you the truth, Nick," he said before suddenly stopping.

"What?"

"Nah, it's too mushy. You'll laugh at me."

"Too late now. I promise I won't laugh."

He sighed again. "Well, to be honest, in spite of everything—the company we work for, the fact that this company is doomed and that we'll all be jobless soon—when I look into that little girl's eyes, all seems right with the world.

"You got to get yourself one of these, dude."

I gasped. A baby? Hell, I still wasn't sure I wanted to get married, and Sam wanted me to be a father? I couldn't even visualize such ridiculousness.

"Eh, someday," I said. "I'm not ready."

"Nick, no one's ever ready. Look at me. Could my timing have been any worse? But she's a gift from heaven."

"No, thanks. Let me and Nicole be selfish and married for a few years. Then, I'm sure she'll drag me into parenthood, too."

"Hey, that's right—your big day isn't too far away, is it?"

"Thanks for reminding me. Actually, come to think of it, thanks for reminding me. Nicole's been nagging me to do this, so here goes. Will you be one of my groomsmen?"

"Hell, I'd be honored. Just please don't partner me with the fat chick. That's my only request."

"That's not my department, but I'll put in a good word for you."

It was nice, the conversation we were having, except, of course, for the fat-chick slamming. Still, it was heartwarming, two friends talking about babies and weddings, the good things in life, while all around us various coworkers were either lying to prospective clients, hoodwinking established clients, or sneaking sips from whiskey bottles stashed in their desks in order to get through the day.

My vice was Chapel Fox, and I was heartened by my coworkers' positive reactions to the introduction of a love interest for Chapel. Unfortunately, when I returned to my office, I had actual work to do. The invention was called 'Scrip Trip, and I was well past the point of anger to even work up a good throat clearing.

Client: Reggie Sandoz

Idea: 'Scrip Trip

It seems as though a light bulb has gone off in Mr. Sandoz's head, and he just has to share his idea with the universe. He explains in his application that his wife, God bless her, is taking so many different medications that it's easy for her to forget which one to take when. So, he continues, he got to tinkering and came up with an idea that will save lives!

You see, it's a device that holds up to 10 different medications, and when it's time to take a particular pill, an alarm is tripped (hence the name), and the person is reminded.

The only thing I wonder, Reg, is this: Does your wife have a medication that protects her from the ails of being married to a fucking idiot? Okay, I guess I could still get angry, and it felt quite delicious, actually, screaming at this man's NPR.

I decided to stay in angry mode as I wrote up his report:
Product Highlights:

- *If you find any, let me know*

- *This is nice, thick paper; it can be put to good use, I'm sure*

- *So sorry for wasting your time*

So, yes, another pill-timing device. In the off chance you're reading this, I hope you're having a better day than I am. You see, I work for an invention-marketing company. How dishonorable is this company? Well, let me put it this way: I look up to people who sell weed to schoolkids. Does that give you an idea? Oh, and if you actually give a fuck, this "invention" will save thousands, possibly tens of millions, of lives, so if you don't pursue it and make a prototype within 48 hours, you will be up to your nuts in the blood of those who can't remember to take their fucking prescriptions. I mean, really, how hard can it be? Write it down somewhere, on a Post-it, perhaps? Write down, I don't know, 10:00, 2:00, 4:00. Cross the time off when you've taken your pill. Get on with your life. And get the fuck out of mine.

Hey, you have a good day now.

Yeah, I sent it out that way, and no one was ever the wiser. Later that day, Andrea announced over the p.a. system that everyone's salary was being slashed 15 percent. She sounded drunk and on the verge of tears. Apparently, she didn't feel up to having a rah-rah meeting and plying us with cake and a show before cutting our already meager salaries. I suppose the move saved a few jobs, maybe even mine, but still. I was making a whopping $16,500. Minus 15 percent, that took me down to barely more than $14,000. And I was getting married in four months.

I was becoming accustomed to the thought of marriage, finally. Our engagement seemed to have lifted a dark cloud that had been hovering over our relationship, and the past several months between us had been terrific. At times, I was even looking forward to moving on to the next stage of my life and all that it had to offer. And considering my current state of economic affairs, I took great solace in the part of the wedding vow that goes, "In richness and in poorness."

By the halfway point of July, we had 13 new clients. Loretta was the only Mousetrap employee who was busy. She put in a legitimate 40 hours a week, lying to new clients and dragging along old ones. It was a hellish job, but she was just the person for it. And she was good at it, to be honest. If she wasn't, our office would at some point have resembled the scene in "Frankenstein" where the natives, all bearing lit torches, decide to attack the beast.

Every day, I expected an angry mob, or at least some pissed-off, bankrupt dude, to burst through our front doors and start shooting wildly, taking out as many of us as he could before turning the gun on himself and ending his dream. It never happened, in no small part due to Loretta's ability to sweet-talk when she had to.

I figured I'd swing by and ask if there were any updates on Luckit. She had just gotten off the phone and was encouraging an old client to stay focused and "dream positive." I thought I might be able to catch her while she was still in pleasant-phony mode.

"Well, Loretta, any word yet on Luckit?"

"Nick, are you retarded? You hide it well, and yet I fucking wonder sometimes."

It was startling to see her go from sweet talk to longshoreman in literally five seconds. I figured for a change, I'd respond in kind.

"Loretta, believe it or not, you hate-filled harpy, Luckit is a good idea. Hell, it's *the* good idea in the history of this company, and maybe, just maybe, you could feel an ounce of redemption in your crust-filled soul if you helped bring to market an actual product that could make someone money."

She was stunned. I had never mouthed off at a coworker before, but I figured there wouldn't be any repercussions. Yes, Andrea seemed to like Loretta, but I assumed that Andrea, no dummy, saw through her like the rest of us.

"For your information, Nick, five of our successful clients came through me. Secondly, where do you get off telling me how to do my job, you good-for-nothing idiot?"

"Wow! Five successful clients? Out of how many, Loretta? That's a great batting average. Do me a favor and fuck off, okay, Loretta?"

I stormed out of her office. I was furious, but I had no idea what I had unleashed. Actions have consequences, as we're often told, and one of the victims of my ranting would be completely innocent.

The next day, Andrea laid off six more employees, including Rachel. None of us, not even Sam, saw it coming. Sam was to take over Rachel's responsibilities, and we tearfully bid her adieu. We didn't even have time to have a goodbye lunch, seeing how Andrea dropped the ax at the end of the day, and by then, Sam, the responsible father, had to get home.

We made plans, though, to have lunch soon, seeing how Rache wasn't able to pack up her personal effects. We promised we would give her everything when we met.

Later that day, Loretta poked her head in my office door and said, "Sorry to hear about Rachel. Maybe that'll teach you not to fuck with me."

I was taken aback and still beholden to the notion that Andrea saw Loretta for what she really was.

"Well, if I pissed you off so much, how come I'm still here?"

"Because I wanted you to know that you were 100 percent responsible for Rachel's dismissal. You seem like one of those nice, caring people, and I know how awful you'll feel for, well, possibly forever."

She was smiling as she said this, and it took every ounce of decency I had not to grab my stapler and attack her with it.

"Have a good day, Nick." She blew me a kiss and walked away.

She was right, of course. I felt like throwing up. I hadn't even bothered telling Sam about laying into Loretta. That's how sure I was that nothing would come of it. Now, though, I needed to tell him the whole story, partially because he had a right to know and partially to absolve myself of the terrible guilt of which I was now in possession.

I walked into his office and just blurted it out. "I got Rache fired, Sam. It's all my fault.

"Nick, remember I'm functioning on much less sleep than normal, and it helps me not in the least when people talk crazy."

"No, I'm serious. Yesterday, I swung by Loretta's office to get an update on Luckit. She was her usual hateful self, and so I let her have it. I screamed, I hollered, I ranted, I called her names. It felt great at the time."

"She's longtime buddies with Andrea, Nick, and she's a vengeful person."

"I figured, wrongly, that Andrea saw through her bullshit."

"She does, but they go back years and years. Damn it, Nick."

"Sam, anything you say to me can't make me feel any worse than I already do."

I hate to admit this, but at this point my voice started cracking, and I felt like weeping. Rachel didn't deserve this. She was decent and kind, and I always figured the three of us would make it to the end together.

"So why didn't Loretta recommend that you get fired?"

"Well, because, in her words, 'I'm one of those nice, caring people.' She knew I'd feel like shit if I was the one responsible for Rache being let go."

Sam just shook his head. He was pissed off at me, but he wanted to kill Loretta.

"Are you going to tell Rache when we see her?"

"I have a moral duty to do so, don't you think?"

"Well, it's your call, but I appreciate you telling me the truth."

"I fucked up, Sam, and there's no way I can make it up to Rachel."

"Nick, these are pretty shitty, low-paying jobs we have, if it's any consolation."

"Yeah, but they're our shitty, low-paying jobs, and if Andrea walked in right now and fired the both of us, we'd be sick about it."

"Point taken. We need to teach Loretta a lesson, though."

"I couldn't agree more."

It didn't take us more than a half-hour to come with the perfect plan, but we knew we had to wait for the right time to execute it. Too soon, and we'd be joining Rachel in the unemployment line.

I anticipated lunch with Rachel as much as I would have the chance to relive puberty. She seemed to be handling her jobless situation fairly well, and the three of us made pleasant small talk, with Sam occasionally shooting me a glance, as if I needed a reminder of what I had to do.

"Rache, it's my fault you were let go." I fairly yelled it out, and my directness caught her off guard. So off guard that she figured I was being a goof and chuckled.

"No, seriously, there's something you need to know." I then pro-ceeded to tell her the entire story, not leaving out a single detail, in an effort to cleanse my conscience. Fortunately, although at first she seemed like she wanted to slap me, she ultimately was more pissed off at Loretta than at me.

"Don't lose sleep over my job, Nick. Look, guys, I have some po-tentially good news, anyway. My fiancé is a finalist for a job in North

Carolina. He seems very hopeful about it. Chances are, I'm outta here anyway. And besides, how long do you think the company's going to last?"

"I have November 8 in the office pool, while Nick—and correct me if I'm wrong—is going for the pre-Halloween beatdown date of October 29," said Sam.

"You are correct. By the way, Rache, what was your date?"

"Actually, I took the long view and picked January 15, 1992. Remember, boys—it's hard to kill a tumor."

We all had a good laugh at the thought that our company was nothing but a vile tumor, and I think Sam and I envied Rachel because even though she was jobless, she was free of the trap.

And when Sam and I returned to the trap, we envied Rache even more than we had five minutes earlier.

"Wow me!" screamed Andrea at us from her office as we walked by. Alice waved for us to enter.

"Listen, you two," Andrea began, "as you may have noticed, morale around here could use a boost. Lord knows I can't give anyone a raise. So Alice and I were talking, and we want you two to come up with something we call a 'Wow!' It's just a pat on the back that employees will give to each other when they think someone's gone the extra mile."

If either Sam or I had made the fatal mistake of making eye contact with the other, we would have immediately joined Rachel in the outside world, sans the benefit of a significant other with a good job prospect.

Alice picked up for our nutcase leader.

"We want you to design and write something that can be handed out to employees. It'll be a 2-copy thing. One the employee can keep, and the other will go into his permanent file. We'll incentivize everyone by saying that after a certain amount of Wows! are collected—say, 20—they'll be eligible for some reward or prize."

"Of course, that's just bullshit, but don't let that stop you," said Andrea, as Alice bowed her head in what I'm hoping and assuming was soul-piercing shame. I guess they don't call it truth serum for nothing.

"Sounds like a plan" was all Sam could muster before he and I headed back to our offices.

"So, Sam, should we like the fact that we're in on Andrea's relentless 'wink-wink' bullshit or be further horrified that, in a sense, we're an active part of the shenanigans?"

"I don't know, but I'm bestowing the first Wow! on you for using the word 'shenanigans.' And I plan on giving you 73,000 Wows! tomorrow just because I'm sure I'll like your tie."

I started batting around ideas as to what could "Wow" stand for:

Whip Out Willy

White On White

Where's Our Work?

Whitey Owns Wendy's

Wrecked Over Work

Weaseling Our Way

I finally came up with one that might actually please Andrea: Wicked On Work!

Sam and I got together to devise the cursed thing. He drew a smiley face brandishing a trophy, while I added the tagline, "Mousetrap, Inc.—where the special 1 percent always go the extra mile." We left blank lines for the recipient's name, the witness, and the date.

I ran it by Alice first, figuring she usually had a pretty good read on Andrea. When I handed it to her, she started shaking her head. "Nick, I'm sure whatever you and Sam did is fine. I just . . ."

She wasn't laughing; in fact, just the opposite was occurring. "What the hell am I doing here?" she said, trying unsuccessfully not to cry. "And then she blurts out what she said to you guys. I wanted to die. I'm so sorry, Nick."

"Sorry for what, Alice? Look, if it's any consolation, Sam and I are quite aware of what goes on here. Andrea's confided in us before. And if it'll cheer you up any, I was directly responsible for Rachel being fired."

"Yeah, I know. I was there when Loretta stormed into Andrea's office. Boy, did she want your head. It was Andrea who—I shouldn't be telling you this."

"No, you know the rules of this game, Alice. When you start a sentence and then say, 'I shouldn't be telling you this,' the jig's up. Proceed."

"It was Andrea who figured you would hurt more if you knew you were responsible for Rachel being let go."

I shrugged. "What, am I supposed to have less respect for Andrea now?" Alice laughed, and for the first time I was actually glad to hear her do so. "It makes sense. Andrea's a lot cagier than Loretta. Wait a second. You're not best pals with Loretta, too, are you? Should I go tell Sam to clean out his desk?"

"No, Nick, no worries there. I find Loretta as repugnant as you no doubt do."

So, Alice was a comrade, after all. I figured I'd see how far I could take it. "I have October 29 and Sam has November 8 in the office pool as to when this company goes full-on belly-up. What date would you like?"

"Oh, it'll survive until early '92. Put me down for, I don't know, January 23."

She said this with great certainty and much too quickly, and seeing how she probably had access to not only the company's numbers but also Andrea's personal finances, this gave me a feeling of relief and finality. What a great visit this was—Alice turned out to be human, and I could tell Sam it was likely we would be employed at least till the end of the year.

I headed straight to Sam's office and said, "January 23."

"Nick, again, I'm gonna say it. I'm working under constant sleep deprivation, a condition that is not helped in the least when people say disjointed things to me. Is there a full thought connected with the random 'January 23'?"

"Well, that's Alice's pick in the office pool for when Mousetrap meets its maker."

"What the hell prompted you to let her in on our thing? I don't have to remind about the Loretta incident, do I?"

"No, she's cool. Trust me. And, oh, thanks for reminding me about Rachel. I had almost forgotten about it for five full minutes. Alice actually apologized to us."

"About what?"

"About Andrea mouthing off during our 'Wow' conversation. She was even crying. Plus, she used the word 'repugnant' talking about Loretta."

"Turn around, Nick."

I looked at him quizzically but did as he asked. I heard him scribbling furiously at his desk and wondered what he was up to.

"Okay, turn around."

He handed me my first "Wow." (He never did get around to giving me one for using the word "shenanigans.")

"Good work finding out about the date, Nick. I believe this will be the first of many bestowed upon a worker of your exquisite caliber."

"Frankly, I'm too humbled and awed to respond to this unprecedented honor. To be blunt, my fervent desire is to swallow the sacred parchment before me, thus letting its inks be a permanent part of my bloodstream."

We were having a good laugh, and I noticed Loretta walking by Sam's office and then heading backwards and into his office. "What's so damn funny?"

Oh, what an opening she gave me:

1. Your outfit, for starters.

2. The company we work for.

3. This whole "Wow" campaign. By the way, Loretta, I'd like to give you one for being the saltiest, most unlikable, cynical human I've ever known.

4. Did I mention your outfit? (Actually, my knowledge of women's fashion could fit comfortably inside a mousehole; I'm just assuming that questioning a woman's fashion sense is a surefire insult.)

And oh, how chicken I was to say anything but the following: "Come on, Loretta. I'm not going down that road again. Do you really expect me to say anything out of line?"

"No, Nick, I don't." She smiled, pivoted, and left Sam's office, triumphant once more.

I looked at Sam.

"Not yet, Nick. The time will be right, but it's not today."

I grudgingly agreed and went back to my office to see if any real work had appeared. It hadn't. Fortunately, my office was located in an offshoot perpendicular to the main hallway; thus, I avoided all traffic unless someone wanted to visit me. This meant I always knew when someone was coming and didn't have to pretend like I was working, in case Andrea or some higher-up was walking by. So I just sat there and stared at my computer monitor. I took a deep breath and weighed my options. I was now quite certain that Mousetrap would last at least through the year. This didn't mean I would stop sending out résumés, but it did help calm me a bit.

Plus, I didn't have much faith in landing a new job, anyway. The economy was in a recession, and the dozens of résumés I had been sending out for several months had all fallen on deaf ears.

Anyway, I did have a great interest in seeing if Luckit could redeem our souls, and Sam and I had to exact our revenge on Loretta. These were not great reasons to stay (well, the latter one wasn't, anyway), but at least I had a sense of purpose now.

By the end of July, Mousetrap had lured 23 new clients, fewer than half of what the consultants had managed to suck in as recently as May and about a 25-percent drop from last month. Somehow, the machinery chugged on. I'd attribute most of this to Andrea's "indomitable spirit," but that clichéd phrase usually is applied to positive role models ("Jackie Robinson was no doubt blessed with a natural affinity to play the game of baseball, but it may well have been his indomitable spirit that enabled him to break the game's color barrier and propelled him to immortality"), not garden-variety sleaze like my boss. So let's just attribute it to Andrea's inability to see reality and cut her losses, which had to be mounting on a daily basis. The math was becoming downright ugly: There were 23 of us left, and this month there was an equal amount of new clients. Plus, unless I missed it, none of our old clients' ideas hit the market lately, thus denying us a fresh batch of profits.

It didn't take a mathematician to figure out she was paying us in part from her own pocket. "Indomitable stupidity" is a phrase not heard often, eh?

August 1991

*It is now time to present the one-act, never-before-published play, titled
. . .*

It's Like a Fish Market in Here!
(Or Beautiful Memories of a Nice Salmon)

Written by Nick Adano
Lyrics by Nick Adano

Characters
(all appearing as themselves)

Sam Wiatt, the talented but artistically frustrated department manager

Nick Adano, Sam's equally frustrated assistant

Loretta Welles, a mendacious account executive

Andrea Bianco, the aging, skanky owner of a duplicitous and dying company

Stan, a security guard

Setting

*A once-bustling downtown Pittsburgh office that has fallen on hard times,
summer of 1991.*

Act 1

A routine August day.

"It's Like a Fish Market in Here" will be performed with as many intermissions as you desire. If you gotta pee, pee, damn it.

Scene 1

Sam and Nick, mostly honest employees of a vile invention-marketing company, have had enough of coworker Loretta's escalating nastiness. Her latest bit of cruelty resulted in Sam and Nick's friend Rachel getting fired.

It is an early Monday morning, and we meet our protagonists as they put the finishing touches on their revenge against Loretta.

Sam: This is the week. Did you see the weather forecast?

Nick: Funny. I thought the exact same thing. Shall we take a trip to Wholey's for lunch?

Sam: Sounds like a plan. You notice how odd it is that the temperature of this building goes up everywhere on really hot days except in Andrea's office, which remains its tundral* self?

Nick: And this surprises you how?

Sam: I didn't say it surprised me. Anyhow, I'm thinking a nice salmon.

Nick: Does it really matter what kind?

Sam: No, I suppose not. I just wanted to say, "I'm thinking a nice salmon." It has a dastardly ring to it.

Scene 2

Loretta Welles, the corrupted, foul-talking account executive, is having a conversation with a new client. She is at her sweet-talking, unctuous best, and it takes every bit of will they can muster for Sam and Nick not to vomit as they eavesdrop.

Loretta: Yes, everything has been processed, and it's a go!

*Yes, it is a word. Deal with it. Okay, actually, it isn't. But it really should be.

No, we're as excited—hell, we're more excited than you are, if you can believe it.

Well, to be honest, it can take time, sometimes months. Remember, Rome wasn't built in a day.

No, there definitely is a need in the marketplace for your pill timer. It's a wonder no one's thought of it before.

Yes, of course. Call me anytime. I'm here to help you.

No, thank you for your business. Never a bother. Don't be ridiculous! Hang up and call me right back if you think of something new to ask. I *am* serious! Okay, talk to you soon—hopefully with big news!

(She hangs up the phone).

Fucking imbecile!

Scene 3

The boys head off to the Strip District, a Pittsburgh landmark that's not what you think it is, you gutter-minded readers. No, the Strip was initially home to numerous factories and foundries, later becoming a wholesale destination. Eventually, while the wholesale aspect still remained, merchants began opening retail stores and restaurants.

If you've ever seen a "Monday Night Football" game on TV from Pittsburgh, you no doubt have seen a Strip District eatery's famous sandwiches. Primanti Bros. is known for putting everything—coleslaw, onion rings, French fries—directly on its sandwiches. For some reason, unbeknownst to the locals, this fascinates the hell out of the likes of John Madden, et al, who inevitably proclaim at some point during a telecast, "They put French fries on the sandwich!"

Now, where was I? Oh, yes, the boys were headed specifically to Wholey's, a fish wholesaler, where they promptly purchased, much to Sam's delight, a nice salmon.

Scene 4

The boys return triumphant from the fish market, and Sam quickly drops the fish in a bottom drawer of his desk.

Sam: I'll meet you at 7:00, right?

Nick: Sounds good to me. I can't imagine anyone would be here at that hour.

Sam: Are you implying that business is slow? Maybe Loretta will be there, talking to her nervous clients through the night, assuaging the fears they no doubt possess that they possibly were mildly retarded in giving us thousands of dollars. Maybe Andrea herself is here till the wee hours of the morning, figuring out new ways to entertain us.

Nick: I'll meet you at 7:00.

Scene 5

The boys meet, as planned, in front of the building, punch in the after-hours security code on the door panel, and enter with ease. Living up to the adage that "all great minds think alike," both are wearing black T-shirts and black jeans. Were it winter, no doubt, our heroes would be wearing matching black skull caps and gloves to finish their robber ensembles.

They exit the elevator and quietly tiptoe around the office, making sure no one's around. The coast appears to be clear.

Nick: (whispering) What's our story if someone shows up?

Sam: (shouting) Hadn't thought about it. You tell me, word boy.

Nick: What the hell's your problem?! We don't want to be caught, remember?

Sam: Yeah, I'm aware of the basic nuances of the plan. But listen. Silence. There's nobody here. And who the hell's gonna show up?

Nick: All right, let's get to work, then.

Sam: Would you fucking relax? We work here, remember? We're allowed to be here.

Nick: We're dressed in black, and we're about to deposit a cut-up salmon underneath Loretta's wall-to-wall office carpet. That's not in my job description.

Sam: Well, believe it or not, it's in mine! I'm in charge of the graphics department and—get this—if a fish needs a-choppin', I get to do it.

Nick: Let's just get this over with.

Being city lads, the boys had scant experience cutting up a dead fish. The process turned out to be not only surprisingly difficult, but gross as hell. After an hour, though, the boys had chopped up the salmon into the size specifications laid down by Sam, who now, with Nick's assistance, was going to cut damn near invisible holes in Loretta's carpet and then fill the holes with, ahem, a nice salmon.

Nick: I have to admit, I'm impressed. (Running his hands over Sam's latest carving). I don't see a difference. I don't even feel a difference.

Sam: Ah, but in a few days, Loretta will smell a difference.

Nick: And she'll never figure out what it is.

The boys were admiring their handiwork and basking in the glory of a well-played practical joke when they heard the footsteps approaching. Come on. You knew at some point there had to be footsteps approaching, right?

Sam: Any ideas?

Nick: Freezing seems to work. Look. Let's just grab this by the horns. Like you said, we're allowed to be here.

Nick gets up and exits the doorway before Sam can stop him.

Nick: Evening, Stan.

Stan: Hey, I thought I heard something. Glad to see a familiar face. What's keeping you here so late?

Nick: Just tying up some loose ends before my vacation.

Stan: Oh, yeah. I hear you. (Sniffing) What's that smell?

Nick: Oh, don't get me started on that. My fiancée packed me dinner. I'm starting to rethink the whole marriage thing.

Stan: Give her time. She'll learn. Believe it or not, when I got married, I was as skinny as you. Now look at me.

Nick: (forcing a chuckle) Well, I better get back to work.

Stan: Yep, me too. Have a good one.

That bullet dodged, the boys finished up their work as quickly as they could, made sure they left nothing incriminating, and departed separately, being cautious not to arouse any suspicions that Stan may possess.

Scene 6

It's 93 degrees today, and it feels like a swamp—just what the boys ordered! In an effort to save a few bucks, Andrea has raised the thermostat office-wide, leaving it barely tolerable. It's early Tuesday morning, and Loretta has just arrived in her office.

Loretta: (sniffing) That's odd.

She departs and heads in the direction of Nick's office.

Loretta: Nick, you have an oversized Italian nose. Follow me.

Nick: Good morning to you, too. And could you be more offensive?

Loretta: Just shut the fuck up and follow me.

As they go past Sam's office, Sam gives Nick the universal sign for "play it cool" by raising and lowering his hands from his chest to his waist. Nick gives him a sly "thumbs-up" in return.

Loretta: Do you smell anything?

Nick: (sniffs) New perfume?

Loretta: You're such an asshole.

Nick: (chuckles) It is a bit musty. I don't know. Maybe it has something to do with the a.c.

Loretta: Well, once again, thanks for nothing. Get out of here. Some of us have work to do.

Scene 7

It is now Wednesday, and for the third day in a row, temperatures are in the 90s. What started out as a vague unpleasantness has now blossomed into a full-blown stench. Loretta has tried everything—deodorizers, perfumes—but the smell always returns. And now Andrea has showed up.

Loretta: (forcing a smile) Andrea, what brings you here?

Andrea: (sniffing) What the hell is that smell?

Loretta: I'm not sure what you mean, Andrea.

Andrea: You're not sure what I mean? It smells like a fish market in here! What the hell is wrong with you?

Loretta: Andrea, I don't know what it is. It's been getting worse every day this week. It's driving me crazy.

Andrea: We'll have our meeting in my office—now. And when you get back here, get rid of whatever the hell is causing my eyes to water.

Loretta: Yes, right away.

Scene 8

The next day, Thursday, was the peak stench day. The temperature reached close to 100, and Loretta spent the better part of her day scouring every inch of her office, completely oblivious to the source of the odor. Sam and Nick took several trips past her office and did their best not to laugh. That night, a cold front pushed through the area, and by Friday the temperatures were back into the seventies. The smell lessened with each passing day and within a few weeks was gone entirely. The only thing that remained were beautiful memories of a nice salmon.

Scene 9

The entire cast gets together for a rousing song that ties up any loose ends.

"A Nice Salmon"

(mid-tempo introduction)

Nick: They say revenge is a dish that's best served cold.

Sam: But somehow we must teach that tiresome scold.

Nick: Patience, friend, or we'll suffer Rachel's fate.

Sam: Don't worry, chum. It's coming off a plate.

(tempo quickens)

Nick: You mean . . . ?

Sam and Nick: A nice salmon will do the trick.

We'll cut it up, but not too thick.

Below her feet it shall go

Revenge is sweet

The stench will grow

Should we put some ham in?

Nah, let's just stick with a nice salmon.

Loretta: As if I don't hate this place enough,

as if my job doesn't suck enough,

what the fuck is that smell?

Have I died and gone to hell?

Andrea: My binge drinking dulls my senses completely,

but even I know when someone isn't keeping office neatly.

Stan: I knew those boys were up to no good,

but I shut my mouth.

Why?

'Cause I like a prank as much as the next guy,

and also I never speak in rhyme.

Entire cast:

A nice salmon will do the trick.

We'll cut it up, but not too thick.

Below her feet it shall go

Revenge is sweet

The stench will grow

Should we put some ham in?

Nah, let's just stick with a nice salmon.

So, yes, the great Salmon Caper went off largely without a hitch, and dumbass Loretta never figured out that we would want to exact revenge on her. Of course, it could be she figured that any number of employees were seeking revenge on her, and that left her incapable of launching a proper investigation.

The only person we ever told of our escapade was Rachel, who not only loved it, naturally, but also had good news: Her fiancé landed the job, and they were in the process of moving to North Carolina. I felt good about the salmon success, but I was downright elated that Rachel was getting on with her life.

So, at least, that little story all came together nicely: I mouth off at Loretta, Loretta fires back by getting Rachel canned, we get away with our salmon installation as revenge, and Rachel lands on her feet in the Tar Heel state. Wonderful.

I got the feeling, though, that the demise of Mousetrap wouldn't be so clean and tidy. Work was getting slower. The only thing I had done so far today, for example, was give Sam a Wow! for our fish-capade. A few minutes later, he returned the favor.

Seeing how I had no actual work and still feeling a salmon buzz, I decided now was as good a time as any for my latest Chapel Fox escapade.

Chapel Fox awoke the next morning in the arms of his smiling lover and felt as though a new chapter had opened in his life. In the past 24 hours, his secret double life had been exposed by his secretary, whom he feared would drop a dime on him the second she came to her senses. Goodbye, life.

And yet, oddly, he never felt more alive. The rust around his usually black heart seemed to be melting (actually, he wasn't sure if rust melted, but it was early in the morning, and that was the best he could come up with.) And what was even more shocking? He actually felt a glimmer of remorse for the murders he had committed and thought perhaps that he had gone too far defending his hometown.

And therein laid the problem. He had to kill again. There simply could be no other solution. Why? The only way he could be sure of remaining a free man was by making Beth complicit in his misdeeds. After all, she indicated that that's what she wanted. He just needed one more murder.

After that, he told himself, he would live like regular folk: Ask Beth for her hand in marriage, get a house on a nice leafy street, maybe have a couple of little Chapels running around in a handsome, fenced-in yard. Yes, Chapel Fox was willing to hang up his trusty Terrible Towel and replace it with a baseball glove and a pair of Rollerblades.

The minute he considered his "one more murder" approach, though, a steady stream of bad movie ideas ran through his head, all premised on the "this is our last heist" or "this is Ramirez's last day before retirement" approach. And Fox, like all movie viewers, knew that premise always laid the foundation for disaster. Sometimes, granted, comedic disaster co-starring Joe Pesci, but disaster nonetheless.

Beth snapped him out of his introspective stupor with a delicious kiss, and the rust further melted.

"We need to get to work, Beth. Remember? Um, are we a public item, or should we keep it low-key?"

"Oh, we're an item, Chap, but let's keep it low-key for now. You do know what I want, right?"

"A fabulous diamond and a trip to Rome?"

"I want in next time you commit one of your deeds. And listen. If I pick up the paper next week and read an article about a mysterious murder that has flabbergasted local authorities, I won't be happy."

"Well, why would you be happy? Murder is an awful thing, Beth."

"You know what I mean."

"Yes, I know what you mean, but—but." He sighed. "Have you ever even killed a spider, Beth?"

"Chap, please lose the psychobabble—and sexist, I might add— bullshit, all right? We have a deal. You let me in, or I call the cops."

"I understand completely. I'm just looking out for you. Besides, you do understand that months can pass before I do this, right?"

"I don't care if it takes six months, but I want in."

For the next several weeks, Fox and Beth behaved like any new couple in love—dinners, shows, weekend trips—and they eventually told everyone in the office what was obvious to all: They were officially dating. There was no harm in everyone knowing, seeing how Fox was the owner. These were happy times for the couple, and only once in a while did Beth inquire as to the prospect of any new side jobs. When this line of questioning arose, Fox would always answer in the same way: "You'll be the first to know. I promise."

Truth be told, Fox wasn't actively looking, and, even more shocking, he no doubt passed over chances to add to his collection. For the first time in his life, he was in love, and, ironically, the beautiful woman who had eased his rampaging heart was forcing him back into his secret life. Yes, Fox realized one morning while shaving, it was exactly as he had feared: His life had become one of those awful movie premises.

Yet, he felt so positive about life that there were times he even considered turning himself in for his heinous acts. He didn't, of course, seeing how his confessions wouldn't bring any of his victims back to life. He did realize, though, that no matter how long he lived, he could never atone for his ghastly sins. Still, when dark thoughts of roasting in hell for eternity filled his mind, the smiling face of Beth assuaged his fears and almost made him believe in goodness.

One night over dinner, she point-blank asked him, "What's it feel like?"

They didn't need to play games anymore, and he knew exactly what she was talking about.

"It's exciting, especially when I know I'm the only one leaving the room alive."

Even talking about it gave Fox a thrill. The embers still burned, apparently. Beth pressed him for more details, but Fox changed the subject, not wanting to ruin a fine dinner by bringing up his wretched past. He also knew that his black heart hadn't entirely healed, and by the look of eagerness on Beth's face at the mention of his part-time job, she couldn't wait for his return engagement.

After dinner, they made furious love, no doubt spurned on by the talk of murder. Again, reader, feel free to add your own details; I'm not your smut supplier. Maybe they went for a swim in Fox's pool and fucked in the water. Who's to say? I've never even mentioned that Fox owns a swimming pool. Use your imagination and fill in the naughty details to your delight.

The brief discussion with Beth over dinner proved to Fox that the beast within him still had a pulse. The next day's paper, though, would beckon him back to the dark side. According to an article in the paper's entertainment section, a certain young actress by the name of Tanna Colson was in town filming a movie. Unfortunately for Ms. Colson, in the course of the article, she referred to Pittsburgh in a very unflattering way. I would document the severity of her crime here, but I would hate to enrage Fox even further by repeating her sacrilege.

When Fox reached his office, a copy of the article was awaiting him on his desk. He didn't have to think twice as to who had done it.

"So, is this the one, Chap?" asked his very eager lover.

Fox sighed. He was straddling two worlds now, so close to a respectable life, he could smell it. And yet it smelled like Beth's lavender perfume. The only nearly perfect way out of this would be to do away with Beth. But he knew he couldn't do that. The rust had completely melted.

He tried reasoning with her.

"Beth, this isn't you. Yes, my first instinct was to fluff up my Towel and make sure it was in good working order. But—but—"

"Chap, if we don't do this, you know what happens."

"How about I kill you instead, then, Beth?"

Beth laughed the worst kind of laugh—the all-knowing one, the one that says, "I hold all the cards." Fox hated that laugh, especially when it emanated from the mouth of the woman he loved.

"You don't have the guts to turn me in, Beth."

"Maybe I do and maybe I don't. But wouldn't you hate to find out you're wrong . . . again, lover?"

And with that, she turned heel and went back to work.

What made the whole situation worse, of course, was that Tanna Colson was somewhat famous. His previous victims had been private citizens, missed by loved ones, of course, but no one else. This murder would make front pages of newspapers all over the country.

Fortunately for Fox, the next day's filming took place downtown, and by performing simple surveillance, he easily ascertained which hotel she was staying at. He also knew that the crew would be filming downtown for another week. He had time to prepare, and the black-hearted part of him wanted to kill everyone associated with the movie—even the best boy and gaffer, whatever the hell they do—so appalling were Ms. Colson's hateful words.

After contemplating the situation for a few hours, Fox devised a plan: He would revive the Pittsburgh Tourism Bureau gambit that worked well with the two clowns from Chicago. This time, however, he would also have a lovely assistant by his side. Together, they would seem so harmless.

He told Beth the details that night over dinner. She was ecstatic.

"So, you think this will work, then?"

"Yes, I've been doing surveillance for a couple days now. She returns by herself to her hotel. We 'bump into her' tomorrow and explain that we're from the tourism bureau and that we'd like to show her the beauty of our city. She accepts our offer because right now, she's Public Enemy Number One in our fair town. She needs us."

As soon as Fox got done detailing their plan, Beth literally cleared the dining-room table and lunged for her lover. They made crazed love on the spot, punctuated by these occasional declarations by Beth:

"I want to drink her blood."

"I want to gain strength from the anguish of her tears as her life is extinguished."

There were several more such declarations, but you get the general idea. And so did Fox. Sure, he was a killer. But Beth? She was fucking psychotic. He had no room in his tidy life for a madwoman.

Tanna Colson would escape Pittsburgh alive and go on to make more movies. Sure, Fox despised her, but he knew he couldn't let Beth be a part of his world. She was a loose cannon. She would have screwed up, and they both would have wound up in prison.

He made sure that they missed Tanna on their daily stakeouts. Beth was mightily disappointed, but Fox gently explained to her that there would be other victims.

He neglected to tell her, though, that she was next on his list.

I made copies of my latest murderous tale and distributed it to my ever-shrinking fan base. I had ample time on my hands to write the stories, and I had no doubt my coworkers were looking for something to do to kill the time, as well. As I walked past Loretta's office (who, needless to say, was not on my distribution list), I overheard her say the following:

"Look, Mr. Gardner. The wheels sometimes turn slowly."

It took a few seconds to register, but finally a switch flipped, and I realized who Mr. Gardner was. He was the Luckit inventor. I decided to eavesdrop.

"No, there's no reason to get upset at all, sir. Yes, we all think it's a wonderful idea, but like I said—No, I don't see how bringing in lawyers will help anything, to be perfectly frank.

"As I've said to you, the wheels turn slowly. Let me make a few calls, and I promise to get back to you this week, okay?

"Really, sir, we adore your product. In fact, I can personally assure you that a few of our young up-and-comers went the extra mile on your behalf. Trust me. I feel this one in my bones, okay? And I've been doing this for years."

Aw, how nice. Loretta thinks that Sam, Rache, and I are up-and-comers. I used my brain this time and didn't confront her, though I did at the moment wish to possess the ability to belch on cue. Or, to be more blunt, projectile-vomit on cue. If I had that power, Loretta and her desk would have been drenched in a sea of warm puke.

Instead, I marched into Sam's office mad as hell and told him of the conversation I'd overheard. I was about 30 seconds into my story before I realized that his daughter was sitting in her little seat, asleep and perfectly innocent.

"Sam, are you sure she belongs here? She's not even two months old. I think babies need to build up an immunity to sleaze their first few months, don't they?"

"It's okay, Nick. She's in the Zone of Goodness. About Luckit—we actually did do our level best, you know?"

"Yeah, but our reputation precedes us, doesn't it? What realistic chance did it have? If the Washington Generals go on a 2-game winning streak, it doesn't change the perception, does it?"

"Got any ideas?"

"I want to talk to him, but I have no idea what I'd say."

"Hi, Mr. Gardner. I'm Nick. My department put together a terrific, snazzy prototype of your card game, and we all really felt great about it. Of course, we also knew that there wasn't a damn chance of your idea ever seeing the light of day. Gee, now that I think of it, the proper thing to do would have been to call you before you sent your check over to that fat bastard Sheldon, who, I might add, is a total sleaze, kind of like the entire company."

I wanted to smack him with his baby. Yes, I realize how horrible that sounds, but I was furious, largely because Sam was right. We had an opportunity to stop Jack Gardner, and we chose to be deluded into thinking that Luckit would redeem our souls.

"But it seemed right, didn't it? I mean, Sam, didn't you think that maybe this was the one?"

"Yeah, Nick. We all were on the same page. Don't be so damn hard on yourself."

I gave the baby's foot a gentle shake and came face-to-face with an upbeat-looking Andrea.

"Young man, get to work! I just put three NPRs in your 'in' bin. Chop-chop!"

And now allow me to don the royal headgear of Carnac the Magnificent, place the NPRs to my cranium, and declare, "Two perpetual-motion machines and a pill-timing device."

Sadly, unlike Johnny Carson, I have no funny follow-up here. What I possessed was anger, and what most upset me was Andrea's triumphant air, as though she had accomplished something worthwhile. I might not have been as angry if she had said to me, "Nick, I just hauled in a fresh batch of nonsense, and I don't feel very good about it, but do the best you can."

But no, she just added three more pelts to her collection, pulled in at least 20 grand in the process, and seemingly didn't give a damn. I browsed the victims' NPRs and noticed two of them contained exclamation points, which always added, I felt, a nice touch of desperation. It was as if some of our clients knew their ideas were half-brained but figured that an exclamation point would somehow brighten their prospects. The pill-alarm device was given the admittedly cute name "Rexie!" I'll spare the details, other than to say it followed the pattern of most of the other similar submissions: This particular story involved a concerned granddaughter and a loving, yet forgetful, grandma. These pill-timer stories were almost becoming urban legends—similar outlines, but with the occasional wrinkle thrown in to make it seem more believable. I was eagerly awaiting a pill-timer submission that involved a hitchhiker, werewolf, nubile coeds, or some combination thereof.

Then there were the two perpetual-motion ideas: One was named Thrust!, which struck me as just plain sad, and the other was named Energetia. What it lacked in exclamation, it made up for in unpronounceability.

It didn't take me long to get through my stack of work. By this time, I had developed a template for the prescription alarm clocks, and I zipped through the perpetual-motion ideas as fast as I could and felt like I needed a long, cleansing shower after having completed them. Helping defy the laws of science was brutal, soul-killing work.

I decided I needed another dose of innocent baby, so I headed over to Sam's office and made it in just in time. Sam's wife, Karen, had arrived and was getting ready to depart, newborn in tow.

"Rough day, Nick? You look like you're not all here," said Karen.

"Rough day? Hell, Karen, doesn't your husband talk about work much?"

"Hey, I have an idea. How about the four of us go to dinner Friday night?" said Karen.

"The three of us and the baby? That's just weird, honey," said Sam.

"No, smartass, I meant Nicole and Nick and the two of us. Lord knows we could use a night away from the princess."

"I'll see if Nicole has anything planned, but, yeah, it sounds like a plan."

It was a great idea, actually. Nicole and I needed to do something that didn't involve wedding planning, and Sam and Karen probably could use a few hours of nonbaby time. Granted, Nicole would probably prattle on about the wedding nonstop, and Sam and Karen would blabber endlessly about how their baby is the Second Coming. It would be up to me to steer a third, happier path.

Within minutes of our double date, I received a complete rundown of Sam and Karen's wedding, interspersed with the ideas Nicole had for our upcoming nuptials. Karen and Nicole debated the merits of a band versus a deejay and what flowers would work best for a November wedding. The next few minutes were dedicated to all things baby. Finally, after the appetizers were served, there was a pause, and I took advantage by declaring, "You know, ladies, Sam and I work for the worst company in the history of America."

Okay, granted, this wasn't the happier path that I had planned on navigating us toward, but it was a third path, and I was happy to be out of the Land of Babies and Weddings.

After repeating our standard woes—the company's days are numbered, it's a sleazy outfit, Andrea is a drunken lunatic—I mentioned Luckit and how we thought that maybe, naively, it could have redeemed us.

"Then call him," said Nicole. "Seriously, I'm not sure what you have to lose. Honey, we're young. What, you'll never find another job as fulfilling as this one? You, too, Sam. You know you're better than this."

And that, in 35 words, is why I was marrying Nicole. Above all, she was honest, and not just in the traditional sense, in that she didn't lie. No, it went deeper than that. Nicole was frank—brutal, even—in her evaluations, and woe be the person who ever crossed her. She forgave nothing, which maybe was an attribute I didn't love but did secretly admire.

"But what do we say to the guy, Nic? Sam and I had this same discussion. We should have known better."

"Look. You told me the other day that Loretta was spouting the usual nonsense. You think he deserves better. Do something about it or quit whining."

Nicole was right. She was also beautiful. And the best part? She was going to be my wife in less than three months. Within seconds, the conversation turned back to babies or weddings or babies getting married—really, I wasn't paying attention—but my bride-to-be had convinced me that my first order of business Monday morning was going to be placing a phone call to Mr. Jack Gardner.

I prepared all weekend for what I was going to say to him, which was a good thing, because when I arrived at the office Monday morning, a well-dressed, elderly gentleman was sitting in our lobby. He introduced himself as Jack Gardner. Our receptionist, Connie, told me that he was waiting to see Andrea but that Andrea was indisposed for most of the day.

"Indisposed" was Connie's way of saying "drunk off her ass," which was alarming even by Andrea's standards. It was Monday morning, and Andrea was already in the tank?

"Sir, I'm Nick Adano, and I worked on your product, which we all think is terrific. But I'm probably not the person you want to talk to most. Let me see if Andrea's second-in-command is in yet. I'm sure she would very much like to speak with you."

There was no way in hell I was going to let Loretta sweet-talk Mr. Gardner in person. It was bad enough to watch it happen over the phone. To see it happen live would have been unbearable.

I noticed Sam arriving through the doors and waved him over to me as I dashed off to Alice's office.

"Where's the fire, chief?" Sam said.

"That man you just passed? It's Jack Gardner. He wants to see Andrea."

"Oh, it's way too early on a Monday to be fucking with me, Nick. Please tell me that it's Bring Your Grandparents to Work Day and that's Grandpa Vito in the lobby."

"No, Sam, there is no such holiday, both of my grandfathers are dead, and neither of them, if you care, were named Vito."

"So where the hell are we going?"

"Well, according to Connie, Andrea's already shitfaced, and it's my opinion that Loretta shouldn't be allowed within 100 yards of the poor man. That leaves Alice."

We arrived at Alice's office and gave her the quick overview.

"And what do we say to the man?" Alice asked.

"Alice, you're on the side of goodness here, right? I mean, this guy has every right to be pissed," I said.

"Nick, yeah, I'm aware of what's going on here. At the same time, Andrea pays me as her legal counsel, and we are in compliance with the governm—"

"Fucking stop it, Alice," said Sam. That got her attention.

"Sam, I don't think—"

"Stop it. You know what Nick and I worked on the other day? Another pill-timing device and two—two!—perpetual-motion machines. You think that's in compliance with governmental regulations?"

"All right, fine, guys. Let's bring in Mr. Gardner and tell him everything. What will that accomplish?"

Sam and I didn't have an answer.

"I'm sorry, Alice. I was out of line," said Sam.

She chuckled. "No, Sam, this company's been out of line forever. Don't sweat it. But, seriously, what do we say to the man?"

"Well, we can't let him see Andrea. Nothing good can come from that," I said. "And I really hate the thought of Loretta sweet-talking him in person."

"Then let's just see where our consciences take us," said Alice, who buzzed Connie to say she'd be in the lobby in a minute.

Alice returned to her office quickly with Mr. Gardner in tow, and Sam, who had gone to his office to fetch our original Luckit prototype, arrived shortly thereafter. So, there we all sat, not quite knowing what to say or how to approach a potentially dangerous situation.

"Mr. Gardner, it's a pleasure meeting you. My name is Sam Wiatt, and I'm the manager of the graphics and production department here. This is the original prototype that Nick and I made for your product. It's similar to the one we sent out to the manufacturer."

Mr. Gardner examined the deck closely and seemed pleased at Sam's work. "It's lovely, young man," he said, "and I'm sure you and Nick put a lot of work into it."

"Yes, we really did," I said, trying to delay the verbal boom that Mr. Gardner was about to lower on us. "I mean, Sam and I and a former employee—Rachel was her name—did our level best. We adore your product."

"But where are the results?" Mr. Gardner said. The question hung in the air like a puffy cloud on an otherwise clear day, just sort of hovering and not really going anywhere.

"I'm sure Loretta, your account executive, has been in contact with you, right?" asked Alice.

"Oh, on more than a few occasions, yes. But she seems to be—well, how can I put this gently?—a person for whom the truth is a rather flexible notion."

"Sir, I'm going to be honest with you," said Alice.

Sam shot me a glance. This was Alice's moment to prove she wasn't a member of the dark side.

"Loretta is a sweet-talker extraordinaire. But you're right. The truth isn't her strong suit. But these boys did their utmost to make your product a reality, and I've never seen them so excited about a product idea in all the months I've worked here.

"The problem, sir, is that the Mousetrap name doesn't exactly engender a lot of enthusiasm in the manufacturing world. Yes, we've had a few successes, but mostly what we've been successful at is perpetuating clients' false hopes. I will talk to Andrea as soon as she's available and see to it that you receive a full refund. You have my solemn word on this."

"That's not good enough, Ms. Legato. What you're telling me is that my product never had a chance."

"True, but you were well aware of the risks before you gave us your check, and we put forth 100-percent effort on behalf of your product. Sir, as bad as I feel that your product didn't succeed, you have no legal recourse."

"The hell I don't, Ms. Legato. Listen to what you're saying. The Mousetrap name is so tarnished that no product—not even, by your admission, a good one—has a chance at making an inventor a profit. I'm sure the FTC would love to hear your admission."

And with that, he stood up, bowed in our direction, and showed himself out the door.

We pressed Alice on the legal ramifications of their conversation, and she assured us that while we were probably on safe legal ground with Mr. Gardner, the notion of him taking his complaint to the FTC made her worry.

"Alice, whatever happens from here on, let me just say I really admired your performance today," I said.

"Ah, don't mention it. I'll just have to have a conversation with Loretta to let her know that her usual bullshit won't work with Mr. Gardner."

So, in addition to everything else, the specter of the kindly but mad-as-hell Mr. Gardner going to the FTC was now hanging over our heads. It was beautifully ironic, though: The one product for which we went the extra mile and were genuinely excited about might just be the one to drive the final nail in our mousehole.

As I sat in my office, contemplating Mr. Gardner's visit and feeling genuine sadness, a drunken Andrea swayed into my office and handed me a new NPR. "I'll never quit," she slurred before taking two tries at making it through my doorway.

The product, beautifully, was something called Captain Barleyhook. Allow me to further explain:

It seems as though Stanley Morningside is incapable of detaching his hand from his beer can when downing a few brews, and he's damn tired of the warmth of his hand transferring to his beverage. So one night, during a poker game with some pals, he had his eureka moment, and Captain Barleyhook was born.

Client: Stanley Morningside

Idea: Captain Barleyhook

Who doesn't love a crisp, cold beer? But what happens when your favorite brew gets warm? Hell, this isn't Europe! We live in America, and we like our beer cold. Well, as any fifth grader can tell you, our hands generate warmth. And what do we inevitably use to pick up our bottles and cans of beer? Our hands! Until now, that is.

Captain Barleyhook—its genius lies in its simplicity—allows beer lovers never to come in contact with a bottle or can again. Simply attach this hook to fit any standard bottle or can, lift it from the hook, and voilà, no more warm beer ever again.

This product can be manufactured in any number of colors and, in addition, could be made in professional and college team colors. It would also be a great corporate trinket. Really, how many more pens and ballcaps do we need?

Product Highlights:

- *Keeps beer always cold*

- *Great for sports fans*

- *Limitless marketing potential*

This one fell under the heading of harmless but stupid, which was better than insanely stupid. Still, it wasn't exactly empowering. Captain Barleyhook would be August's last product. Amazingly, Andrea and the few salespeople left managed to snag 25 new clients, an increase of two from July. The inevitable demise of her company hovered around those remaining with relentless intensity, yet Andrea would trumpet this barely noticeable increase in sales as though the company was turning the corner.

September 1991

I'LL JUST GET IT out of the way: Labor Day was just as fucked as the Fourth of July. At least this time, we saw it coming before Andrea announced her decision to us via memo, which read:

Fellow survivors,

I can think of no better way to celebrate our national day of labor than by working toward our goal of keeping Mousetrap on firm financial ground. So I ask you, not as the person who signs your paychecks, but as a loyal friend who truly believes that you are all members of that special 1 percent to please join me on Labor Day, as I roll up my sleeves and get down to the business at hand—a business, I might humbly add, that saw a nice bump in sales over last month.

I salute your diligence and dedication. It's people who like you who made this country the birthplace of ideas that it is.

Warmly,

Andrea

No, we assumed our three-day weekend would be vanquished as soon as the anger of working the Fourth of July had dissipated. What we didn't see coming, though, was Andrea dressed in a Rosie the Riveter outfit. Her getup might possibly have worked were we manufacturing something or even had reason to use a hammer or drill. On the positive side, at least the outfit was new and stain-free.

Labor Day passed with little labor being exerted by any of us. Fortunately, Andrea spared us the rah-rah meeting that was usually part of her holiday festivities. Unfortunately, that also meant there would be no cake to dull the pain of working for free on a holiday.

Cake can go such a long way in healing wounds. Sadly, though, this day brought no cake, little work, and a whole bunch of time on our hands. I used mine to put the finishing touches on the short, psychotic life of Beth L. Park:

Fox had hoped, perhaps misguidedly, that if enough time passed, the love of his life, Beth, would forget about her desire to kill. They would marry and live a long, happy life together. After all, it had been a while since the aborted Tanna Colson mission, and, to Fox's delight, Beth hadn't reminded him of their arrangement.

For Fox, everything was coming together nicely. He was putting his past behind him, guided by the love of his beautiful girlfriend. He felt more alive and hopeful than he ever had in his entire adult life. Plus, if Beth had decided to drop their agreement, then he wouldn't have to do the thing he dreaded most: kill her.

Then, one night over dinner, polite talk about the office abruptly turned to the subject Fox foolishly hoped was behind them.

"What about Becky?" said Beth.

Fox, enjoying the hell out of a succulent pork tenderloin, truly had no idea what she was talking about.

"What about Becky?" he repeated.

"You know, your other life."

"Becky, one of our paralegals? Becky, who has a couple of kids and a husband? Beth, honey, are you out of your mind?"

"Oh, yeah, Chap, I'm out of my mind. You've killed Lord knows how many people for insulting your hometown, but I'm the one who's nuts."

"Yeah, you are, dear. You see, there's always been a reason."

"Chap, listen to yourself! You've killed people—killed people!—for ridiculing Pittsburgh. But I want to off a coworker, and I'm the crazy one, right?"

Fox had to admit she had a point, but only to a certain degree. Yes, he had killed people. But they were strangers to him, and they had stupidly run off their mouths about his favorite city. They had it coming. His beloved, on the other hand, wanted to kill a well-liked coworker whom Fox had known for almost a decade. The very thought of it made him damn near throw up.

Up to this point, he had been enjoying a lovely meal. Now he was convinced there was no hope for Beth. Still, he gave it one last shot.

"Honey, let's just live our happy life together—no more killing. Trust me. You don't want to travel the road I've been on way too many times. Since I fell in love with you, I have strong feelings of remorse for what I've done. I know my soul will pay the price someday. Please, honey, don't make me do this."

"Chap, we had a deal."

"To hell with our deal, Beth! I love you. I think you love me. Maybe I'll call your bluff. Go ahead. Call the cops. Send me to jail forever."

"Don't think that I won't, Chap."

"That's exactly what I think, Beth. You won't. You love me."

The rest of dinner and the remainder of the evening were spent in cold silence.

It was around 10:00 a.m. when the Pittsburgh detective showed up at Fox's law firm. As Fox led the man into his office, he caught Beth's eye. She was trying not to laugh.

"Mr. Fox, I received a tip late last night that you may know something about Inez Gutierrez. I believe she was a client of yours?"

"Oh, yeah. That was a real shame. To be honest, I met her only once, and then . . ."

Fox's voice trailed off, trying to convey to the detective how heartbreaking the whole story was.

"But I'll be willing to tell you all I know. Like I said, I met her only that one time. She seemed pleasant, maybe a little distraught."

"What do you mean by distraught?" said the detective.

"Well, sir, you know how it is. Most people who come here are distraught. Divorce is hell. You married?"

"Was, yeah. I know what you mean. It was hell. How about you?"

"Me, married? Are you kidding? I'd have to be insane. You should hear some of the cases I've had to deal with over the years.

"Listen. How about we grab some lunch around 1:00? I have some clients to meet this morning, but I'd love to talk with you in-depth."

"Yeah, that sounds good. Look. I'm sorry for barging in here. But we hate having unsolved murders on our hands, and I gotta tell you. That was a pretty weird phone call I got concerning Mrs. Gutierrez. But yeah, I'll come back here this afternoon."

Perfect, thought Fox. He had softened up the detective with a little bit of charm. And over lunch, Fox would ply with him with salacious tales of divorcees. By the end of the lunch, the detective would think Fox had about as much to do with the Gutierrez murder as did Mother Teresa.

After the detective parted, he beckoned Beth into his office.

"So, Beth, I'm still a free man. Look"—he thrust his hands toward her—"no cuffs."

"Don't fuck with me, Chap. Maybe you can weasel your way out of this, but we had a deal. You break the deal, I keep on harassing the cops until you break. I'll call them every day for six months if I have to."

She left in such a foul mood that Fox wondered if he should give Becky the rest of the day off, for fear that Beth might embark on a solo project. He had a horrible vision of Beth detaching the paper-cutter blade from the unit's body and wielding it like a pirate in the direction of Becky's head and torso.

Like clockwork, the detective returned at 1:00. The two men went to a nearby deli, and Fox, as he planned, had the detective in hysterics over his clients' many antics through the years. The detective returned the favor by regaling Fox with stories of inept criminals. To any observer, it would have seemed the two men had been friends for decades.

By the end of lunch, the detective gave Fox his card and apologized for wasting his time. Fox assured him humbly that there was no need to apologize and told him if anything else about the late Mrs. Gutierrez popped into his head, he would let him know immediately.

Instead of heading back directly to the office, Fox took one detour. Over lunch, he decided that tonight would be the night that he and Beth would part as a dating couple. But it first involved one small purchase.

Upon returning to the office, he told Beth he would like to meet with her in private. She looked at him skeptically but followed.

"Fettuccine Alfredo tonight, dear. And you can't say no." Fox was smiling as he said this, which further confused Beth. Fettuccine Alfredo was a Fox specialty, but he made it only a few times a year, seeing how calorie-laden a dish it was.

"You're not mad at me?"

"Hell, no. I think it's kind of funny, actually. You called my bluff. I had to spend the past hour and a half charming a stranger, and I won't see a dime's profit out of it. Now, that pisses me off, to be honest. But the rest? Let's just forget it and celebrate with dinner tonight. Does 7:00 work for you?"

"Sure." Beth smiled. "But you do realize our original deal is still in place, right? No amount of fettuccine can change it."

"Enough about the deal, Beth. Tonight we relax, open a couple bottles of wine, and have fun. Now get back to work. I don't pay you just for looking good, you know."

They kissed, and she departed, leaving Fox time to jot down plans for the evening. Everything had to be perfect.

Beth arrived at Fox's house around 6:30, looking as beautiful as ever. They had a pre-dinner drink while Beth put the finishing touches on setting the dining-room table. Fox had decided to use the good dishes and the family-heirloom tablecloth he had inherited from his loving grandmother. Beth had given him a quizzical look upon entering the dining room, but after a relaxing cocktail or two, she was now quite calm and ready for sustenance.

Dinner was wonderful, but not half as good as the time the couple was having. They laughed and enjoyed themselves so much that Fox knew he would never love another woman as much as he did Beth.

"Are you ready for dessert, dear?"

"Ooh, you made dessert, too? What is it?"

"You'll have to close your eyes. And no peeking."

Fox hopped into the kitchen and placed a small velvet box on a beautiful dessert plate, also a family heirloom. He also grabbed the sharpest knife he owned.

He returned to the dining room, placed the plate in front of her, popped open the box, and told her to open her eyes.

She was astonished.

"Beth, I want you to be my wife, and I want to spend the rest of my life with you."

Beth was too stunned to move, and Fox continued.

"But the only way we can marry is if you drop the terms of our agreement. I don't want to live that life anymore, and I don't want you to live it for a second. So you have a choice to make. Say yes to my marriage proposal, or I slit your throat right now from ear to ear."

And with puma-like grace, he put the tip of the knife right under her left ear and pressed it in ever so slightly to show he meant business.

"You wouldn't, Chap."

"Beth, we don't want to play the call-your-bluff game again, do we?"

She stared at the ring, which was a stunning 2-carat diamond. It cost Fox a small fortune, but, after all, with the exception of the occasional Larrimor suit, he rarely spent much on material goods.

Every passing second felt like a decade. Fox knew that the next word out of Beth's mouth would forever alter their destiny. He was hoping that she would say—

"Yes, Chap. Let's do it."

He pulled back the knife and gently placed the ring on her finger. He had never been so happy. A lifetime with the woman he loved, no more killings, maybe some kids down the road—it was time to throw in the Towel.

Maybe my judgment had been clouded by my own upcoming nuptials, but I just couldn't have Fox kill the love of his life, could I? Plus, I was hoping my female coworkers would enjoy a tale of romance, albeit one that involved a knife and potential death by slicing, instead of the usual Fox tale.

My own wedding plans—picking a deejay, helping select flowers and a dinner menu—were coming along nicely and, in addition, gave my mind something to think about other than the state of my employment.

I deferred to Nicole's opinion on everything except for this: I insisted on wearing a black tuxedo. From this I would not budge, and Nicole didn't seem to care one way or another. Why was I so insistent? Have you ever seen a wedding album from the seventies? Often, in those less-enlightened times, menfolk thought it a good idea to wear pastel-colored tuxes. No man should ever wear peach anything, under any circumstances. I figured that one could never go wrong with black, and I didn't want to provide hours of amusement for future children laughing at pictures and video of their father in his lavender tuxedo and wondering if I was celebrating Halloween or my wedding day.

You always have to look toward the future, like our latest client: local victim Rob Pilar, who wants to prevent what happened to a buddy of his from ever occurring again. Let's let Rob explain.

"Man, you shoulda seen Jimmy's car. I mean, the thing was totaled, right? And why? A freakin' deer. I mean, it must have been a 12-point, the way it destroyed everything. And Jimmy? He was pretty messed up, too. It took him months to breathe right."

Okay, the letter goes on and in further, grosser detail—"the blood had mixed with the gas and oil, and I swear it looked like chocolate pudding, though I wouldn't want to eat it, you know?—but I'll be kind and forgo the rest. Here's the deal: Every fall in Western Pennsylvania, thousands of cars are attacked by our large deer population. It's really not a laughing matter—the collisions are sometimes fatal—though Mr. Pilar's solution is.

He's "invented" two small plastic devices that attach to the front end of the car above the headlights that create a high-pitched whistling sound that our inventor swears will ward off any oncoming deer.

Here's the big problem with this product: It already exists, and it's known to be completely ineffective.

Ah, but Mr. Pilar has seen through this obstacle and has raised me . . . flashing lights. Again, Rob Pilar:

"So, sure, the whistle thing already exists, but here's where my idea gets great, if I do say so myself—blinking lights. You see, the second my devices sense a deer, a set of blinking lights is activated that will really annoy the deer. That way, if the whistle doesn't work, the lights will. It's a backup."

You see? Two 5-cent lumps of plastic will magically "sense" when a deer is approaching. This event will trigger lights to blink, and everyone will live happily ever after. Who knows? Drivers may be so relieved at avoiding a collision, they may hop out of the car with a bucket full of carrots and spend some time frolicking in the woods with their newfound sylvan friends.

This company needed to get mauled by a herd of deer. Right now. Seeing how that probably wasn't going to happen, I banged out Mr. Pilar's idea and spent the rest of the day compiling a list of songs I wanted played at my wedding. I also mulled an invitation problem I had been ruminating over for weeks: Do I invite Andrea and her husband? From an etiquette standpoint, I suppose inviting the person who signs your paycheck, paltry as it may be, is the proper course of action. But . . . boy. The combination of Andrea and free booze and my family watching the spectacle unfold sent chills down my body, the likes of which I hadn't felt since the last time I visited Andrea's lair.

Of course, Nicole kept reminding me that it was the right thing to do, so in the end, the beast and her hapless hubby would probably get an invite. And I would probably regret it. On the other hand, what's a wedding without at least one drunk doing something memorably stupid?

As I was contemplating my options, who should walk in but ol' Drinky herself. She was seemingly sober, though, and possessed a determined look, which scared me more than the thought of her destroying my wedding.

"Young man, this company is moving in the right direction again. Our sales increased in August, and I feel great about September. But we need to promote ourselves and put this company back in its proper spotlight. I want you to come up with something like you did with that 1-percent idea. I still love that! Maybe you and Sam could devise a newsletter and talk to some of our awesome clients. You could interview the guy who created that card game that you and your buddy were gushing over.

"Anyway, get back to me by the end of the week with your ideas. That's all!"

The swagger, unbelievably, had returned. Our sucker count increased from 23 in July to 25 in August, and she was parading around like a titan of industry. And now I had to take time out of my ridiculously unbusy schedule to promote Mousetrap. And yeah, Andrea, I'll be sure to give the Luckit dude a call pronto. If I'm lucky, I'll catch him in between meetings with his team of lawyers.

Nonetheless, as much as I hated the idea of promoting that which I never believed in, I was given my marching orders, and I promptly told Sam about our directive.

"So, let's get Jack Gardner on the phone posthaste!"

"Yeah, Sam, go right ahead. I'm sure he'd love to hear from us."

"So, got any ideas?"

"Yeah, actually, and I think it works in two different ways: Andrea will love it, and the press might actually bite."

I could tell Sam was intrigued. I was slightly disgusted with myself, but the fact was this: I was given a task—a challenge—and I was going to accomplish it to the best of my abilities.

"Our economy's in a recession, right? But we're Americans. We love the big dream. How about this: Mousetrap sponsors an inventors' showcase. We invite the press, pushing the American Dream angle."

"And which inventions would you propose we promote?"

"Not the perpetual-motion machines or anything that's ridiculously stupid, of course. Just the harmlessly stupid ones. You know, like Captain Barleyhook."

"So you're proposing that we prop up this rotting-flesh corpse of a company by giving additional false hope to our hapless clients."

"Yes, Sam, that's exactly what I'm proposing, you miserable s.o.b."

Sam's earnest logic stopped me dead. I actually looked away in shame.

"Nick, it's a good idea. Don't get me wrong. I just wish I believed in the cause."

"Andrea's on a mission, Sam, and she gave us her demand. What are our choices?"

Sam threw up his hands. "I'll leave it up to you to coordinate everything. Just keep me posted."

I returned to my office, somewhat deflated by Sam's lack of excitement but fully aware that he was right. Still, I had something constructive to do, and my first order of business was finding a half dozen or so inventions that fit the requirements I was looking for.

After a few hours' research, I decided to resurrect the following creations:

SpeakerPlanters, by Liz Orosco

Fabrocs, by Beth Sewickley

State Pies, by Marcy Hackwell

Captain Barleyhook, by Stanley Morningside

Spice-tisserie, by Sue Labeck

And to represent the countless prescription-timing devices that passed my way, I selected Prescript-i-Clock, by Allison Park. Ms. Park had little idea that she would be the ambassador of an entire non-industry.

I met with Andrea at the end of the day and told her my proposal in terms I knew she would lap up. "We'll call it something like the American Dreamers Showcase and entice the local media to come."

"I think I love it, Nick! Have Loretta contact the clients and arrange for it to happen ASAP. Great!"

Yay, I pleased the beast. Now I had to face my next unpleasant task: visiting Loretta.

"What the hell do you want?"

"And a pleasant hello to you, too, Loretta. Listen. Andrea asked Sam and me to come up with some promotion ideas for the company. We've decided to host six inventors to tell their stories in what we're calling the American Dreamers Showcase."

"Nick, don't take this the wrong way. Actually, take it any way you wish, come to think of it. You realize that's retarded, right?"

"Look, Loretta. Andrea loves the idea. If you want to give her your two cents, don't let me stop you. All I'm asking you to do is contact the six clients we've chosen and get them all here on the same day ASAP."

"Consider it done, Nick."

"Thank you, sunshine. Just let me know what date you've all agreed upon."

My next job was writing a press release that would hopefully attract the attention of local media. It wouldn't be much of a promotion if the press didn't show up.

Local dream factory to host American Dreamers Showcase

Pittsburgh—No amount of economic bad news can ever slow down the American Dream. And on September __, local invention-marketing firm Mousetrap will host its first-ever American Dreamers Showcase, featuring six clients, from all walks of life, who are the very embodiment of the American Dream.

Liz Orosco, an inventor from Boston, has come up with something she calls SpeakerPlanters. Are they plants that talk? No! She's simply tired of how ugly conventional stereo speakers look and has devised a way to hide them by making them appear to be planters.

Or how about Marcy Hackwell? This inventor has devised not only a tasty invention, but one that might also help children learn geography. Her idea? Individually sized healthy pot pies whose tins are in the shape of our 50 states.

Then, there's Stanley Morningside and his fun invention, Captain Barleyhook. Stanley, like many of us, is "hooked" on a certain amber beverage but has grown tired of transferring the warmth of his hand to the bottle or can of his favorite brew. The solution? A hook that enables the user to enjoy a hands-free cold one that stays cold.

These ideas and others will be featured at Mousetrap's headquarters in an all-day affair, where you will have access to our inventors and staff and be able to witness the American Dream in action.

There will also be a catered luncheon, so please RSVP by September ——.

Okay, the catered-luncheon bit I was going to have to clear with Andrea. After all, such an expenditure was no doubt beyond the company's budget, but my reasoning was this: Free food attracts reporters.

I presented the press release to Andrea, and she loved it, except for the last sentence.

"Scratch the lunch part, Nick, and it's a go."

"Andrea, we want to attract the press, right? Nothing attracts people like free food."

She shook her head.

"Andrea, believe me. Besides, who's to say it has to be professionally catered? Why don't you get the staff to help? I'm sure there are people here who are decent cooks."

"Okay, now you're talking. But what about servers?"

"Andrea, the reporters aren't going to know a Mousetrap employee from a waiter. We'll all pitch in."

She smiled, Grinch-like, and I knew now that my plan would be approved entirely. And while the staff chosen to be waiters would no doubt hate my guts, I would remind them that being a waiter for a day was better than standing in the unemployment line.

Loretta got back to me by week's end and informed me that Tuesday, September 17, would be the day. I faxed the press release to all local media outlets immediately and then held my breath, hoping for at least three or four positive returns.

By the next day, I had received confirmations from 10 local television stations and newspapers. Without the promise of free food, that number would have been half as much, if that.

And here's the beauty part about the food: Over the years, Loretta has constantly boasted about what a wonderful cook she is. To be fair, she actually is pretty good, having sampled some of the concoctions that she's shared with her coworkers. But cooking for a luncheon that's supposed to generate positive buzz for our flesh-stripped cadaver of a company? I knew it would make her even grumpier than normal.

A few hours after all the plans were finalized, I found myself walking by Loretta's office, hoping to witness a meltdown. I wasn't disappointed.

As soon as I entered her field of vision, I heard something about "poison" and "enough stuffed chicken breasts to feed a fucking army."

I poked my head in and asked her if everything was okay.

"Don't play games with me. I've just been commissioned to cook for your dumbass idea. Thanks a hell of a lot."

"Hey, no problem. It's all about teamwork, right?"

"If I were you, I'd really skip eating that day."

"Now, now, Loretta. Poisoning our clients and a bunch of reporters would do nothing but give our company a black eye. And we'd hate for that to happen, wouldn't we?"

"How about I give you a black eye right now, idiot?"

I smiled and kept on walking. You know how some people put up a false-combative exterior but are really marshmallows inside, once you get to know them? Loretta wasn't one of those people. And now she was stuck putting her cooking skills to the test in an effort to prop up a company that she detested. Life, temporarily, at least, was good.

Finally, the big day arrived. Since every remaining employee used the same excuse—"Oh, Loretta, you're a great cook. What I do can't compare"—Loretta got stuck preparing everything except the salad and desserts. And, I have to admit, she came through—stuffed chicken breasts, a beautiful scalloped-potato dish, and various vegetable side dishes, all of which were worthy of the pages of a food magazine.

The reporters did their jobs and interviewed the chosen six, but what really made them linger was the food. Andrea couldn't have been more pleased. And our inventors? They were ecstatic and presented themselves and their ideas better than I ever could have wished.

Andrea, seemingly sober the entire day, was in her element, giving encouragement to her clients while at the same time sucking up to the press.

At one point, she said to Allison Park, our pill-alarm representative, "You know, Ms. Park, I can't tell you how many ideas we get in a year that are similar to yours. But there was something special about your submission that really caught our attention."

"Maybe it was the trigger device for the pill drawers?" suggested Ms. Park, who, in spite of her inability to sniff out a scam, seemed to be an otherwise lovely human.

"Yes! That's exactly it! You see," said Andrea, turning to the reporters, "it's the little details that we look for here. It's that—dare I say it?—extra 1 percent that our clients possess."

The reporter standing closest to Andrea took the bait.

"What do you mean when you say 'that extra 1 percent,' Ms. Bianco?"

"Well, it was an idea first brought to me by young Nick over there, who organized this event, too. It's no secret that our success rate isn't high. In fact, as you know and have reported, it's less than 1 percent. But where you see negativity, we see beauty. That special 1 percent has the stuff of dreams. They are passionate about what they do. They want to make the world—maybe only in some small way—a better place. They are the American Dream. They are our special 1 percent. And we love them and do everything we can to make their dreams reality."

The reporters couldn't scribble this shit in their notebooks fast enough. They ate it up quicker than they had Loretta's lunch. Sure, I had come up with the idea, and Loretta came through in the food department. But make no mistake. This was Andrea's stage, and like Reggie Jackson in October, she delivered.

All three local 11:00 newscasts gave us about a minute of positive airtime. But the best surprise was waiting for me on my desk when I arrived at work the next day. The front page of one of Pittsburgh's two dailies featured a picture of Andrea and inventor Liz Orosco.

The cutline read: *Mousetrap, Inc. owner Andrea Bianco discusses client Liz Orosco's invention, called "SpeakerPlanters." The local invention-marketing company hosted its first-ever "American Dreamers Showcase." Story on B-1.*

Section B-1 was adorned with the following: "Thank you, Nick! With Love, Andrea."

The story was nothing but flattering, as if the company's sins had been washed away with a nice stuffed chicken breast:

Local Company Dares to Dream Big

No economic downturn can kill the American Dream.

At least that's what the folks at local invention-marketing company Mousetrap, Inc. are hoping. The company hosted its first-ever American Dreamers Showcase, which featured six of its clients and their inventions, ranging from a way to keep beer cold to a tasty treat that will not only entice youth but get them to learn geography, too.

Owner Andrea Bianco, while admitting that her company sees less than a 1 percent rate of success, says she sees beauty in what she calls "that special 1 percent."

"That special 1 percent has the stuff of dreams. They are passionate about what they do. They want to make the world—maybe only in some small way—a better place," said Bianco. "They are the American Dream, and we love them and do everything we can to make their dreams reality."

The story went on, quoting the inventors and discussing their ideas. There wasn't one negative note to be found, and the article ended with a sentence that must have made Andrea's heart skip a beat:

Who knows? Maybe that idea you have—a brand-new product or an improvement on an existing one—is worthy of being in that special 1 percent, too.

Wow. An innocent reporter, just going about her job, was doing Andrea's bidding for her. For free. In a newspaper read by tens of thousands of local people.

And, as it would turn out, at least one non-local person.

Did I mention that Mr. Jack Gardner, our favorite inventor, the man who hovered around us like Banquo's ghost, resided in Wheeling, West Virginia? Well, that's where the man lived. And occasionally Mr. Gardner picked up a Pittsburgh newspaper. You're smart enough to see where this is headed, so I'll spare you the seconds and come out with it: Mr. Jack Gardner, inventor of our favorite product, picked up a Pittsburgh newspaper on a certain day in September and damn near had a heart attack.

Okay, I don't actually know if his heart almost stopped working, but I gathered—as you will, herewith—that upon reading the glowing account of our first-ever American Dreamers Showcase, something unwell happened to any number of Mr. Jack Gardner's bodily functions.

Two days—48 hours, 1,440 minutes, 86,400 seconds, a mere blip in the universe—after the paper ran a ridiculously positive account of our event, the following article appeared on the front page:

"American Nightmare?"

Mountaineer Inventor Claims Fraud

Wheeling resident Jack Gardner couldn't believe his eyes when he read the paper two days ago.

What caught his attention? An article about local invention-marketing company Mousetrap, Inc. and its American Dreamers Showcase.

"I mean, these people all but admitted they would never be able to get my product to market, and now they're having a showcase?" said Mr. Gardner.

Mr. Gardner's invention, a card game called Luckit, was accepted by Mousetrap and embraced with much enthusiasm, he says.

"Their two graphics guys did a great job of putting together a prototype, but when I met with the company's legal counsel, she was very apologetic and admitted, in her words, that the company's name is so 'tarnished' that my idea never had a realistic chance," he says.

Alice Legato, the company's lawyer, said that while Mousetrap has had legal entanglements with the FTC in the past, the company is now in full legal compliance and wants to look toward the future.

"We feel our showcase is a first step in a new direction we hope to take this company, and we see Mr. Gardner's product as a part of our future," said Ms. Legato.

When asked if Mr. Gardner's allegations were true, that the company's reputation is so poor that his product had no chance of succeeding, Ms. Legato said, "We love Mr. Gardner's product, and, as I said, we see it as part of Mousetrap's future."

But Mr. Gardner remains unmoved from his original notion.

"When the muckety-muck of a company tells you that your idea is dead in the water, you tend to believe them, right? I just want everybody to know what not to do if they think they have a great idea."

So, what will he do with his card game now?

"Well, I'm not really sure, to be honest," he said. "Maybe I'll try to contact game companies myself. Heck, what do I have to lose at this point?"

So, that was that. We had nearly one day of relative happiness and hope. The day after the initial story ran, Alice poked her head into my office and told me that a reporter wanted to ask her a few questions concerning Jack Gardner. It's funny. Although we all knew that Mr. Gardner was right, we got caught up in the apparent, though fleeting, success of our Showcase.

There was more to the article—a rehash of the fines we've paid to the FTC, a nice slamming of Loretta by Mr. Gardner, though she remained nameless, even the Mousegoyle incident of many years ago—but what you read pretty much sums it up.

There was one positive thing, though, that emerged from an otherwise bleak account: Alice from now on would be called, affectionately, "Muck" by Sam and me. Yeah, she sounded quite weasel-like in the article, but what choice did she have? She did the best she could under the circumstances, and the best we could hope for was that the two articles would cancel each other out and our status, shaky as it was, would remain unchanged.

What we forgot to factor in, of course, was the undying spirit of the American Dreamer. Between September 19 and the end of the month, Mousetrap, thanks in whole part to a positive article in a Pittsburgh daily, received 33 new client submissions, all from the tri-state area. These 33 folks either didn't see the article that appeared two days later or, more likely, chose to ignore it and focus on the positive.

By month's end, I had received so many unsolicited hugs from Andrea that I actually became concerned of contacting lung cancer through osmosis. We had received a mere 17 new submissions prior to our event. Add in the 33 post-Showcase stooges, and September gave us a nice, round total of 50 new clients, our best numbers since April and double what we received in August. None were rejected, even though two were perpetual-motion machines (EternaMotion and No Quit!), three were "improvements" on inventions featured at the Showcase (Country Cakes, Lady Barleyhook, and—hold on to your hats—Pill Buzz), and most of the rest fell into the "What the Hell Were These People Thinking?" category. To wit:

- "Notch Mate," a special tool just perfect for adding extra holes to a belt—ideal for people whose weight fluctuates. Okay, two things here: One, buy a new belt, or, if you're really in love with a belt, purchase an awl, a tool that's been around since, I don't know, forever?

- A local woman wants to eliminate the scourge of sour milk from the earth. Her idea? Something called Milk Safe. Now, granted, her idea is actually a good one and could truly help people. The problem, though, is that what she really has is an idea for an idea. Let's let her explain:

"My idea, I think, is a simple one, and don't they always say that the simple ideas usually turn out to be the best ones? Well, anyway, wouldn't it be great if milk turned a different color—like blue or green or whatever—when it went bad? That way, you wouldn't have to rely on your nose anymore."

Yes, ma'am, it would be great if milk—or any food, really—turned a nonfood color when it was spoiled or bad from the get-go. The problem, is, ma'am, that you're not a chemist or a scientist of any kind, and what you've submitted is the full extent of your "idea." And for this, you've given Andrea how many thousands? Believe me, ma'am, buying the occasional bottle of Pepto-Bismol would have cost you a lot less.

- Cat Lites. What, you ask, might a Cat Lite be? Well, it seems that a local cat lover thinks cats have trouble seeing at night. Thus, she proposes a series of decorative night lights, all in whimsical shapes that cats will adore—fish, a ball of yarn, mice—to be used when Mr. Whiskers goes on his nighttime prowls. Apparently, the inventor has never seen an actual cat at night, because if she had, she would have realized that cats' eyes, as is the case with most animals, glow in the dark. Or perhaps our new client thinks that cats' eyes give off light just to fuck with humanity. Whatever the case, it's clear that our latest sucker skipped that day in science class when the rest of us learned that cats see as well in the night as they do in the day. Therefore, no need for kitty nightlights.

I shouldn't have been complaining, though. At least the new clients kept me busy and, unknown to them, gave me a few chuckles. And Andrea's good moods and sobriety, coupled with this steady flow of work, made Mousetrap a reasonably pleasant place to spend eight hours a day. Plus, the leaves were changing, pro and college football finally had returned, and I was about to become married.

Life was good, right? So let's say we end our story here and leave our plucky employees in a state of happiness. Sure, they're misguided, and yes, one of the reasons for their happiness is the fact that they just snookered 33 local "inventors" out of some hard-earned cash. But the characters you've read about are good people, for the most part. Wouldn't you agree?

So, yes, then it's agreed. We'll end it here. I become happily married. Mousetrap carries on and even thrives, due in no small part to my American Dreamers Showcase idea. Sam and Karen raise a wonderful family. Andrea sobers up and actually starts rejecting clients again and leads Mousetrap on a more virtuous path.

Nah, I can't lie to you. Allow me to finish this soul-cleansing, and I promise to spare you no truth, no matter how ugly it gets.

October 1991

IN WHICH THE LONG-AGO promised rampant, embarrassing nudity finally will take place.

The first directive of the month from Andrea was a simple one—include the positive newspaper article highlighting the American Dreamers Showcase in all future potential client packets—but one that ultimately would doom her company. Alice tried to stop her but was met, she said, with the following declaration:

"The paper ran a great article about my company, right? Damn right! And why shouldn't my potential clients be aware of the positive force we are, for once? What do they say about newspapers? They're the first draft of history, right? Damn right! Well, my company will make history, and I want everyone to see that article."

Alice told Sam and me that she tried to explain to Andrea why this was such a bad idea. Yes, she said, a positive article ran in the local paper. But two days later, a less-than-flattering article, featuring the angry quotes of an extremely dissatisfied customer, ran in the same paper. The FTC might not like the fact that we're including the positive and burying the negative, particularly considering that Jack Gardner's points are correct.

Of course, in these resurgent days, Andrea would hear none of it and rejected Alice's legal advice. Alice figured that Andrea wanted to keep the momentum going and acquire as many new clients as she could before the FTC came in and gave her a fresh, and possibly fatal, smackdown.

Alice had been talking to us for several minutes, and I couldn't help notice that not once in the whole conversation did she even smile, let alone punctuate a sentence with a chuckle.

"What's wrong, Muck?" I asked.

"Well, Nick, I'm paid to give legal advice to a woman who has lived for decades skirting on the edge of legality and sometimes stomping all over that edge. I didn't work so hard in law school to become some corporate Tom Hagen."

"Whoa right there, missy," said Sam. "It's been decided that 'Muck' is your nickname. We can't start calling you Tom Hagen, too. It'll confuse the hell out of us."

That elicited a slight, forced smile on her face.

"And besides," I said, "it's not like Andrea raised you. Clearly, you're not Tom Hagen."

She looked at both of us. "Why are we here?"

I wasn't sure if she meant it in the big-picture, stoned-college-kid question way or not, but I figured that she meant, "Why are we at Mousetrap?"

"Well, Alice, I'll take a stab at it. See, I pretend I'm a copywriter for a successful ad agency and that I'm surrounded by creative types who wow me all day long with their bottomless creativity.

"And when I'm in a more realistic mode, well, to tell you the truth, I just want to see how this all ends."

"Yep," added Sam, "Nick and I have the same delusions, except where he's the awesome copywriter, coming up every day with slogans that are on the tongue of every American, I'm designing images that are unforgettable and the bottomlessly creative people or the creatively bottomed people, blah, blah, blah.

"Also, I smoke a good deal of peyote."

Alice laughed out loud on that one, as did I. Nothing like a good peyote reference to bring a smile to someone's face.

"Besides, Muck," I said, "you told me several weeks ago that this sucker will stay afloat into January, right? Hell, there's plenty of time for us to find new, better jobs."

"Come on, Nick. Don't b.s. me. If you had a better job offer tomorrow, you'd be gone, and you know it," she said.

"Hey, we're trying to cheer you up, damn it. Don't bring the truth into this."

She chuckled, thanked us both, and returned to her office, possibly less glum than when she arrived.

"Hell, Nick," said Sam, "I'd settle for any job offer tomorrow. It wouldn't necessarily have to be a better one."

Both Sam and I had sent out numerous résumés over the past several months, and neither of us had gotten as much as an interview.

"I try not to think about it too much, Sam."

"Well, then, start thinking about this—your bachelor party."

"Yes, I have thought about it, and here's what I propose: We—you, me, my other groomsmen—have a nice dinner and then go to a Pens game."

"Hey, Nick, that sounds great, if by 'dinner' you mean tits, and by 'Pens game' you mean excessive tits."

Sam grasped both my shoulders with his hands and looked me squarely in the eye, as though he were a drill sergeant and I had just passed basic training.

"Don't deny me this, Nick."

Well, so much for dinner and a hockey game. Bring on the "excessive tits." How could I prevent a friend—not to mention my boss—a night of stupid, drunken revelry? Besides, my other groomsmen and my brother, who was to serve as my best man, would no doubt echo Sam's sentiment.

"Anyway, Nick, I've been in touch with your brother for weeks now. I wasn't really looking for your approval, just merely informing you of what's in the works."

"Oh, well, since you put it that way, I guess what I have to say is irrelevant."

"Exactly! And, friend, this serves two purposes: First, as I mentioned already, who isn't a fan of 'excessive tits'? Second, your words being irrelevant? Welcome to marriage!"

I laughingly flipped him off and headed back to my office, where I was welcomed with a nice pile of work. Andrea's second act was still in progress, and, skimming through the stash, it occurred to me that the well for bad ideas was bottomless, as was Andrea's lack of a conscience.

The truth was, Sam and I could have done nothing all day. Truly. Seeing how our NPRs never saw another set of eyes after they were sent out to potential manufacturers, we could have stuffed envelopes full of dirty limericks, for all that it mattered. So why did we persist in writing words and drawing images that nobody would ever see? I guess it beat staring at four walls all day long. Plus, we both figured that Andrea was paying us, meager as our salaries were, and that we owed her our best effort.

So, I spent the next few hours transforming our latest batch of inept dreamers' words into coherent paragraphs, while Sam changed their pencil-drawn images into something that came to life, and for the moment we felt as though we were contributing something to the fabric of American commerce.

Even though work had picked up, I still had plenty of time to contribute to the fabric of Chapel Fox's story, too, so after finishing up my actual work, I turned my full attention to my favorite blood-lusting, psychotic Pittsburgher.

Neither Chapel Fox nor his bride, the lovely Beth L. Park, had come from a very big family. Because of this, Fox had suggested sneaking off to a justice of the peace—no fuss, no attention, just the way Fox liked things. Beth, however, had other ideas, and so on a crisp Saturday in October, in a historic Downtown church, surrounded by what little family they had, the law-firm staff, and some friends, Mr. and Mrs. Chapel Fox legally became husband and wife.

Fox had to admit, when he saw her walking up the aisle toward him, that Beth looked more beautiful than ever. He may not have been able to say what the white gown was made of or what style of gown it was, but he knew beauty when he saw it. He also had to admit that he was glad she finally convinced him to wear a tuxedo. Standing there, in front of family and friends, waiting for the love of his life to become one with him, it felt right wearing a tux.

The ceremony went off without a hitch; the reception that followed, at their favorite Italian restaurant, was equally wonderful. (Do the details really matter to you? If I say, "The guests ate penne in vodka sauce and artichoke-stuffed chicken breasts," does that add anything? I didn't think so).

From the restaurant, they bid farewell to their guests and hurried back home to pack for the honeymoon: a two-week tour through Europe.

"This is a new beginning, in so many ways, Beth. If I'm half as happy throughout our marriage as I am right now, I'll still be pretty damn happy, Beth," said Fox, whose ears couldn't believe what his mouth was uttering.

"I know exactly what you mean, Chap," said Beth, fighting back tears of joy.

The first destination on their honeymoon? London, a city neither had ever visited. Their excitement was palpable, the joy in their hearts measurable, and nothing—truly, nothing—could return Fox back to his old ways.

Well, except this . . .

As the two lovebirds entered their hotel room, luggage in hand, they caught the eye of a man departing the room next to theirs. Fox and he made eye contact, and Fox offered a friendly hello.

"Ah, Americain," said the man.

"Oui," said Fox, smiling and extending his hand.

"Where are you from?" said the stranger.

"Oh, we're from Pittsburgh. It's in the Northeast part of the States."

"Ah, iz Peetsburgh the armpeet I 'ear it is? Is it 'ell with the lid removed, as someone once said?"

Without thinking, and before anyone knew what had happened, Fox kicked in his rude neighbor's door and found himself atop the man, punching him in the face.

Beth immediately grabbed a paperweight from the desk, smashed it at least three times into the man's head, and within 30 seconds, there was a passed-out Frenchman lying on the floor of a London hotel, done in by two pissed-off Pittsburghers.

Fox walked to the bathroom, grabbed a glass of water, and threw it in the man's face until he recovered.

For a moment, he was bewildered, and then he started stammering apologies.

Fox laughed at him, opened up his suitcase, procured his Terrible Towel—this really confused the hell out of the Frenchman—and fulfilled his initial promise to Beth. Within a minute, the Frenchman had breathed his last, and after a moment had passed, Beth and Fox went off to their own room, where they made such mad, passionate love, they feared they had done damage to the room, if not the foundation of the 'otel itself.

It was, of course, the perfect crime. Why would that nice American couple—remember, just hours ago, Fox was light of heart and had even engaged in pleasant banter with the hotel staff—kill a complete stranger in cold blood? The bobbies would never put the pieces together, and Fox and Beth would be in the clear, as long as they acted completely normal.

The next morning, Beth and Fox awoke to the screams of a cleaning lady. Fox felt bad about that, but what was he going to do? Chop the bastard's body up and place various parts in wastebaskets around London? No, of course not. He and Beth had to go about their day like the carefree tourists they were. When the police did question them later the next day, Fox, drawing on his years of courtroom experience, was at his believable best. Beth, meanwhile, merely sobbed throughout the questioning, occasionally shaking her head. She was so convincing that the policeman reassured her that London was quite a safe place and that there was no need for her to be worried as a foreign tourist.

The interview finally done, Fox and Beth enjoyed the next three days seeing all that London had to offer. (Again, do you really want details? Hell, this isn't a travelogue, and I've never been to London. Okay, um, they saw

Big Ben and Westminster Abbey. Let's see. They had tea and crumpets with Prime Minister Major and also took in Stonehenge, which may or may not be anywhere near London. Do your own damn research if you want the answer).

Next, they were off to Paris. They were having such a wonderful honeymoon that the ugliness upon arriving in London hardly merited a mention. But it was there, in Fox's mind, and no amount of mind-altering sex and great food could remove it, try as he may.

"Beth," he said, as they walked down a fashionable street in Paris (not a travelogue, folks), "I want that to be a one-time thing."

"The hell you do, Chap." She smiled in a way that seemed to say, "I want to have sex with you right now in the middle of this street, and, seeing how we're in France, I think it might be legal and go unnoticed."

She was right, of course. Like any addict, the thrill was still there. Any alcoholic, no matter how long sober, would kill for a cold beer or a shot of sweet, bone-penetrating whiskey. Any smoker, even one who's kicked the habit for 20 years, would do anything to inhale the smoky goodness of a cigarette even one more time.

Of course, Fox reasoned, what happened in London was a fluke. They were in Paris now. Who would insult Pittsburgh here?

Two dumbass American tourists—that's who!

So, there they were, enjoying the Eiffel Tower, taking in the views, when a couple near them struck up a conversation. They introduced themselves—Bob and Susan—and said they were from Philadelphia.

"Oh, what a small world—we're from Pittsburgh," offered Fox.

"Sorry to hear that," said Bob, laughing.

Fox and Beth chuckled, too. Fox was willing to let this pass. Maybe Bob was one of those "jokey" salesman-type guys. No harm.

"So," said Bob, "I imagine you guys are Steeler fans."

"You bet," said Fox, hoping he didn't insult—

"Boy, maybe you can explain it to me, 'cause I can't figure it out. What's the deal with those stupid Terrible Towels? I mean, you got to admit they're pretty moronic."

Yeah, Bob had crossed the line. Unfortunately, it seemed his wife would have to pay the price, too, for her husband's bottomless stupidity. After all, she did marry the knuckle-dragging asshole, didn't she?

Fox politely explained the history of the Terrible Towel, mentioning, in as gentle manner as he could, that the Steelers had won four Super Bowls, compared to Philadelphia's big, old goose egg in Super Bowl wins.

Bob showed a hint of anger at these troublesome facts, but, like Fox, was playing it coolly.

Fox suggested the four of them go to dinner. Bob and Susan agreed but said they needed to go back to their hotel room first. Thinking quickly, Beth told the couple that she had a lifelong interest in hotel rooms—in fact, she was even thinking of turning her love of amateur photography into a coffee-table book of hotel rooms—and would love to see their room. Bob and Susan, of course, agreed.

Again, like in London, it was over in the blink of an eye. As soon as the four entered the room, Fox seized a letter opener from the desk, secured it in Bob's right hand, and plunged it deeply into Susan's neck.

Before he could utter a word, Bob found himself knocked to the ground by a series of perfectly landed punches.

Susan was dead almost instantly. Bob was alive and would be kept alive long enough to know the error of his ways.

"You stupid Philadelphia fuck," Fox kept muttering over and over again. Perhaps he was fond of the alliteration. Or perhaps he was mad at himself for getting dragged back into a life he thought he had escaped.

Fox and Beth instinctively knew they couldn't just kill Bob. Somebody would put the pieces together, and words like "extradition" and "monsters" would suddenly be splashed across every newspaper in London, Paris, and most of the U.S. The USA Today would probably even run a pie chart about them.

Beth propped up Susan's lifeless body and began licking the blood from her neck.

Before Bob could finish the sentence, "You sick bi-" Fox grabbed his hand—Bob was still stupidly holding the letter opener—and plunged it into his neck.

Perfect—a murder-suicide. In Paris, no less. How tragic . . . yet romantic.

Again, Fox felt bad for the cleaning people—yoy, what a mess—but it had to be done. It took great self-control on both Fox and Beth's part not to have sex on Bob and Susan's bed—they realized what a mistake they would be making by leaving behind evidence—so they waited patiently until they felt safe that nobody would see them depart.

Within a few minutes, they found themselves back on the street, completely undetected, just two American tourists enjoying the sights of Paris. They hurried back to their own hotel room, where, again, they feared getting a bill from hotel management informing them of the lovemaking damages, and then had a sumptuous feast of a meal. After all, they had earned it after a long day of exercise—walking around Paris, killing idiots, making crazed, furniture-splitting love.

The next day, Paris newspapers featured headlines like "Tragédie Americain!" (This may or not be proper French. If you're that concerned with language accuracy, really, that's your problem.) Just like Fox and Beth figured, it would be seen as a murder-suicide. Again, they were home-free.

The last leg of their trip took them to the Eternal City, Rome. They were delighted to discover that what's been said about Italians was true: They were ridiculously friendly. In fact, not only were there no insults directed Pittsburgh's way, but a few Italians that Fox and Beth engaged in conversation told them that they had relatives who had emigrated to Western Pennsylvania decades earlier. (Okay, if you must know, they loved the Colosseum, were stunned at the beauty of the Sistine Chapel's ceiling, and ate some delicious fettuccine.)

As they headed back to the States, Fox knew that while technically their honeymoon was over, their honeymoon of righting the wrongs of those who would dare insult their fair city was just beginning.

And when he was being honest with himself, Fox was none too displeased about it. Now he had a partner in life who was also his partner in crime. And in both "incidents" across the pond, Beth had behaved with instinctive good sense, allaying Fox's earlier fears that she would act out of control and get them both placed on death row.

No, Beth was just the right amount of crazy, and Fox knew that he had chosen the perfect life partner. Plus, they could still have all the "normal" things that Fox craved—the fenced-in yard, the kids, the summer barbecues.

In addition, Beth could no longer threaten to call the police on him. She was just as guilty as he was. It was all perfect—the smart, beautiful wife, who was sensible when his other line of work arose, their future as bright as the sun, the respectable, well-paying job.

Then, why, much to Beth's surprise, did Fox have tears in his eyes as they headed home from the airport?

"Is something wrong, dear?" she asked.

"No, it's just that I'm so happy," he said, clearing his throat to prevent any additional spillage.

Fox was lying, but he knew he had to suppress the feeling—the deep, soul-crushing feeling—that he had been given a chance to escape his past life, only to give in to old habits at the first sniff of a Pittsburgh insult. Why didn't he just shrug off the Frenchman? Was it necessary to do? No, of course it wasn't! The man probably had a wife and kids. Or even if he didn't, even if the man led the loneliest life on Earth, it was still his life to live. And the couple from Philly? Good heavens! They had lives, too. And family—family that will be confused the rest of their lives as to why Bob went batshit and plunged a letter opener into his wife's neck before taking his own life. ("It doesn't make any sense," said Gladys Funkhouser, the dead man's aunt. "They had been planning their dream vacation for months. They have two beautiful children and everything to live for. When I think of Ashley and Madison," she said before convulsing into tears.)

Fox, like the fictitious Aunt Gladys he had conjured in his mind, was sobbing now, too, but Beth was completely clueless as to the inner workings of her husband's brain.

This couldn't go on. Fox had to change before it was too late. As he pulled into his driveway, he wondered if he would get another chance.

Certain things are inevitable—the demise of this company, snowy winters in Pittsburgh, the return of Chapel Fox to his killing ways. Plus, unlike the arrival of snow, I was giving the people what they wanted. How did I know this? Well, to a person, my readers told me they were glad to see Fox back to doing what he did best. They ignored the inner anguish that my protagonist was facing, and which he clearly addresses at the story's end, and focused on his European killing spree. What are you gonna do?

Also inevitable—my bachelor party, which was scheduled for the last Friday in October. My groomsmen were at least smart enough to plan the event a few weeks before my wedding. I guess none of them wanted to go through my wedding day with a pounding headache and a mouthful of regurgitated nachos and beer.

So the day Sam had had been so eagerly awaiting finally arrived, and we met my other groomsmen after work and all walked over to the Steel Pussycat. My brother, seven years older than me and my best friend, shared in Sam's excitement, as did John, my best friend from high school, who, when not visiting strip joints was leading a respectable life as a dentist. I was sad, though, that my other groomsman, who was a dear friend from college, could not attend. It's not that he had prior commitments or anything. Well, actually, that may have been the case, but I had instructed Sam not to bother asking Bill. Why? Bill was a minister, and I had a hunch he wouldn't approve of such shenanigans. Or, even weirder, he may have said yes, solely for the purposes of preaching to the leering heathens.

The first half-hour of our trip to the demimonde went as expected: naked college-age women cavorting about the stage, beers drunk, junk food eaten, jokes about marriage filling the air. To wit: A man recovering from a heart attack asks his doctor if it's okay for him to have sex again. The doctor replies, "Yes, but only with your wife. I don't want you to get too excited."

All in all, what you'd expect from a bachelor party. Then, the emcee took the stage, to loud booing, and announced that, as was tradition, the last Friday of the month was amateur night. The boos turned to cheers, as we all realized we were going to get to see actual women shed their clothes for our approval and the chance to win 500 bucks.

The beers started to kick in, and I had to admit to myself I was having a pretty good time. It had crossed my mind that "amateur night" was just a gimmick, that we'd simply be seeing a parade of professionals acting like first-timers, but after the first two performers had left the stage, there was no doubt that these were real women. They were nervous. They fumbled with their outfits. Their dance moves weren't exactly crisp. But in spite—or perhaps because—of this, they were a thousand times hotter than the pros.

And then the third amateur came out following this introduction: "Ladies and gentlemen, our third lovely contestant is currently out of work, and while she may be down on her luck, if you're lucky, and hiring, she may be going down on you. Please give a warm welcome to Laney."

Laney was a tall, attractive brunette who was wearing a conservative business suit—gray pinstripe jacket and skirt, white blouse, black shoes, and a silver mask. She was clearly nervous, but, unlike the first two, seemed to have a sense of ease as she glided across the stage, first losing the skirt, which revealed her long, athletic legs, then quickly the jacket. She even did a spin around the pole, which elicited whoops from the audience, and then doffed her blouse, revealing her small yet perfectly firm breasts.

The last item to go was the mask, and when she did so, her hair also fell to her shoulders, and at that moment, Sam and I almost fell out of our chairs, and had we not been completely frozen, we no doubt would have. Laney, it turned out, was Elaine, our former coworker. Unfortunately, when she rid herself of her mask, Elaine's eyesight quickly improved, and not only did we see her, but she saw us. She audibly gasped and tore back into the dressing room. Sam and I both ran after her, not really sure what the hell we were doing, and before the bouncers could punch the hell out of us both and throw us to the curb, we caught up with Elaine, who was making a valiant attempt to cover herself.

So, there we were, in the strippers' dressing room, not really sure what to say. The bouncers, thanks to Elaine, didn't deposit us on the street and let us stay, much to the chagrin of the other strippers, who started calling us perverts and pelting us with various articles of underwear.

"You must think I'm"—Elaine tried speaking, but it was difficult through the sobs. She had trouble even making eye contact. "Please don't tell anyone."

"Of course not," I said. "And no, we don't think anything. This is incredibly awkward for all of us. Why don't we get the hell out of here?"

"But, Nick, what if she wins the 500 bucks? I think we should stay to the end."

Sam's joke made Elaine chuckle, and we told her we'd meet her outside in five minutes, which, coincidentally, was the exact amount of time the bouncers informed us we had before they "bashed in our fucking skulls."

We quickly informed the other two members of our party what had happened, which they found to be hysterical, and then informed them that our night was going to have to be cut short, which was probably a good thing for Pittsburgh-area drivers.

In the minute we had before Elaine joined us, Sam and I debated what we should say.

"If it's any consolation, she was the best of the three amateurs we saw," said Sam.

"Do you think that's really what she wants to hear?"

"Well, yeah, maybe. She chose to do this, after all."

"Hell, I don't know. Let's just wing it."

Elaine finally arrived, dressed in the business suit. The three of us stopped at the nearest bar/lounge, and, oddly, it was Elaine who was the overdressed one this time.

"Dinner's on me, guys. I'm $500 richer right now," she said.

"You mean you won?" I asked, so glad that she broke the ice.

"Yep."

"That's . . . nice?" I asked.

"And the owner asked me back for an audition. This might become a full-time gig for me."

Sam and I both looked at her blankly.

"Come on, you two. I've been working up the courage to do this for a long time. Like I didn't see your eyes pop out of your heads every time I showed you a little something."

"Oh, that," Sam said. He turned to me. "God, I wish Rachel were here right now. This is complete validation."

"You mean Rachel knew about it?"

"Well," I said, "she walked in on a conversation we were having one day about how you seem to like exposing yourself to us, and she thought we were just being typical male pigs."

"But why, then," I asked, "did you burst into tears when you realized we were in the audience?"

"Well, the enormity of it all hit me. I mean, come on. You guys—my former coworkers, my friends, people that I know—just saw me completely naked. Psychologically, I was able to do what I did when I had it in my head that it was just a roomful of strangers. But then I saw you, and, well, wow."

"If it's any consolation," I said, "we didn't realize it was you until you lost the mask."

"Really, no need to apologize. Look, as I was getting dressed afterwards, and after what the owner said to me, I realized that it was a good thing you guys were there tonight. Now I have no fears, unless my father were to be in a future audience. Then, I'd have to kill myself."

So, there it was. Elaine was no longer, and Laney had taken her place. She asked us about Mousetrap and expressed surprise that it still existed. We had a few laughs, and, as she promised, our dinner was paid for with stripper money.

Both Sam and I kept telling her, in different ways, before we parted, that we hoped she would always be careful. She thanked us both and gave us a peck on the cheek, and then reminded us what the two bouncers looked like and what they threatened to do to our skulls.

We were temporarily assuaged by her confidence, and she vanished into the dark, off to pursue a new life in which she would likely earn more in one night than either Sam or I did in a week.

The next night, Sam, Karen, Nicole, and I went out for dinner, and we spared no details of my abbreviated bachelor party. Sam had managed to hold his wife at bay, telling her that the main story of the evening would be worth the wait.

We told them that it was amateur night, and no, it was for real, not just a gimmick. We told them how the third amateur had quite the act going on. We told them what happened when she removed her mask.

"Elaine?!" both Karen and Nicole exclaimed.

We proceeded with our tale, talking about our trip to the strippers' dressing room and our encounter with those friendly bouncers.

"Elaine?!" they exclaimed again, seemingly unable to get past that part of the story.

"Yes, Elaine," I said.

"You saw your former coworker naked?" asked Nicole in a not-too-pleasant voice.

"Yeah," chimed in Karen, equally unpleasant.

"Ladies," I said, "it's not like we knew she was going to be there taking off her clothes. And I think I speak for Sam, too—the second we realized who it was, we stopped looking."

I was being honest, but Karen and Nicole found my answer so ridiculous that they started laughing.

We then told the rest of the story—she won, paid for dinner, will now be pursuing life as a professional stripper—and the ladies sat there, still not quite believing what they were hearing.

"Do you think that's smart?" asked Karen.

"Hell, no, Karen, but she's a grown woman. It wasn't our place to try to dissuade her," I said.

"Plus, honey," said Sam, "she won. Perhaps she has a gift. Would it be right for her to deny the world of her talent?"

It occurred to me that Sam had had one beer too many, based not only on his smartass response but also on the fact that the fire of hatred emanating from Karen's eyes was making him laugh hysterically.

This, of course, made Nicole and I start to laugh, too, which prompted Karen to turn her heat vision on us, which made us all laugh even more. Fortunately, Sam possesses an infectious laughter, and it was only a matter of time before Karen broke and joined us.

Before we parted, I gently encouraged Karen to take the wheel, which she assured me she would do. I also told Sam to enjoy the couch.

On Monday, Sam and I had a brief meeting and contemplated whether we should tell anyone about Elaine's new line of work. We decided to be gentlemen about it and keep the secret to ourselves. Work had been progressing at a normal pace. Actually, it was possible that October's numbers were slightly better than September's had been. Apparently, the

Jack Gardner article hadn't yet defeated the American Dreamers Showcase and its evil mastermind, Andrea Bianco.

Okay, yes, I was the mastermind of the damn Showcase. But I'm not evil, and I'm certainly no mastermind.

Thursday of that week was just another day for me. My wedding was a few weeks away, work was at least stable, and I truly had forgotten what day it was. Andrea, however, didn't.

The second the elevator doors opened, I was ensconced in what I thought was smoke. The first thing that popped into my head was that Andrea torched the place for the insurance money. But then I heard cackling. And then I started to make out a cauldron beyond the lobby doors. Cautiously, I opened the door and was greeted by a paddle-wielding Andrea, dressed in her finest witch regalia—she even had a giant wart attached to the end of her nose—cackling as she stirred the contents of the cauldron.

"Welcome," she said, in a voice barely indistinguishable from her own tar- and nicotine-ravaged sound.

I was about to speak, but then I noticed that the office had been inundated with black cats. There were at least two dozen scampering around the office, fighting with each other and rubbing up against the furniture.

"You can rent cats, Andrea?" I asked, more stunned by the cat flood than the rest of the goings-on.

"Anything's negotiable, young man. You just have to know how to ask. Now get to work. Meeting in the conference room at 1:00."

I eventually made it to my office, having to dodge at least a half dozen cats. When I finally made it, there was a cat nestled on my chair, who promptly hissed at me when I tried to shoo it away.

"Maybe we can get them to gang-pee in Loretta's office!" yelled Sam from his office.

"Hey, Sam, how many cats do you have in your office?" I asked.

"Oh, just three, but two of them are sleeping directly under the vent, and the other one's looking out the window."

"Oh, that's right. You have a window, unlike us peons."

"Yep, that's right. I'm a captain of industry. The industry's worthless, of course, but I am a captain."

"Seriously, Sam, this is fucked up even by Andrea's standards, and yet I look forward to 1:00."

"Oh, hell, yeah. I wouldn't miss it for—"

"I've never seen so many damn black cats in my life." Alice joined our conversation. "I have six in my office, and they seem pretty content to stay there forever."

"Elaine's a stripper," said Sam.

"Sam!"

"What did you say, Sam?"

"Nick, the owner of our company is dressed as a witch and is stirring a giant cauldron in the lobby of our office, which is overflowing with fog. There are dozens of black cats roaming the halls and offices. We are all due at a meeting in a few hours that no doubt will put the current oddities to shame. If these aren't signs that the apocalypse is nigh, then I don't know what is. Telling Alice the truth about Elaine just feels right."

He had a point.

"Are you serious? How did you find out?"

"Well, Nick insisted on a naked slut-fest for his bachelor party, and he forced all his groomsmen to go along with his awful, soul-tainting plan."

"Alice, allow me to translate for Sam. Sam is a sad, horny shell of a married man who, in his words, didn't want me to deny him a night of, ahem, 'excessive tits.'"

"You know, Sam," said Alice, "Nick's story rings truer to me for some reason."

"Who's right? Who's wrong? What does it matter anymore? The point is this: Elaine is a stripper, and, if I may add, a pretty good one. Wouldn't you agree, Nick?"

"Frankly, yes, I would."

"Are you guys pulling my leg?"

"Nope. She won amateur night, and, in fact, she was so good, the owner is considering hiring her on a full-time basis. If you don't believe us, hop into the Pussycat some night and see for yourself."

"No, Sam, that's okay. I'll take your word for it."

"Sam and I had agreed a whopping three days ago to keep it a secret, but now you're in our club, too, I suppose. Could you keep it a secret?"

"Of course. Besides, we have a different kind of pussy to deal with today, don't we?"

"My gosh, Alice. You really have become one of us. Now you're making naughty word jokes. I'm shocked," said Sam.

"Shut up and get to work."

She laughed as only she can and departed.

"The only other person we should tell is Rachel," I said.

"Nah, she'd never believe us. We'd have to go back with cameras."

"Oh, yeah, the bouncers would love that."

"Well, I guess we'll just have to be satisfied in the knowledge that we were insanely right about Elaine."

We returned to our offices, and I eventually got rid of the cat slumbering in my chair. The first new idea I had to deal with was a comic-book submission titled "The Righteous Invaders." It was by now well-established that Andrea was accepting 100 percent of client submissions, but this struck me as reaching a new level of wrong. The illustrations were awful; even my untrained eye could ascertain this. When I showed Sam, he couldn't stop laughing. Trimbolo is drawn, poorly, in the standard superhero outfit: blue unitard, white cape, with a giant R.I. on his chest. He wears no mask but does seem to be sporting a beret of some sort.

And the writing? Well, here's a sample, and please allow me to set up the clip. In this episode, the Righteous Invaders, led by Trimbolo the Munificent, are attempting to run some drug dealers out of town. In the climactic scene, Trimbolo, along with his sidekicks, Red Hat and Inscrutable Inga, is just about to lower the boom on the bad guys, who are led—really, I can't make this stuff up—by T. Thuggary.

Trimbolo: You people make me sick.

Thuggary: Why? Because I give the people what they really want?

Trimbolo: Is that what you think? You're giving the people what they want? There's an elementary school not 20 feet from where we're standing.

Thuggary: Heh-heh. Those are my future customers.

And this apparently is when Trimbolo loses it, because in the next panels, Red Hat and Inga appear out of nowhere and proceed to blammo and pow Thuggary and his cohorts onto the next page. Why the name Red Hat? Well, Red Hat possesses a magical red hat that when thrown produces a blinding flash of light, enabling Trimbolo and Inga to get the jump on bad guys. Weirdly, Red Hat wears a business suit, navy blue pinstripe, with a white shirt and deep-red tie.

And why is Inga inscrutable? Well, from what I could tell, she's not, but apparently the client was fond of alliteration. Also, the client, true to comic-book form, is fond of giant breasts, because he bestows a giant pair on Inga. Perhaps he should have considered Inflatable Inga. She, like Trimbolo, is drawn in the standard superhero fare: a bright red unitard unzipped low enough to highlight what's certainly not inscrutable.

So, in the end, Trimbolo cleans up the neighborhood, and the bad guys go to jail. And why is Trimbolo called "Munificent"? Again, I'm not sure. It's not alliterative, but I'll admit it does have a nice ring to it. I was expecting that at the story's end, he would buy some supplies for the drug-zone school or at least plant some new trees in the schoolyard or do something, you know, munificent. Nope. He just vanishes back to wherever he lurks, sidekicks in tow, warning us, on the last page, that "Wherever a wrong needs to be righted, Red Hat, Inga, and I will be there before you can say, 'Help.'"

As bad as I felt about being a party to this submission, a part of me couldn't help but wish that the Righteous Invaders would burst through the lobby right now and kick Andrea's ass to the curb. Well, after the meeting, anyway. This, I wanted to see, and, fortunately, reading through the comic book had put a serious dent in my workday. It was, blessedly, meeting time.

When we arrived in the meeting room, the first thing that struck us was that all the cats—and there were more cats here than employees remaining—were here, contentedly rolling around the carpet. For a second, I thought perhaps Andrea really did possess magical powers, and I was slightly worried. After all, who could possibly round up two dozen cats without a good dose of sorcery to help? Then I took a closer look at the cats and realized that Andrea had plied them all with catnip. So now we had two dozen stoned cats moping around stupidly and lolling on the floor around us.

And at the front of the room stood Andrea, stirring the cauldron. She was being assisted by Loretta, who was also attired in standard witch wear. It took every ounce of self-preservation not to yell out some smart-ass remark to her, but I held my tongue.

"As you all know," Andrea began, "today is Halloween, the spookiest of holidays. Lord knows we've been through some spooky times here, but we—you—have soldiered on bravely, like the 1 percent you are."

Oh, like a razor blade in an apple, those words.

"So I wanted to celebrate a little today and have some fun, seeing how the last few months have been so much better for the company. But I also wanted to tell you about tomorrow."

She paused here for effect, and there was so much tension in the room that it seemed even the cats' rolling momentarily ceased.

"Tomorrow, as you may know, is All Saints' Day, which is followed by All Souls' Day. Now, All Saints' Day, as you may gather, is a Catholic celebration of all the saints. But All Souls' Day is a day of prayer for those souls trapped in purgatory so that they can reach heaven.

"Now, you might be saying, what does this have to do with us?"

We all were mesmerized. There, Andrea stood, addressing us, her employees, and giving us a lesson about the Catholic Church. In the background stood the hopeless Loretta, stirring the bubbly cauldron, nodding in agreement with everything that Andrea said.

"Well," Andrea continued . . . and quick as a flash, a dove emerged from a sleeve of her witch's dress and flew high toward the ceiling. "The American Dreamers Showcase was like prayers for those souls trapped in purgatory, and, like this bird, we will rise again!"

This performance was better than anything you'd see in Vegas. At the release of the bird, the cats started jumping on us and onto the table in an attempt to end the bird's life. Apparently, even a stoned cat will charge a bird.

In spite of the mayhem and nonsense that ensued—the cats never stopped trying to get the bird, Loretta never stopped stirring the cauldron, and Andrea kept going around the room, telling each of us how much our dedication meant to her—there was, blessedly, cake served, and it, like most cakes, was delicious. Also, by the time the meeting ended, so had the workday.

All in all, this wasn't a bad way to end the month: a free, memorable floor show followed by cake. But November was nigh, as were my days of bachelorhood.

November 1991

SURPRISINGLY, I WASN'T NERVOUS when the day arrived, as though a sense of calmness upon the beginning of a new life had enveloped me. I joked with my groomsmen, chatted with guests, and eventually had to be led into the chapel at the left of the altar to await the arrival of my bride. You were beautiful, Nicole. And I was glad to say that instead of crying, like most brides do, you were all smiles. It made me happy. I never quite understood the crying bride. Was it simply part of a tradition that women felt they had to follow? Were some brides flat-out sad at the realization that they were, in all likelihood, marrying a dork?

Who knows? But the only bride I cared about was the one approaching me up the aisle, and she was smiling the whole way.

The ceremony was long but beautiful. My 3-year-old niece performed wonderfully as our flower girl, pacified by gum as the ceremony dragged on. But then, finally, I was a married man. A married man with a dead-end job. A married man full of fear that the end of Mousetrap was not merely possible or probable but a cinch, in spite of Andrea's new-found hope.

But for today, I would put those fears aside and enjoy my wedding. My family was here. My friends were here. Rachel and her husband even made it. And, after much deliberation, we decided to invite Andrea and her hapless husband. As I had mentioned, the thought of Andrea plus free booze causing a scene in front of my family worried me to no end, but, blessedly, with the recent uptick in business, she was focused and sober, at least during business hours.

Rachel played nice and shook Andrea's hand; Andrea, to her credit, seemed genuinely happy that Rachel had landed on her feet, after being so unceremoniously dumped because I had mouthed off to Loretta.

The reception was a hell of a good time, and, much to our relief, Andrea behaved and acted as though she didn't have a care in the world.

Sure, she drank, and may possibly have been legally drunk, but it was a happy version of tipsy, not the scary "Days of Wine and Roses" version that I had seen firsthand more times than I'd care to remember.

We danced, we ate, we laughed, we reminisced with old friends. At the night's end, my parents seemed bittersweet at their youngest born leaving. Were they happy for me? Yes. Did they like Nicole? Yes. But as Nicole and I bid them farewell, they were supplying the tears that Nicole had so bravely cast aside eight hours earlier. Someday, no doubt, I'll understand how hard it is to let go, to comprehend that that little child you still see in your mind's eye is a full-grown adult, ready to tackle the world on his own.

Someday I will understand it, but not today, when I'm 24 years old. Another thing that I didn't comprehend on my wedding day: It's probably the only time in many, if not all, of our lives when the people we care about the most are all gathered in the same room. No, 24-year-olds aren't exactly the go-to people for deep, emotional thinking. What Nicole and I were thinking about was our wedding night, our honeymoon, and, in my case, escaping Mousetrap for a week.

We honeymooned in Key West, Florida, and enjoyed the warmth, the fabulous sunsets, and everything about being newlyweds. And, unlike Chapel Fox's honeymoon, no one died at our hands, which was a nice bonus.

Oh, how I didn't want to return—not to the impending winter weather that awaited us, not to a job that I hated, though had to admit was damn entertaining, not to the reality of being a married man whose job security hinged on the bad ideas of people willing to stupidly fork over thousands of dollars to a company run by a woman who just a few weeks prior spent the day dressed as a witch to celebrate the company's purported rebirth.

But there I was, sitting at my desk, a handful of NPRs awaiting my mastery. Sam quickly caught me up to speed; this took about five minutes, as nothing much had happened in my absence.

And what better way to greet my arrival than that all-time favorite among the inventor community but . . . Well, let's let Sidney Delba explain not only his product but the inspiration for his genius.

"Here's the thing. My mother isn't doing so well, so she has to take a lot of pills. And she forgets things now. So, I was sitting on her porch one day, having a lemonade"—

I'm sorry. I can't put you through this. I think we all by now know where Sid Delba's going with this, don't we? Ah, but there's a difference this time. It seems ol' Sid wants to add a musical component to this number-one-with-a-bullet idea. So instead of an alarm ringing when it's time for Grandma to take her arthritis pill, this little device will play a song. (Sid suggests "Bad Case of Loving You.")

And the name of this can't-live-without-it product? Medi-Song. Gotta love it. Only a few days earlier, I was enjoying Key lime pie under a gorgeous sunset with my beautiful newlywed wife. And now, here I sat, trying to find the positive aspects of a product idea that had come through my office as often as Charlie Brown lined up to kick that infernal football.

I pulled up the template for the product, made the few necessary changes, printed it out, pulled up the list of potential—who was I kidding?—manufacturers, and thus did my part in unwittingly sealing the company's fate. Sid Delba would be one of the few Mousetrap clients to meet with success; not in the money-grubbing way Andrea would define success, granted, but—well, we'll get to that in a while. For now, let's check in with our favorite psycho killer, Chapel Fox. We last left our antihero in a state of confusion. During the course of his honeymoon, he had offed three people with the assistance of his lovely newlywed, Beth. This left him torn and saddened . . . yet also thrilled.

Chapel Fox stood at a crossroads. On one hand, his life was perfect. He was owner of a lucrative business. He was considered a respectable member of his community. He had married a woman who was everything he could have hoped for in a partner. He envisioned all the good things that life had to offer: starting a family, opening his heart to let the love shine in, basking in the success that his professional work had granted him.

On the other hand, his was life was a disaster. Sure, he was successful, but material things meant little to him. With the exception of an expensive wardrobe, which was a necessary cost of doing business, Fox had led a pretty Spartan existence until becoming married. And that woman who was perfect in so many ways? She was also his accomplice in his latest series of murders, and she was good at it. Kids? How could Fox burden the world with his progeny, knowing full well that there was a chance any offspring could grow up to be as homicidal as he and his wife were? Plus, he wondered, was his blackened heart capable of loving something as innocent and pure as a newborn?

On the surface, all seemed well. Fox didn't get away with murder by wearing his emotions on his French-cuffed sleeve, after all. The first few months of marriage had passed uneventfully. Fox and Beth worked together, commuted together, loved together. By all appearances, they were the happy newlyweds. And the ugliness of their secret lives hadn't had to make an appearance since the incident in Paris. But Fox knew it was only a matter of time before something happened that would prompt Beth to twitch with excitement.

What was making his situation even worse was that the subject that would make his wife spasm with homicidal hope was his beloved Steelers, who had lost five of their last six games, an uncharacteristic swoon for a team that had given Fox and his hometown so much vicarious pleasure over the years. Fox and Beth had even seen the latest defeat—a 41–14 shellacking at the hands of the Redskins—in person and witnessed various obnoxious Washington fans insulting both the Steelers and Pittsburgh. Beth cocked her eyebrows at her husband numerous times throughout the game, trying to elicit a response, but Fox ignored her as best he could. He was trying so desperately to shed his old life.

On the way home, Fox was furious about the way the Steelers had played. Beth, however, was more upset that he ignored her eye signals.

"You do realize why I was giving you the sign, right?" she asked.

"Yes, of course. I assumed you weren't flirting with me, dear."

"Oh, so you think it's okay to ignore me, then? You didn't hear those fat bastards in front of us?"

"Yes, I heard them, and yes, I was ignoring you. Beth, don't you get it? I don't want to do it anymore."

"Please! Tell me you didn't love what we did on our honeymoon. Look me in the eye and tell me."

"Honey, I'm driving right now. It wouldn't be prudent for me to stare into your lovely, homicidal eyes."

The rest of the trip was silent, save for the morons calling in to the postgame Steeler show, lamenting the fact, yet again, that the Steelers didn't draft Dan Marino when they had the chance.

When they got home, Beth repeated her request: "Okay, look at me in the eye and tell me you didn't love what we did on our honeymoon."

Fox grasped Beth by the shoulders and said, "Honey, Europe was beautiful. I loved taking in all the sights with the person I've chosen to spend the rest of my life with."

"Stop being an asshole, Chap. You know what the hell I mean."

"Yes, honey, all right. I fucking love it, okay? Must I tell you something you already obviously know? Hell, I was willing to kill you before you accepted my wedding proposal. Remember? I like to end the lives of those whom I feel deserve it. But that doesn't mean I ever want to do it again."

He began sobbing, desperately trying to fight back a flood of tears.

"And you can't threaten me by saying you'll run to the police anymore. You're just as guilty as I am, dear."

Beth looked startled, as if she hadn't until this moment realized the truth and gravity of what Fox just said. "But you've killed more than I have," she said.

Fox chuckled. "Beth, do you think that matters in the eyes of the law? You've been an accomplice on three murders. I've killed many more than you have. The end result? We'd both get the gas chamber."

"You're wrong, Chap. You know the law goes easier on women. All I have to say is that you forced me into doing your awful deeds with you. I'll say I was brainwashed. I'll get six months and community service. But I promise to visit you while you're on death row, awaiting yet another rejection of yet another pointless appeal, you psychotic animal."

She said this with a smile on her face, so happy was she that she once again held the upper hand. Fox wanted to plunge the nearest sharp object straight through her graceful neck and end it as only he could. But, of course, he couldn't. This was his wife. She had some family and many friends who would notice her missing. His head was throbbing now.

"I'm going for a walk. Don't wait up," said Fox, who quickly threw on a coat and embraced the autumn wind that awaited him on the other side of the door.

As he walked around his neighborhood, he mulled his options:

A. He could turn himself in and admit to everything, helping the police, both in Pittsburgh and internationally, clear a lot of cold cases and bringing some sense of closure to his victims' loved ones.

B. He could off his newlywed wife, whom he loved dearly but was much too eager to continue his murderous ways.

C. He could stop for a root-beer float at Cal's Custard Shoppe, a block from where he was standing.

D. He chose "C," and while he was enjoying his float, he considered further options:

E. *He could string Beth along, like he did when the unpleasantness with the insulting actress arose, and feign interest in pursuing what he hoped was his past life.*

F. *He could face reality and admit that he wouldn't know what path he was going to take with the rest of his life until the next Pittsburgh insulter pushed him over the edge.*

Some obnoxious Washington Redskin fans are breathing today because they didn't tip Fox into homicidal territory. This may have had something to do with the afterglow of his honeymoon. Or maybe Fox was genuinely changing. He hoped so, and the float, as usual, was delicious and calmed him down a bit.

He returned directly home, gave Beth a pleasant peck on the cheek, and apologized for the argument.

"Honey, let's just take it day by day, okay?"

"Hey, Chap, that's all any of us can do, isn't it?"

The newlyweds made up and awoke refreshed the next morning, filled mostly with hope but unable to shake a sense of foreboding.

As fate would have it (and there again is our tale's friend, fate), the new day brought a new client, a man by the name of Arnold Burrell, who, despondent over his wife's infidelities, entered Fox's office angry at the world. To break the ice, Fox brought up the Steelers' current woes, figuring that a little male bonding over sports would pacify his new client.

"Fuck them, too," snarled Burrell. "Everything sucks in my life right now, even the Steelers. Fuck 'em all. They should fire Noll, too. He's not too much of a genius without the talent he used to have. Know what I'm saying, chief?"

Fox took this verbal barrage of hatred aimed at his beloved team . . . shockingly well. He was more upset that this virtual stranger had referred to him as "chief." And he was furious that Beth happened to be in the office to witness this clown tee off on the Steelers. As soon as Burrell finished his tirade, Beth started shooting him looks.

Fox chuckled. "Well, Mr. Burrell, I'm sure there's no need to do anything hasty"—he glanced quickly in Beth's direction—"like fire Chuck Noll. The team is merely going through a rough patch. It happens. Now let's get back to your case, shall we?"

The tedium of the rest of the meeting was broken only by spikes of cursing. Burrell was an angry man, and Fox assured him he would do the

*best he could to gain a fair settlement. The second he left Fox's office, the seat
across from Fox's desk was filled with the eager visage of Beth.*

"Well, Chap, did he do it?"

"Did who do what, sugar buns?"

"Stop it. Did he push you over the edge?"

"No, but you're starting to. Listen, Beth. Yes, I was slightly annoyed
at our newest moron of a client pontificating stupidly about the Steelers.
But I've come to the conclusion that perhaps—perhaps—doing so shouldn't
warrant a death sentence."

"You're not the man I married, Chap."

"Then get a divorce. I know a good lawyer."

"No, you know what I'll do."

"God, Beth, listen to yourself. You're blackmailing me into murder. So,
we kill Burrell, right? And then next month, you decide someone else should
be offed. And then next month and the month after that. Beth, eventually,
we would slip up. You can't do this."

*Beth seemed to grasp what he was saying; at least Fox wanted to think
this was the case.*

"I'm going back to work. We'll talk later," she said.

*She wasn't happy, but at least she was out of his face, which gave him
time to ponder . . . the imponderable, the one thought always present in the
deep recesses of his brain that he never wanted to promote to the front. The
ugliness of the thought made him wince, made him tear up. He thought they
had an agreement, forged at the tip of a knife on the night he proposed. But
then the honeymoon murders happened, and that unleashed an insatiable
bloodlust in Beth, one that only Fox could extinguish.*

Ah, leaving my faithful readers with a little fictitious suspense,
which, I hoped, would supplant nicely, at least for a few minutes, the
actual suspense we were enduring, being the last survivors on the *SS
Mousetrap*. The unmistakable fact that hardly anybody wanted to confront, especially not our Dear Leader, was that the company had fallen
back to pre-Showcase numbers. It was three weeks into the month, and
we had taken in a mere 17 new clients.

Next week was Thanksgiving. Sam and I, blessed with time on our
hands, envisioned one of Andrea's holiday festivals: Andrea dressed as
a pilgrim, Loretta grumpily donning a Native American outfit, turkey
for all, or, even better, live turkeys running through the offices. Instead of cake, there would be pumpkin and apple pies. All in all, a nice

pre-Thanksgiving bash, filled with the entertainment we'd grown accustomed to.

Unh-unh. The Tuesday before Thanksgiving, we all received the following memo:

To: The Survivors

From: Andrea

Re: Celebrating Thanksgiving

Date: Nov. 26, 1991

My dear survivors, I invite you all to spend Thanksgiving Day with me, here at our corporate headquarters, as we head toward the end of calendar year 1991, a year that has been at times a roller coaster, but a roller coaster that now is headed magically in only one direction—up, up, up!

Make no mistake—this will be a working holiday for us, the survivors, the believers, and, yes, that special 1 percent. Do not expect to smell turkeys cooking and the sounds of football emanating from the meeting room's television set.

You can, of course, choose to stay home and smell all the turkeys and watch all the football you want. This memo in no way is making demands. But I know you all, and I know how much you want this company to prosper for the rest of 1991 and beyond.

I would be nothing short of shocked to not see every one of you here by 9:00 Thursday.

Onward!

Andrea

"This has to be illegal, no?" asked Sam.

"I'm guessing no. She says in the memo that she's making no demands of us."

"And what do you think will happen to those who don't show up?"

"They'll be canned Friday, but the fact is, is that she's saying clearly that attendance is not mandatory."

"It's not a total loss, actually. Karen's family is coming in, and this gives me the best kind of excuse in the world to see them only minimally—a legitimate excuse!"

"Yeah, isn't that the best when you actually have genuine reasons to not do something that you hate doing? I remember I was visiting Nicole's parents once, and an ice storm hit. I spent I don't know how many hours chipping ice off sidewalks and cars. It was so much better than being stuck in the house with Nicole's parents."

"I can even bring home the memo as proof."

"Why not get it notarized, too? Then laminate the damn thing and parade it around your house, proclaiming your freedom."

"I just might. Do you think we'll still get a floor show?"

"No, I'm guessing this is Andrea in serious mode, by the tone of the memo. She'll actually expect us to work on a holiday at a time when we have virtually no work."

As it turned out, I was more right than wrong. There was no floor show, no pilgrim outfits; sadly, Loretta was dressed in her usual personality-appropriate drab work clothes. Until meeting her, I was never aware how many shades of gray existed on Earth's palette. Andrea did, however, gather us for a meeting around lunchtime, which, regrettably, featured no lunch.

There were 17 of us; amazingly, we had six no-shows. I admired their courage but questioned their sanity.

"November has not been a good month. You don't need me to tell you that. But my hope for this company is bottomless. I think by now, you know that. Sadly, due to the sudden drop-off in business, I've decided to let six of you go."

She then read off the names. The six no-shows would never show here again. Quel coincidence!

"That's right. Your six former employees are home right now, enjoying second helpings of cranberry sauce while they root for their favorite teams. They're spending quality time with loved ones, maybe around a fireplace, enjoying each other's company. You folks, meanwhile, are here, in a dull corporate office. You're not eating turkey. You're not watching football. There's not a fireplace anywhere I can see. No, you're stuck in a windowless room with a crazy old lady who forced you to be here.

"And for that, I give you my endless thanks and my pledge: This company won't go down without a fight, without sweat, without blood. Now get the hell out of here. Go home and enjoy the rest of the day with your families. But come back here tomorrow with a renewed passion for what you do."

"Nick, let's grab a beer at the Pussycat. I'm in no rush to get home."

"Sam, it's a holiday. Nothing is open. No one is on the streets. You have two choices: sit in your office for the next four hours by your lonesome or go home to your waiting in-laws."

He looked blankly at me.

"You're seriously considering staying here, aren't you?"

"No! Well, yes. It's not like Karen will ever find out we got an early dismissal."

"Yeah, she will."

"You're gonna tell her?"

"No, but I'm going home now, and our wives talk, and at some point, in some otherwise boring conversation, Nicole will mention that we got out early Thanksgiving Day, and Karen will say something like, 'That's funny. Sam got home at his usual time.' Then she'll think about it for a few minutes, call you a bastard, and you'll spend the rest of the week sleeping on the couch."

"I don't like your scenario at all. I reject it fully. Sometimes a man has to make a stand. This, friend, is one of those times."

"No, it's not, Sam. Go home. Karen will be happy to see you. Your in-laws will admire you for being so dedicated to your job and important to your employer that you had to work at all on Thanksgiving."

"I don't care what they think."

"Okay, have it your way. In fact, make it even better: Call Karen around 4:30 and say Andrea asked you to pull a double shift."

"No," said Sam. "That would seem crazy. She'd know I was lying then."

"Whatever, pal. I'm outta here. Have a great Thanksgiving."

As I was putting on my coat, I saw Andrea approaching. In my mind, I cursed Sam. If it weren't for his silliness, I'd have been heading home by now. Instead, I found myself about to converse with Andrea, and I was never prepared for what came out of her mouth.

"What are you still doing here, young man?" she said as she got to within five feet of me.

"I was just leaving, Andrea."

She peered into Sam's office.

"And what the hell are you still doing here? Wait. Let me guess. In-laws?"

I laughed. "Bingo, Andrea," I said.

"Ah, I'm an old married hand. I know all the tricks. It's fine by me if you want to stay here. Hell, there's a couch in my office. Spend the night if you wish."

Sam shot me a look, as if to say, "See? The boss understands," to which I replied in my mind, "Yeah, but the boss is out of her fucking mind. Remember?"

"All right, Sam, I'll see you tomorrow. Let's go, young man. I'll walk with you out the door."

I casually flipped Sam off and departed with Andrea, who decided to hook her hand inside the crook of my elbow, no doubt much to Sam's delight.

"Nick, your favorite client really thwarted our momentum."

"Andrea, we never figured"—

"No, Nick. I'm not blaming you. Hell, you're responsible more than anyone for our brief resurgence. But damn it, that second article shot a hole in our balloon, didn't it?"

She sighed. "Well, my parking lot is right up the street. Enjoy the rest of your day, Nick. And come armed tomorrow with ideas. I know what you're capable of."

"I'm capable of shoving you into traffic," I wanted to say. But, unfortunately, it was a holiday, and there was no traffic. Besides, spending the rest of my life in prison for shoving an old woman into traffic probably wasn't the best idea I'd ever had.

The bus ride home seemed longer than normal, perhaps because I was the only passenger. Even the bus driver, who obviously was working on a holiday, would occasionally shoot me a sad glance from the rearview mirror. He probably deduced, from my appearance—I was wearing khakis that had seen better days and a green dress shirt that should have been retired a while back—that I was working because of a crazy boss and not because I was a vital cog to my company's success.

I arrived through the door of our apartment and was greeted by hugs from Nicole. All thoughts of the lonely bus ride immediately evaporated. "Come on," she said. "We're due at your parents."

For a moment, I had forgotten it was a holiday. And what did my mother prepare for our Thanksgiving feast? The usual—well, the usual for us, anyway: stuffed rigatoni, breaded chicken in wine sauce, veal cutlets, and various side dishes. I asked my mother where the turkey was, and she laughed, as she did every year at this question.

I ate ravenously, trying to fuel my brain for a great idea to impress Andrea with. Okay, yes, I would have eaten ravenously regardless. My mother is a ridiculously good cook. Andrea merely provided me with a nice excuse to be a glutton.

As I walked past Andrea's office the next morning, she shouted, "Well, Nick? What do you have for me?"

"Okay, Andrea. Since it worked out so well the first time, how about this? 'American Dreamers Holiday Showcase'? We'll feature inventions that have a Christmas theme. In addition . . ."

I paused to build up her excitement, which was already substantial.

"We invite Jack Gardner as a show of decency."

She frowned. "Fuck him and his horse."

"No, Andrea. Hear me out. He won't show. He thinks we're scum. But we can make a point to the reporter that we went the extra mile to get back in his good graces."

"I like the way you think, Nick. It's on! Round up the inventors, have Loretta contact them, pick a day, and it's a go!"

I then walked into Sam's office and confessed my sins to him.

"Nick, don't be so damn hard on yourself. She asked you to come up with an idea. You did. It's that simple. I stayed here last evening till 6:00. I meant to leave at 4:00, but I was so fucking bored that I fell asleep. By the time I caught a bus—they were running on a holiday schedule, which had slipped my mind—it was 7:00. I walked through the door at 7:23 and was greeted by Karen with a growl."

"Okay, you're a heel of a husband, but I keep doing things to keep this rancid tumor of a company afloat."

"The few of us who remain thank you, except for Loretta, who will again have to cook a feast."

"Yeah, it's not all bad, I suppose."

I went to my office to round up the next batch of Showcase contestants. They would be . . .

Phil Marston, inventor of Bell Tonez, the programmable doorbell that can contain up to 10 different tunes. And who wouldn't want a doorbell that can play up to 10 different Christmas carols?

Jane Schiffman, inventor of the coolant-filled potholders she calls FrigiPots—just in time for that holiday baking!

Missy Briscoe, inventor of Cat Lites, whimsical-shaped nightlights for cats. We all have a pet lover on our Christmas list, don't we?

Ken Burchfield, inventor of Radio Stay-tion, the radio that emits the signal from only one station. Electronics and gadgets are big at Christmas. Plus, we all have a moron on our Christmas list, don't we?

I banged out a press release, figuring that reporters would once again not pass up a free lunch, despite the bucket of reality that Jack Gardner had doused us with following the first Showcase.

American Dreamers Showcase—the Sequel!

Pittsburgh—Based on the success of local invention-marketing company Mousetrap's inaugural American Dreamers Showcase, the company has decided to host a follow-up event to promote more promising ideas that have yet to find their way to the marketplace.

"We were thrilled with the coverage of our first event, and we figured, why not bring more of our clients' ideas into the public eye?" said Mousetrap president and CEO Andrea Bianco.

The company's second Showcase will have a holiday theme, and the product ideas being featured will include:

Phil Marston's Bell Tonez. Aren't we all tired of the same, old "ding-dong, ding-dong"? Well, this inventor has devised a doorbell that can play up to 10 different songs. What better way to put someone in the holiday spirit than by hearing a different holiday tune every time the doorbell rings?

Jane Schiffman, like millions of others, plans to spend a lot of time this holiday season in the kitchen. Her idea? FrigiPots, the potholders with an internal coolant that will avoid painful kitchen burns 100 percent of the time.

Missy Briscoe has an idea that's the perfect gift for cat lovers. And who doesn't have at least one cat lover on his list? Cat Lites are whimsically shaped nightlights for cats. They could be made in the shape of a fish or a mouse or a ball of string and will delight cats and cat owners alike.

Ken Burchfield has designed a radio that every parent will love. His Radio Stay-tion promises that any adult who has a favorite radio station will never again have to worry about someone—say, a teenager—changing the dial. Why? Well, because, like the name says, the station stays in place. How? It receives a signal from only one station. It's a simple idea, and people love buying gadgets for holidays.

These ideas and others will be featured at Mousetrap's headquarters in an all-day holiday affair, where you will have access to our inventors and staff and be able to witness the American Dream in action.

There will also be a catered luncheon, so please RSVP by December 6.

The dirty part of my job now complete, I now approached Loretta with the news that once again she would have to prepare a feast for a bunch of hungry reporters. This gave me joy, and when my smiling face was greeted with the words "I already know why you're here, you fucking retard," my heart, not unlike the Grinch's, grew three sizes, almost bursting out of my chest, so overflowing with joy was it.

I kept smiling. "Now, now, Loretta. The bitterness you possess could infect the food you're going to prepare, which, in turn, could permeate the entire event, prompting the reporters, through your innate nastiness, to give the event a poor write-up."

"So, how is Rachel these days, Nick?"

"Is that supposed to scare me, Loretta? Look. In case you haven't noticed, what, with your 8-hour-a-day lying spree that you call a job, there are 17 of us left, and the company is hanging on by its nose hairs.

"But just so you know, Rachel's doing great, thanks."

"Maybe Andrea would be interested in hearing our little conversation."

"Okay, Loretta, listen to me clearly. First of all, I'm going to tell you to fuck off. Fuck off. Secondly, I'm going to leave your office, march right into Andrea's ice dome, and tell her that I told you to fuck off. She will find this to be hysterical. End of discussion. We want the Showcase to be held no later than December 9. If you have any problems with your duties, please address them with Andrea."

And then I marched into Andrea's office and said, "Andrea, I just told Loretta about the upcoming Showcase and what you expected her to do. She was her usual nasty self, and I told her to fuck off. Sorry."

And Andrea, just like I had predicted, proceeded to laugh hysterically, to the point of resting her head on her desk and howling into her blotter.

"I've never heard you use language like that before, young man," she said.

"Well, Andrea, Loretta brings out the worst in me."

"Don't sweat it. I appreciate hearing it from you. Get out of here."

There was, however, one final dirty part of this upcoming Showcase that I was saving for last: inviting Jack Gardner. I liked Jack Gardner. I liked his invention. And I hated using him as a defense for the media: "Well, to be honest, we invited Mr. Gardner to the Showcase. We value him as a customer and want to do everything we can to make his dream come true."

But I promised Andrea I would do it. Promised her? Hell, it was my idea.

Dear Mr. Gardner,

Mousetrap, Inc. is proud to announce it's hosting a second American Dreamers Showcase, which will be held in early December in our corporate headquarters.

We would very much like to feature your product in our Showcase as a show of good faith and commitment to your product idea. We'd hate to think there was any bad blood between the company and yourself, and we see this as a first step toward mending fences.

Please let us know by December 6 if you will be attending.

Sincerely,

Andrea Bianco

"So, you think he'll turn the invitation down, right?" Andrea asked me when she finished reading what I had written.

"I can't imagine he wants anything to do with us. But it"—

"Gives us cover. We can make sure every reporter there knows he was invited to show off his idea. Good. And if they don't mention him, make sure you do, and make sure they remember who he is."

"Of course, Andrea."

"Oh, Nick, Loretta came by about a minute after you left my office and told me what you told her. I laughed my ass off again. You should have seen her face."

"Glad I gave you a chuckle, Andrea."

"But don't worry about Loretta. She knows I want her to prepare a feast for the Showcase, and, believe me, she'll prepare a feast."

I departed Andrea's office feeling as though she was my new best friend forever.

December 1991

THANKSGIVING, OF COURSE, HAS come to mean the official beginning of Christmas. As soon as the turkey's done and the last speck of stuffing consumed, out come the lights and decorations. Christmas has become a monthlong celebration, a time of happy tidings, merry smiles, and good-will toward all.

On December 5, Sam received a letter from Jack Gardner. What it lacked in Christmas cheer it made up for in vitriol and rage.

Dear Mr. Wiatt,

I received your boss's entreaty to attend your company's alleged "American Dreamers Showcase" the other day.

Surely, you're jesting, right?

You and your partner seemed to be earnest, talented young men. As an older, and, I hope, wiser man, allow me to impart some wisdom onto you before it's too late: Get out of the company. Now. Quit today. You both deserve better. The company you work for is garbage. The woman who signs your checks is so completely lacking in integrity that it boggles the mind.

The end of Mousetrap is near, Mr. Wiatt. And I'm hoping to take credit for what I sincerely pray is the final nail in its rotten coffin.

You may remember a few months ago you received a product idea from a potential client named Sid Delba. His idea was one your company has tried to promote without any success dozens of times. I've learned this via conversations I've had with that snake you folks call an account executive. If anyone at your company had anything resembling a conscience, Mr. Delba's product would have been rejected promptly.

Unfortunately for you, Mr. Delba's product was accepted, and he—that would be me—was bilked, like all your company's clients, out of thousands of dollars.

Now, for my purposes, I viewed the $5,000 I forked over as an investment on the total demise of your company.

So, you're probably asking, how does one more disgruntled client end Mousetrap? Well, you see, I noticed in my initial application package that you folks included the glowing article from the first Showcase. What you didn't include, however, was the follow-up story. You know—the one that featured me and told the truth.

The FTC, needless to say, was very interested in your selective article choice. They were also quite interested in hearing that my "product" had been accepted by you folks dozens of times over the years.

The wheels are in motion, Mr. Wiatt. Please show this letter to whomever you feel needs to see it. Clearly, the FTC is none too pleased at Mousetrap's latest duplicity.

The end is very near. Leave, today if possible.

Sincerely,

Jack Gardner

After Sam finished reading the letter, I muttered, "Disabled."

Sam gave me a puzzled look.

"Sid Delba—backwards. It spells "Dis Abled."

"Does that mean he's disabling the company, or does he think we're disabled?"

"Who knows? I suppose it works either way," I said.

"He's clever, that Gardner."

"Yeah, I suppose. It's weird. Everything he wrote in that letter is true, and yet—"

"You feel kind of bad for Andrea, seeing it laid out in black and white and knowing we're partially complicit in the misdeeds of this company?" asked Sam.

"Uh-huh. Well, have fun telling Andrea. Bye!" I jumped quickly out of my seat.

"Get your ass back in here! First, we show it to Alice. Then, we follow her lead. If she wants us with her in the lair for support, we go. If she wants to tackle it alone, we let her."

"I know, I know. But you do realize this will be the ugliest moment of our lives, right?"

"Well, maybe Alice won't want us there."

After quickly scanning the letter, Alice looked at both of us and declared, "I'm not doing this alone."

As much as we wanted no part of the spectacle that was about to take place, we both knew we owed it to Alice to give her our support on what was going to be a very unpleasant undertaking.

"Of course, Alice," said Sam, as I nodded my assent.

And then the three of us stood, immobile, almost afraid even to blink, as if that would somehow tip Andrea off that something wasn't right.

Alice managed to give us her trademark laugh, and while the three of us enjoyed a chuckle, we still didn't move any closer to the door.

"All right, I'll lead the way," Alice said, finally, and we cautiously followed her into the tundra.

Andrea looked somewhat nervous at the sight of all three of us approaching her desk but tried to put an immediate positive spin on the visit.

"I bet this is about the Showcase, right? I can't wait. Let's hit this one out of the park like last time, folks!"

"Andrea, Sam received a letter from Jack Gardner today. You need to read it," said Alice.

"What's that bastard want with us?" She knocked the letter to the floor. "What? He turned down our invitation? Good. That's exactly what we wanted. Nick, you knew that."

"It's not about his invitation to the Showcase, Andrea," I said softly.

"Speak up!" she yelled. "Then what the hell is it about?"

Alice picked up the letter and handed it to Andrea. She scanned it, and, as she did, her already pale complexion seemed to grow translucent.

"Get out," she muttered.

"Andrea, listen to me. We—"

"Get out, Alice. Get out, all of you. I need to be alone."

We weren't three feet from her office when the crashing began, followed by the swearing. The showcase was in four days, and that included a weekend. I figured we could still pull off the event and wring at least some positive news from the event. The reporters again would be well-fed, assuming Loretta still cared about her job and still felt it in her to suck up to Andrea for perhaps one final time.

But could Andrea make it through the event and turn on the charm, like she's done so many times? Or would she simply go on a perpetual bender and drink herself into a coma while various FTC agents burst through the office, rummaging through files, laughing at the sight of a drunken, broken-down mess of a woman?

The same batch of reporters had RSVP'd that they'd be attending. Apparently, Loretta wasn't a total fuck-up; they were coming back for seconds. I touched base with all the inventors to make sure they still planned on coming. They all told me yes and seemed thrilled at the prospect of pitching their ideas.

So, with everything in place, that left me the weekend to worry about Andrea's condition. Would she make a spectacle of herself and essentially end the company on the spot? I was sitting in my office late on Friday—none of us had seen nor heard Andrea since we left her office the day prior—and there she was, standing in my office doorway, holding a piece of paper in her hand and looking sober and determined.

"Nick, I want your feedback on this ASAP. If it's a fight they want, then let's have it." She thrust the paper into my hands and promptly left.

Dear client,

There's a reason "patience" comes before "success" in the dictionary, as I'm sure you're well aware. Remember—Rome wasn't built in a day, as the saying goes, and your product won't be built overnight.

But progress is being made each day, and our team of hardworking idea lovers will never stop pursuing the ultimate goal for your idea: the manufacturing of your product and its entry into the marketplace.

Our country was founded on a dream. And my company thrives because of American Dreamers like you. We here at Mousetrap hold you in the highest esteem, and we want to continue to do everything we can to make your dreams come true.

But we need your help.

As you are no doubt aware, our country's economy is not in the best of shape right now, and we all need to do our part and pitch in to make things better. As a result, to better serve you, the board and I have instituted a new yearly maintenance-fee plan for all existing clients. For a mere $50 per year, we will continue to pursue your idea to the ends of the Earth and help make your dreams come true.

If you choose not to participate in this new program, the current state of the economy will not allow us to pursue your idea as much as we'd like to.

If you have any questions concerning this exciting, new path Mousetrap is taking, please call Loretta Welles at 412- . . .

My laughter attracted Sam's attention. His laughter attracted Alice. I shut the door as Alice was reading, not wanting to attract anyone else's attention, least of all Andrea's.

"She's kidding, right?" asked Alice.

"No," I said, "and think it through. Some of these dopes, who haven't heard from Mousetrap in years, will fork over that 50 bucks in the hopes that their idea isn't dead yet."

"Yeah," said Sam. "And if you've already lost 8 or 10 grand, what's another 50 bucks?"

"Why doesn't she just rob a bank or mug a drunk guy leaving a bar?" asked Alice. "It's the moral equivalency."

I shrugged. I was horrified, of course, but no more so than I normally was. Plus, I was relieved to see that Andrea was sober and focused. I could enjoy the upcoming weekend without being distracted by thoughts of a drunken crazy woman fistfighting with reporters or denouncing them while drunk off her ass.

I excused myself from my company and went to Andrea's. I said the letter was fine and told her to make sure whoever sent out the letters didn't send one to Jack Gardner. She winced at my saying his name but grunted her agreement.

"So, is everything set for Monday?" she asked.

"The clients are coming, the reporters are coming, and I assume Loretta has everything under control concerning the food," I said.

"You're assuming with Loretta?" she asked. "Does that mean you haven't confirmed it with her?" She winked at me.

"To be honest, Andrea, at this stage of the game"—and yes, I regretted my choice of words as soon as they escaped my mouth—"I'm trying to avoid her as much as I can." I stood there and grinned stupidly, hoping she didn't catch what I said.

"'At this stage of the game,' young man?"

Well, so much for that hope.

"Do you care to elaborate?"

Words didn't come immediately to me. As soon as my brain was able to compose a believable lie, though, and I began to open my mouth, Andrea came to my rescue.

"Look. Save whatever bullshit answer you were going to give me, okay? I'm a lot of things, but stupid isn't one of them. I know it's fucked. But we're going to have this Showcase and get some good attention again, and if my yearly maintenance plan even suckers in a third of our clients, we might—might—be able to withstand the FTC's next assault."

I nodded. It seemed to be the safest route.

"Now get the hell out of here and rest up for Monday. And, by the way, I checked with Loretta this morning. She assured me everything will be fine for the Showcase."

I left Andrea in fighting trim on Friday afternoon. Nicole and I enjoyed our weekend, and I really didn't worry myself about Monday's Showcase. The first one was probably the highlight of my Mousetrap career. The stage was set for another round of success, which the company desperately needed. The clients would be giddy and eager. The reporters, eating Loretta's delicious food, would be sated and write nice things about us, especially if any of our clients were the least bit interesting. And Andrea would again turn on the charm and make up for any personality deficit the clients possessed.

So, sure, I could see the event going swimmingly in my mind's eye. What I couldn't foresee, of course, was who else was to arrive at Mousetrap's office first thing Monday besides the invited clients and the reporters.

When I arrived early Monday morning, nervous but quite hopeful about the upcoming Showcase, the first thing I saw was a conservatively dressed man in his mid-40s with a dour expression on his face sitting in our lobby. I introduced myself and asked if he was here for the Showcase.

"I'm sorry, no. What's this 'Showcase' you referred to?"

I explained to him what was going to happen, and he laughed mirthlessly and said, "No, that's not why I'm here. I'm from the Federal Trade Commission, and I'm here to see one Andrea Bianco." His eyes seemed to narrow upon uttering her name, as though she were the villain in a poorly acted Western. I half-expected him to throw his cigarette, had he been smoking, to the ground and extinguish it with his spur-clad boot.

"Oh," I said, trying not to vomit, "well, she should be in shortly. Let me check for you, okay, sir? And would you like some coffee? You know, you've come on a good day. Part of our Showcase features a feast prepared by one of our employees."

I was babbling, and the man took pity on me, grasped my shoulders, and said, "I just need to see Ms. Bianco, son."

"Yes, of course."

I sprinted to see if Sam or Alice were in yet. They weren't. Neither was Andrea. But Loretta was. I rolled my eyes and barreled into her office.

"Listen closely, Loretta."

"Good fucking morning to you, too, asshole."

I ignored her. "There's a gentleman from the FTC sitting in our lobby. He wants to meet Andrea. Our Showcase starts in three hours. If you have even a shred of human decency in that dried-up husk of a body, you will help me do everything we can to prevent this guy from seeing Andrea before the Showcase."

She glared at me, but said, "What did you have in mind?"

"I'm going to take him back to my office and give him a tour of the facility. I'll then pretend that I'm contacting Andrea and inform the man that she won't be able to see him till the afternoon. Andrea should be here shortly. You tell her that the FTC is here and to stay in her office till the Showcase starts. That way, at least we can get the event started before she hits the bottle."

I sprinted back up to the lobby, but I was a minute too late. When I got back, Andrea was introducing herself to the FTC representative, assuming, like I did, that he was a client. I got there just in time for her to be informed otherwise.

"We need to speak, in private, Ms. Bianco."

"You need to fuck off, in public, Mr. FTC."

"Your surliness will not help matters in the least, ma'am. Now, we can proceed in a civil manner, behind closed doors, or we can do it the hard way."

"Ooh, I love it when a man takes control. Too bad you're not a man, cocksucker."

"Okay, Mrs. Bianco, let me put it to you another way: We go to your office and discuss the matter at hand, or I padlock this shithole you call a company inside a minute."

Andrea blinked. I think Mr. Uptight Suit Guy's use of the naughty language not only put her in her place but caught her off guard. She waved her hand in the direction of her office, and off they went. I stood, frozen, for a moment before I remembered there was a Showcase to put on, FTC or not. I scrambled back to Loretta's office to give her an update.

"Forget Plan 'A', Loretta. Look. I'll corral the reporters and clients, and Alice, Sam, and I will do everything we can to make the event run smoothly. I think you're the best person here to keep Andrea in control. If she's in the condition I think she'll be in after her meeting, don't let her anywhere near us."

"Sounds like a plan, Nick."

And that's when I realized the enormity of the problem we were facing: Loretta not only agreed with what I had said, but she did so without swearing or insulting me in any way. She was afraid. That should have made me happy, and, no doubt, would have under any other circumstances. Now, though, I was terrified.

Fortunately, when I got to my office, Sam and Alice were both in, and I quickly caught them up-to-speed.

"On a lighter note, don't you think 'This Shithole I Call a Company' would make a great title for Andrea's autobiography?" said Sam.

Alice and I glared at him. "Aren't you a little bit frightened of the spectacle that could erupt in a few hours?" I asked.

"What? You love Andrea's spectacles."

"But those were all private, within-our-walls spectacles. This one will be public, in front of reporters. It will be in the paper. Our families will see and read about it."

Sam looked at the ground. "Oh, now I get it," he mumbled.

"Though, yeah, now that you mention it, that would be a pretty damn good title," I said.

"Okay, you two, do you want to kiss each other to formalize your apology, or can we all focus on the problem at hand?"

"That's just sick, Muck. Look at him. I could do way better than Nick."

"So, what is the plan?" I asked, ignoring Sam.

"We act like everything's fine. We talk to the reporters. We mingle with our clients. We pray like hell Andrea doesn't come near us."

"Well, I told Loretta her job was to guard Andrea and prevent her from reaching us," I said.

"And she listened to you?" asked Sam.

I nodded.

"Wow," said Sam. We're really fucked this time, aren't we?"

I nodded again, slower this time.

"Come on, guys. Focus. Put on your best happy face and let's get out there."

We arrived in our lobby just in time to greet our clients. They all had that eager, first-day-of-school look: hair neatly styled, Sunday-best clothes, polished shoes, pleasant smiles. They really thought this Showcase would produce the breakthrough they've been dreaming about for years. The three of us shot quick glances at each other, and I could read in Sam and Alice's eyes they were thinking the same thing I was: "Shithole you call a company" was way too kind. I wanted to vomit. I also, however, was desperate to see how this played out. I'd gone this far, after all. Just throw a few more soul-sucking hours on my already lengthy tab, and let's be done with it already.

"You must be Phil . . . you must be Jane . . . what a great idea . . . we all really loved that one . . . isn't that true? . . . we're all cat lovers here . . . I don't know how many times I've burnt myself in the kitchen . . . they can't mess with that radio, huh?"

The three of us were all holding our own, and, finally, it was time to lead them into our big meeting room to mingle with the reporters and have lunch. So far, so good. Either Loretta was doing her best to contain Andrea, or Andrea was still in her meeting.

The mingling was going great. The reporters were happy and fed. The clients were the champions of their own products, and each seemed to be talking the ear off every reporter they could find. The three of us mingled around the tables, making sure everything that was said was putting the company in the best light possible.

Then, a reporter crooked a finger in my direction. "I supposed Jack Gardner isn't here today, huh?"

"Well, sir, to be honest, we extended him an invitation to come. We would love nothing more than to showcase his product."

"But he declined, I presume?"

"Yes, he did. Have you tried the stuffed chicken breasts? Our Loretta is a fabulous cook."

"Yes, they are terrific. But about Mr. Gardner—what's your take on that?"

"Well, sir, we have had thousands of clients over the years, and, like any company, not every client is satisfied 100 percent of the time. You know that. I believe your paper runs corrections just about every day, no?"

"Well, Nick, I think you know there's a difference between an honest mistake and willful—"

And then I saw something which, under any other circumstance, would have made me cheer. But seeing it right now unfold in front of not only me but a roomful of clients and reporters, I wanted to run and never stop.

There, in the hallway that led to the meeting room's double doors was Andrea, slapping the hell out of Loretta, who was making a valiant, though futile, attempt to tackle Andrea and prevent her from heading toward her destination. In one last attempt, Loretta tossed herself arms-first to the ground, like a safety trying to stop a wide receiver sprinting toward the end zone, only to have Andrea stomp on Loretta's outstretched left hand, causing her to scream out in pain. If anyone in the room had been oblivious to what was transpiring on the other side of the door to this point, Loretta's horror-movie scream left no doubt.

Andrea threw open the doors and had everyone's rapt attention. In the background, a crying Loretta, holding her bruised hand, was limping back to her office. I may have actually felt bad for her if I wasn't so absolutely horrified at what was happening five feet away from where I stood.

"Look at all of you bastards," Andrea began.

Alice approached her, but before she could utter a word, Andrea stuck out her hand in Alice's direction and said, "Did you see Loretta out there? I'll do the same to you, too.

"So, this is the big, fucking Showcase, eh, folks?" She was crazy drunk. I should have known it the second I saw her pummeling Loretta, of course. How else would she have had the strength to do that?

"Hey, media jackals, here's a news flash for you: The FTC—and oh, I'll let you in on a little company secret here. You know what I say the FTC stands for? You'll love this." She giggled and motioned to the reporters to come closer to her, as though she were about to whisper. "Fuck those cocksuckers!" she yelled, causing the reporters in unison to jerk backwards.

She laughed mightily at this, and a few of the reporters chuckled amiably, apparently fearful of making a bad situation worse.

Sam, Alice, and I each possessed the physical mobility of an ice sculpture, even too frightened to look directly at each other.

"So, where are my clients?" asked Andrea.

Four timid hands raised slowly in the air.

Andrea started crying. "You people—I love you people. You're the dreamers, the believers. And I believe in you. But those FTC bastards—they believe in tearing down your dreams. They're giving me another huge fine"—

"How big a fine, Mrs. Bianco?" asked a reporter.

Andrea marched over to the man and got inches from his face. "Bigger than your fat ass, idiot." She then marched over to the tray of chicken breasts and started to fling them at the questioning reporter, who, unfortunately, was too stunned to move fast enough and took a breast to the face.

At this point, Alice tried to grasp Andrea by the hands and was greeted with a heel stomp to the foot, which made her, like Loretta moments ago, yelp in pain. "Back off, you fucking hyena," said Andrea.

Amazingly, Andrea seemed oblivious to the TV cameras that were capturing every second of her breakdown. I was doing my best to stay out of range. It was bad enough I was here. The last thing I needed was to be seen on the evening news as the owner of my company assaulted a reporter with a chicken breast.

"Let me tell you one damned thing, people," she screeched, pointing madly with her sauce-glazed hands in the direction of the reporters. "This isn't the end. I won't let it die. It's over when I say it's over, and it ain't over, folks. Now print that and get the fuck out of my office."

And with that, she mustered what little dignity she could, thrust her head into the air, and wobbled out of the meeting room. Sam and I turned in unison to face Alice. After all, she was a company muckety-muck. She pursed her lips at us but then tried to wring something positive from this horrid display.

"Well, as you folks can see—both clients and media alike—Andrea is nothing if not passionate about her company. Obviously, she's having a bad day. Really, who among us hasn't?" She chuckled. "But I implore you"—and now she was looking directly at the reporters—"to go easy on her. Who here would want the worst day of our lives captured on film and scribbled down in a notebook? Andrea's had a multiyear battle with the FTC, but I would take her at her word when she says that she's going to fight on. You haven't heard the last from her.

"And our dear clients, please don't get the wrong impression. You see, I hope, that you have a fighter on your side, one who will move heaven and Earth to make your dreams a reality. Take that positive thought from today's meeting and banish the other nonsense you witnessed."

Alice's soothing words had a magical effect on our guests. Within a few minutes, everything returned to normal, as it had been before Andrea made her memorable entrance. Granted, barring a plane crash or some tragedy of that magnitude, there was no doubt in my mind that Andrea's spectacle would be the headline of the local news and splashed across page one of tomorrow's newspapers.

After everyone had finally gone, the three of us sat in silence for minutes, not knowing what to say. Finally, I spoke.

"What just happened—I mean, the bad part—wasn't a nightmare, was it? It really happened, right?"

"Oh, yeah, Nick. But, Alice, you were awesome." She gave Sam a weak smile. "Thanks. But what good is it going to do?"

"Well, the Showcase started strong and finished strong. It's the middle part that was the problem. But Sam's right. You were terrific."

She smiled again, and we began cleaning up the mess that lay in front of us.

I watched the news that evening, fervently hoping that the U.S. had declared war on some country, any country—Canada, Peru, Australia— thus saving me the personal humiliation of seeing my company headline the news. Sadly, there were no declarations of war.

Anchor: Good evening. We lead off tonight's news with the bizarre story of a meeting gone bad. Local invention-marketing company Mouse-trap, Incorporated was holding an event for clients and invited media earlier today when company CEO Andrea Bianco, apparently inebriated, burst into the meeting room and began verbally and physically assaulting assorted guests. Reporter Alex Shields has more. Alex?

Reporter: Thanks, Dennis. Well, it seems that Mousetrap has been having a battle with the Federal Trade Commission for years concerning its practices, and today a representative from the FTC came to visit, unan-nounced, to levy more fines . . .

Now, as the reporter is saying this, there's footage of a drunken Andrea berating the media, followed by the money shot: the chicken-breast toss, which, incidentally, this channel's newscast opened with. If I hadn't been actively involved, I'd be doubled over in laughter and calling everyone I knew to make sure they caught this. It was that funny. Except it wasn't, of course.

Reporter: . . . though they refused to go on record, it's possible, based on the last batch of fines, that Mousetrap could be looking at a 7-figure punishment. Dennis?

Yeah, and based on how drunk she was, I think seven figures seemed about right. The morning paper was no better. There, underneath a head-line that read "Mousetrap Meltdown," with a subhead reading "Company CEO 'tosses lunch' upon hearing FTC decree," was a picture of Andrea throwing the cursed breast at the stunned reporter. Again, if I hadn't been actively involved in the nonsense, I would have found this to be gut-bustingly hysterical.

The story was no more pleasant than the picture or headline, and the reporter focused heavily on the fiasco and only mentioned on the A-12 jump the real reason the inventors and media were invited to our

Showcase. I couldn't really blame the reporter, of course. I would have done the same thing had I been in her shoes. Yet it still hurt and was terribly embarrassing.

The mood at work the next day was even more somber than usual. I thought a visit from Chapel Fox might lighten things up for everyone, and seeing how I had little actual work to do, I continued my story . . .

He awoke with a start. Again, it was the same damn dream he had been having almost every night for two weeks. In the dream, he was sitting in his living room, reading the paper, with Beth snuggled up against him. Suddenly, the front door burst open, and there stood two Pittsburgh cops, guns at the ready, ordering Fox and his wife to hit the floor.

"Don't make any sudden moves!" one of the cops shouted. "Chapel Fox and Beth Fox, you are both suspects in the murders of Jean-Claude Fuqua and Bob and Susan McReynolds. You have the right to remain silent. Anything you say—"

"Who the hell is Jean-Claude—what the hell are you saying?" Fox asked, genuinely confused for a moment before remembering the parts of their honeymoon they neglected to tell friends and coworkers about.

"Anything you say can and will be held against you in a court of law. You have the right to an attorney present during questioning. If you cannot afford an attorney, one will be appointed for you. Do you understand these rights?"

"Yes, I'm a lawyer. And you guys are way out of line. Listen. Stop this nonsense before it gets even further out of hand."

While Fox was trying to put a sheen of reason on the chaos that was descending in his living room, Beth remained almost motionless, trying to convey the notion that this was all a terrible misunderstanding.

Needless to say, Chapel Fox had very vivid, lifelike dreams. Most people obviously wouldn't dream about a cop reciting the entire Miranda rights. But Chapel Fox wasn't most people.

The dream continues with him in a dimly lit room being interrogated by a right-out-of-central-casting detective. The dude's beefy, wearing an ill-fitting tan jacket. His tie is loosened, and he's purposely blowing cigarette smoke in Fox's face.

"This whole thing would go down a lot easier if you started talking, Mr. Fox," the detective said.

Fox chuckled. "Look, Detective. This is crazy. Yes, my wife and I honeymooned in Europe, and we did all the normal things tourists do. Committing cold-blooded murder wasn't on our itinerary."

"We have video surveillance of you and Mrs. Fox coming in and out of both hotels when the murders were committed. That's a hell of a coincidence. Also, the local Gutierrez murder has always hung over your head like a storm cloud, whether you're aware of this or not. You were the last person to see her alive."

"Detective, I'm a lawyer. Do you really think"—

"What, and a fancy-shoed, overcharging lawyer can't be a fucking psycho? Really? Get over yourself. Start talking, or you and your lovely wife will never see each other or the light of day ever again. I'll make sure of it."

Fox froze. He could talk. Good golly, he could talk. He could wipe out about a dozen cold cases in under five minutes. He remembered all their names, or at least the specifics of the cases. Families would at least gain a sense of closure. Maybe if he spilled his guts entirely, he could spare Beth some hard time. He'd take the rap for her. He'd tell them he influenced her.

The detective got within an inch of his face. "Talk."

"You don't know the half of it, sir."

The detective moved back and squinted. "What the hell does that mean?"

"Are you into deal-making?"

"Are you fucking around with me? Confess to the crimes you've been dragged in here for, and we'll go from there."

"No, that's not enough. There have been others."

"More than the three we're talking about?"

"Way more."

"What do you want?"

"My wife—she was involved only in the last two, and it was because of me. She walks."

"You're fucking out of your mind. Murderers don't walk free."

"Okay, how long does she spend inside?"

"It depends on what you have to offer, and if it's true."

"Oh, it's true, all right. Mrs. Gutierrez—I killed her. Remember those two Cubs fans who were killed after attending a Pirates game?"

"You killed them?"

"Oh, yeah." Fox couldn't help but smile at the memory.

"Is there a connection between these crimes, or are you just completely out of your fucking mind?"

"They insulted our town."

The detective was apparently too stunned to blink, even. "They made fun of Pittsburgh, so you killed them?"

"Yes." *Fox then went on to admit to the honeymoon killings and the other solo efforts he had undertaken over the years.*

"I've dealt with a lot of lunatics over the years, but you, sir, take the cake!" *The detective slammed both hands on the table as he concluded, shoved himself up from his chair, and slammed the door behind him.*

It was the dream door-slamming that always startled Fox awake.

"Honey, what is it?" *asked a groggy Beth.*

"It's that dream again—the one where cops burst in, and I confess everything to get you a reduced sentence. Oh, honey, it was so real. I'm terrified that it's some sort of warning."

"Fox, listen to me. You are an exceedingly rational human. Do you really think you possess the power to have psychic dreams? And even if you did at some point, you probably squelched it."

Fox laughed. "Yeah, I suppose you're right. It's just"—

And at that moment, they were startled by the sound of their front door being kicked in. Before they knew it, they were on the floor of their bedroom, protesting their innocence. Just like the dream, Fox found himself a few minutes later in a poorly lit room on the other side of a table from a beefy Pittsburgh detective. And just like the dream, Fox spilled the beans in an effort to give Beth a chance at freedom.

And then he really woke up. Fox, for the first time in his life, had experienced the dreaded and quite uncommon "dream within a dream." This time, when Beth started to offer words of solace, Fox shushed her. He wanted to make sure that he was fully awake. He slapped the nightstand twice and then felt his heart rate finally slow.

"This has been going on for weeks now. It's the same nightmare every night. But tonight—tonight, Beth, I had a double feature."

Beth looked at him groggily, which was understandable seeing that it was 3:08 in the morning and that her husband was speaking gibberish. "What the hell do you mean, honey?"

"I dreamt I was dreaming. See, it was the normal dream, and then I woke up, except I didn't. I only thought I woke up. You were there, saying nice things, and then the cops burst in again. And then I woke up for real. At least I think I'm awake."

"Maybe you should get some professional help," *said Beth.*

"What? And tell them why I'm having the dreams? Yeah, that'll go over great."

"You don't have to be specific. Just say you're having recurring nightmares, and maybe someone can help you work through your problems."

"Honey, it's not a mystery what my problem is. It's not like it's some subconscious memory from childhood I've hidden from myself. I'm a mass murderer. I'm fucking psychotic. And so are you. It's eating away at me. I live every day in fear that the cops—some cops, somewhere—will put together the pieces and throw my ass in jail for the rest of my life. It's not a big mystery."

"Would this be a bad time to mention I'd love to update the dining room?"

Fox laughed and ran his fingers through his slightly graying hair. *"Help me, Beth. I don't want my dark side to overcome me ever again. You got a taste of it on our honeymoon, but that's as far as it ever needs to go. Help me, Beth. Help me become the person"*—

And then the front doors really were kicked in. And then there really were two Pittsburgh cops, guns drawn, telling Fox and Beth to hit the floor. And, just like his dreams, and his dream within a dream, Fox found himself sitting face-to-face with Mr. Beefy, who really was wearing an ill-fitting tan jacket and really was blowing smoke in Fox's face.

"So, you gonna start talking? There's a lot more where this one came from," said the detective, tapping the pack of Winstons resting in front of him.

"I will have nothing to say until my attorney is sitting by my side," said Fox, efforting to appear calm.

"Do the names Bob and Susan McReynolds ring a bell?"

"Not really, unless they're the couple that moved in up the street a few weeks ago—the ones with the obnoxious 10-year-old twins. Is this about them?"

The detective was now literally nose-to-nose with Fox. *"Listen, fucknuts. We have the surveillance videos from the hotel. We can place you and Mrs. Fucknuts at the scenes. Now why don't you tell me about Jean-Claude"*—

And, before he knew what had happened, Mr. Beefy crumpled to the floor, the recipient of a head butt and a perfectly landed straight-arm to the throat. As Fox tightened the detective's tie around his throat until the man's breathing ceased, he couldn't help but think that this would have been preventable completely if the cops had just stayed the hell away from him in the first place.

While the first obstacle had been overcome, there were still many to come. Naturally, he took the detective's gun, and while he sincerely hoped he *didn't have to use it, he knew how to shoot a weapon and felt confident that if used properly, it would be his and Beth's springboard to freedom.*

He opened the door of the interrogation room and clotheslined the first cop he saw. He quickly wrapped his forearm around the stunned cop's throat and placed the revolver at his temple.

"You let my wife go now, the three of us," nodding in the direction of his hostage, "take a little walk outside, and no one gets hurt."

Fox's prior conquests always had been such quiet, secluded matters. This one would be page-one news the next day. Fox hated making such a spectacle, but what choice was he left with?

Fox backed his way to the exit and fired a warning shot at the cops surrounding Beth. "The next one goes through his head, I swear," said a forceful Fox. The cops, figuring their best chance at nabbing the duo was outside, let Beth go. The couple, hostage in tow, made it outside. Fox looked around. He didn't see anyone mobilized.

"Whatever you're doing, it'll never work. You won't make it five blocks past here," said the cop.

"Shut up and jimmy open this car," said Fox, pointing to a silver Toyota Corolla. "And then start it up. Failure to do so won't be pretty."

The cop did as he was instructed, and the car fired up within a minute. "Now put your gun on the passenger's seat, very carefully, and get back inside. No false moves."

"Is Henry dead?"

"If by Henry, you mean that corpulent, black-lunged detective, then, yes. But how much longer do you think he had, anyway, in his condition?"

The cop, now visibly shaken, unholstered his gun, placed it on the seat, and walked back inside.

The second Fox pulled out, he was followed by a phalanx of Pittsburgh's finest. And they were firing. And up ahead, no doubt, lay those tire-ripping strips of metal that cops use to catch rogues like Chapel Fox and Beth L. Park. It had been a hell of a run, but Fox and Beth knew it was coming to a violent, horrifying end.

"Thanks for trying, Fox," Beth said, her beautiful eyes brimming with tears.

"Hey, babe, for you, I'd do anything. Now let's see how far we can make them go."

Now, dear reader, the story could end there, with Fox and Beth meeting a certain death. Sure, I spared the details, but just think about the movie "Bonnie & Clyde," and you'll get the general idea. Bullets—and lots of them—ripping Fox and Beth limb from limb, their blood pooling like vomit on a frat-house floor.

So, yes, it could end there, with a sparing-the-details ending that leaves no doubt of impending doom.

Or, if you're daring—and willing to suspend belief just a little more—I could present you the alternate ending. Yes? You would like that? Well, if you would, read on . . .

The second Fox pulled out, he was followed by a phalanx of Pittsburgh's finest. And they were firing. And up ahead, no doubt, lay those tire-ripping strips of metal that cops use to catch rogues like Chapel Fox and Beth L. Park. It had been a hell of a run, but Beth was convinced it was coming to a violent, horrifying end. And then Fox laughed.

"What the hell's so funny, Fox?"

"Just watch. It's all been leading up to this moment, Beth," Fox said as he expertly weaved around the traffic, which, fortunately, was sparse, seeing that it was 4:00 in the morning.

"If we can make it to the airport—and reach the locker I've had there for years—we'll be in the clear."

"This is crazy, Fox. What the hell are you talking about?"

"Yes, it's crazy, and it might not work, but what's the alternative?"

Beth hushed, and Fox continued to elude the police, at one point zipping between so many alleys that he and Beth were able to ditch the Corolla and jack another car. Now reaching the airport would be a snap.

They reached Pittsburgh International by 5:15 and split up. Fox told Beth to meet him at the locker. Ten minutes later, Beth was wearing a delightful blond wig, while Fox sported a professor-like mustache and goatee. They slipped on some new clothes, stuffed what they were wearing in the locker, and proceeded, as Mr. and Mrs. Robert Pensgrove, to purchase two one-way tickets to the Cayman Islands.

They flew first-class on their way to their luxury beach home. The Spartan living that Fox endured all these years finally paid off. Mrs. Pensgrove was delighted with the new digs.

Even the dining room had been nicely updated.

My readers appreciated the fact that I ended the Fox saga on a happy note, considering the mood of everyone in light of yesterday's events. And in case I was about to forget what had transpired a mere 24 hours earlier, Alice's head suddenly appeared in my doorframe. "I need to see you and Sam."

We walked by Sam's office, Alice beckoning him with her hands. He rolled his eyes at me but followed.

"Look. I just got the lowdown from Andrea—the truth about yesterday. Remember when I said January 23 as my pick for the company's last day?" Sam and I nodded. "Well, we'll be lucky to see December 23. Almost a million, guys."

"Holy!" said Sam. "And she can pay it?"

"She already has, but now there's really nothing left. She was sitting on a nice mountain of money before the FTC started with her. So, barring any new surge of clients—which wasn't likely under the best of circumstances, but now, considering yesterday's events—well, I just wanted to let you guys know."

"Well, we appreciate it, Alice," said Sam.

"And, for what it's worth," I said, "you're one of the good guys here."

"We had some laughs, though, didn't we?" she said, clearing her throat and fighting back tears.

"We can all do better," said Sam.

"I know you're right, Sam," said Alice, "but this still sucks. I mean, in a weird way, don't you feel bad for"—

"Ah, there you are, young man," said Andrea. "Come on. Let's brainstorm."

I followed Andrea to her igloo, unsure what lay in store.

"So, I'm guessing Alice told you about the present the FTC had for me yesterday, right?"

"Yes, she did, Andrea. I'm sorry."

"Well, if it's any consolation, I'm a million times sorrier." She chuckled at her own joke.

"So, what's your take on this, Nick? How do we make amends for yesterday? How do replace the money the FTC just stole from me?"

I was bewildered. Was she serious? "Andrea," I wanted to say, "this is it. You're on the mat. You're down for the count. You made an ass of yourself in public yesterday. You do not pass 'Go.' You do not collect $200."

"Well," I said, trying to come up with empty yet soothing words, "the first thing we need to do is distance ourselves from the events of yesterday while still embracing them. We need to see what happened as an opportunity."

"I like it! I like the way you think. I want you to think about this and get back to me with something concrete." She waved me out of her office.

I didn't waste a moment's time trying to figure out ways to revive the company. It was pointless. The end was here. Amazingly, over the next few weeks, we actually did receive a few new client submission forms. And, perhaps even more amazingly, 73 people sent us $50 "yearly maintenance" checks.

On December 23, we had our office Christmas party. Loretta asked Sam and me to take a trip to her car to help unload the food. We obliged. Loretta and I had been civil to each other since the Showcase. I felt bad about the surgery she had to undergo to repair the damage to her hand, and I think both of us knew we wouldn't be seeing each other much longer. What was the point of the hostility anymore?

It was a miserable, lifeless day. Sam and I trudged to the garage, unlocked Loretta's trunk, and were greeted by a feast—stuffed chicken breasts, side dishes, cheese-and-meat trays. We both looked at each other and thought the same thing.

"Well, the chicken and most of this stuff, I guess, has to be heated," I said.

"But not the cheese-and-meat trays."

For the next 20 minutes or so, Sam and I stuffed our faces and laughed our asses off. It was a pointless revenge—I'm not sure whom we were really sticking it to—but it was fun nonetheless, considering our impending unemployment.

We spread out what was left of the massacre we had unleashed to make the trays appear full, then laughed some more at how ridiculous they now looked.

Our mischief complete, the two of us, arms weighted down with food, headed back into the gray.

Made in the USA
Las Vegas, NV
09 November 2021